"Are we having fun yet?"

Matt frowned at Christie. "Yes, we are."

"Good. I wouldn't want to miss anything." Christie lifted her ponytail and flapped it, trying unsuccessfully to fan herself. "This idea of yours isn't working," she continued. "You're having a miserable time. But you *did* enjoy yourself in New Mexico."

"I'm having a great time. And so are you. You probably haven't been to the Statue of Liberty in years. Just wait until we're on the ferry. Then you'll see. This'll be the best day you ever had in your life."

Christie rolled her eyes and groaned.

"All right, this is it!" Matt looked about expectantly. They'd finally managed to board the ferry and secure a seat. A boy of about eight sat down next to him.

"I'm going to be sick," the little boy announced.

Ellen James has wanted a writing career ever since she won a national short-story contest when she was in high school. *Two Against Love* is Ellen's third Harlequin Romance novel, and the second one set in her home state of New Mexico. She and her husband, both writers, love to travel and they share an interest in wildlife photography and American history.

Books by Ellen James

HARLEQUIN ROMANCE
3052—HOME FOR LOVE
3069—THE TURQUOISE HEART

TWO
AGAINST LOVE

Ellen James

Harlequin Books

TORONTO • NEW YORK • LONDON
AMSTERDAM • PARIS • SYDNEY • HAMBURG
STOCKHOLM • ATHENS • TOKYO • MILAN

ISBN 0-373-03118-1

Harlequin Romance first edition April 1991

TWO AGAINST LOVE

CHAPTER ONE

THE PARLOR WINDOWS were open wide to the summer afternoon. Rich, golden sunlight streamed into the room, and a breeze rustled the curtains as if beckoning Christie outside to the garden. But Christie Daniels didn't have time to enjoy the beauty of the day. She was too busy grappling with a bolt of bright red cotton. The material billowed around her, seeming to have a will of its own. Finally she managed to drape some of it over the ancient dressmaker's form that she'd found in an antique store last week. The form had come with its own nickname, "Old Grace." It possessed a regal yet jaunty posture, as if it had been ruling the parlor for generations.

Christie gathered a corner of the material and flung it rakishly over Old Grace's shoulder. Vivid red was her favorite color—brash, exuberant and aggressive. She knew that she was going to create a wonderful dress. Of course, she'd never so much as basted a hem before, but that was beside the point. Sewing was like all the other goals she'd ever achieved. It was something to be tackled, struggled with and ultimately conquered. She was determined to master this skill, in spite of the fact that she kept stabbing pins into her fingers. It was all part of her brand-new life, far away from the pressures and tensions she'd battled in New

York City as a partner in her father's Wall Street brokerage firm. These days Christie led a simpler, more satisfying existence, running her own business—a bed and breakfast in the small, picturesque town of Red River, New Mexico.

Humming to herself, she rummaged through the cigar box full of buttons she'd unearthed in the attic. Picking out a simple white one, she held it up against the red material. It might do, but it was a bit plain. She smoothed back a strand of her long, honey-blond hair and popped the button into her mouth as if it were a candy. Sucking it thoughtfully, she searched through the cigar box for something more festive. Perhaps a row of small pearl buttons all the way down the front of the dress...

"Excuse me," boomed a deep male voice right behind her. Christie started violently, taking in her breath with a gasp. The button in her mouth shot straight down her windpipe. She couldn't breathe! Heart pounding wildly, she heard the voice go on talking.

"I'm looking for Mary Christine Daniels. Is this the right place?"

Christie tried to yell out her panic, but no words came. Her lungs felt as if they would burst in their struggle for air. All she could do was flap her arms around, like a penguin yearning for flight.

"Does that mean you don't know her?" the voice asked doubtfully. Christie flapped some more, but her efforts began to weaken. It seemed as if time was slowing down, each second of terror stretching out endlessly. Through a haze she saw the pattern of the wallpaper begin to waver—faded cabbage roses expanded and contracted in the most alarming manner. *Oh, no, she was hallucinating.* A man's face interposed itself between her and the wallpaper. Christie had a vague impression of reddish eyebrows drawn together in a frown. The face loomed closer, appearing oddly disembodied.

"Good Lord," it said. "What have you done to yourself?" A powerful hand slapped her on the back, and that made her choke all the more. Fear coursed through her. The man grabbed a vase of buttercups from the coffee table, pulled out the flowers and then shoved it under her nose.

"Water," he said. "You need to drink some water!"

Christie wanted to laugh hysterically. She stared down into the vase and saw the murky liquid there, a soggy flower stem floating in it. She felt as if she'd been hurled into a vacuum. There was no air, no light, nothing to hold on to—

The man's arms caught her from behind, clenching her body like a vise. She knew he was trying to help, but the painful pressure of his arms made her feel more trapped than ever. Terror engulfed her and she fought for escape, all reason gone. Christie kicked back against the man's shin until his hold slackened a little. She tried to wrestle away from him, frantic that he would squeeze the last bit of air from her body.

The man refused to let go. "Stand still, damn it!" he shouted. But they were both off balance now, and together they stumbled against the dressmaker's form. It spun around crazily, like a drunken countess at a ball, and went crashing over on its side. Christie began to plummet into unconsciousness. Then the man's arms tightened again. His fists jabbed up forcefully underneath her rib cage and the button shot right out of her mouth.

At first all Christie knew was the blessed burning of air into her lungs. Only gradually did she become aware of the strong arms still holding her, the solid male body pressed against hers. Suddenly she felt very safe with the man's warmth radiating into her. She slumped back against him, as wobbly as a rag doll. He half lifted her over to the sofa, depositing her on it unceremoniously. She flopped down onto the pillows, gasping with the sweetness of air. Everything seemed so vivid and keen right now. She savored the late-afternoon sunlight splashing in through the windows, and the damp, pungent odor of the buttercups strewn across the table.

The man leaned over her. "Are you all right?" he demanded in his deep voice.

"Yes," she croaked, gazing up at him. He was exceptionally good-looking, with dark, russet hair and rugged features. He had a rather belligerent nose that only added to his attractiveness. The sunlight accentuated the red-gold hair on his forearms, and his skin had a golden cast. A man of copper and gold... Christie blinked, feeling so shaky she wondered if she was still hallucinating.

The man straightened up. "I'll get you a decent glass of water," he said. "Which way is your kitchen?"

She pointed the direction and watched him walk away. He moved with impatient energy, each stride he took long and powerful. A few moments later he returned with a glass of clear, sparkling water. Christie took it gratefully, lifting herself up to drink a few sips. But then she collapsed back on the pillows, a realization hitting her with force.

"You saved my life," she said. "If you hadn't done something, right now I might be—" She couldn't even finish the sentence. She clamped her hands around the glass of water, her fingers trembling.

"You didn't exactly make things easy for me," the man said dryly. "Keep practicing that kick of yours, though. It has promise." He reached down and picked up something small and white from the faded Persian carpet. He shook his head. "What the hell were you doing with a button in your mouth?"

"I always like to chew on something when I'm thinking," she explained. "It helps to clear my mind."

"Damn fool habit," he said. "Maybe you realize that now." He dropped the button onto the coffee table. It landed with a small "plink."

"Well, you see," Christie said, "it's just that you crept up behind me, and it really made me jump—"

"I knocked on the screen door out front, but no one answered. You *are* Mary Christine, aren't you?"

"Christie," she amended, still gazing up at him. He had hazel eyes, and the color made her think of autumn leaves drifting at the bottom of a mountain stream. "No matter what happened," she said, "you saved my life. How can I ever thank you for that?"

"Forget it," he answered, looking disgruntled. "I was supposed to stay here for a few nights. But maybe I should go somewhere else for a little while and let you recuperate. I'll come back later this evening—"

"Oh, no," she exclaimed, turning her head on the sofa pillows. "You can't leave after what's happened.

Don't you see? You saved my life, and that creates a bond between us. I mean, you can't just walk away." Christie saw the man's face tighten warily, as if he needed to protect himself from her sloppy emotions. She didn't care. Her whole body was trembling after the narrow escape she'd had, and she needed human contact—his contact.

"That was quite an experience for both of us," she said through chattering teeth. "I don't imagine you save someone's life every day. It puts everything else into perspective, doesn't it? I was so annoyed today because one of my guests checked out and left an awful mess for me to clean up in her room. But that doesn't matter anymore. It doesn't matter at all. Don't you agree?"

He didn't say anything. He just stood there looking down at Christie the way a scientist might inspect a bizarre species of creature. His eyes focused on her ruffled calico square-dancing skirt, and on her baggy T-shirt that admonished in bold red letters Come Shoot the Rapids of the Mighty Rio Grande. Christie didn't mind the unflattering perusal he was giving her. Nothing could bother her right now because she was so happy just to be alive. She nestled blissfully against the pillows, wiggling her toes in their sandals. He stared at her feet, apparently fascinated by the fuchsia polish on her toenails. Finally he spoke. "How are you feeling?" he asked gruffly.

"Light-headed—not in a bad way, but like somebody shook up my bones and the pieces haven't fallen back into place again."

He retrieved the glass of water and placed it on the coffee table. Then he took both her hands, balancing them gently in his own. "Your skin is a little clammy," he said. "You could be suffering from shock."

Christie nodded. The man's nearness seemed to bring on all sorts of additional symptoms. Her heartbeat began to skip erratically and she felt more light-headed than ever.

Now he pressed his palm against her forehead. "Your temperature is on the cool side," he pronounced. Even though he kept his voice clinical, his touch was warm and Christie felt a sense of loss when he withdrew his hand. Taking the crocheted afghan from the foot of the sofa, he spread it over her. She found the gesture immensely comforting, although his expression was even more disgruntled than before.

He sat down in the armchair across from her. He was wearing jeans that fit well on his lean hips, but the denim was much too stiff and unused. His shirt gave the same impression—it was cut in a casual style that enhanced the breadth of his shoulders, and yet it looked as if he had worn it straight from the package. There were still creases where it had been folded.

"What's your name?" she asked.

"Matt Gallagher."

"Gallagher...oh, yes," she said with satisfaction. "You made a reservation for the weekend. I'll put you on the third floor. You'll have plenty of privacy up here, and a wonderful view of the ski slopes. They're beautiful right now, very green. Of course, they *are* spectacular when they're covered with snow," she rambled on. "And this winter I'm going to learn how to ski. How about you, Matt? Do you ski?"

"Never had the time to learn," came his terse reply. He shifted in his chair, looking uncomfortable.

Then he took a small gold watch from the pocket of his jeans and studied it. He turned it in his fingers with practiced ease, as if it were some sort of talisman. After a moment he glanced up, Christie's presence seeming to register again. There was nothing pleased about his expression as he surveyed her.

Christie was piqued by Matt's unenthusiastic reaction. She didn't consider herself a beautiful woman, yet her looks were certainly acceptable. Her hair was an unusual shade of dark blond, cascading all the way to her waist, and her eyes were a deep blue. Perhaps her cheeks were a bit too round, but her figure was slim. Matt Gallagher didn't need to stare at her so disapprovingly, as if she looked like a plucked goose!

She pushed the afghan away and struggled to a sitting position. "Ouch!" she yelped, as a strand of her hair caught in one of the buttons tacked into the sofa back.

"What is it now?" Matt demanded, stuffing the watch back into his pocket. He was beside her in a second, leaning over her again. He had a clean, masculine scent that mingled with the smell of crisp new denim. Christie saw the freckles scattered across the bridge of his nose and found them much too appealing. She yanked on her hair.

"Here, let me do it," he said. He tugged gently at the strand of hair, without success. Next he tried unwinding it from the button, but ended up tangling more strands. "There has to be a method to this," he muttered. "Let's see..." He sat down on the sofa and went after her hair with both hands now. Christie watched in fascination as he plucked at the strands like a harpist experimenting with an unfamiliar melody.

He had strong, blunt fingers with good knuckles. Christie found it unsettling and most annoying to be attracted to a man's knuckles.

"You should stay away from buttons altogether," Matt grumbled. He went on attacking the problem of her hair; apparently he was not one to give up easily. "I think I have it. Wait a minute…aha, that's it!" He freed the last strand triumphantly.

But Matt didn't let go of her hair right away, allowing it to remain spread out over the palm of his hand. He gazed down at it. "Hmm," he murmured with an inflection of surprise. Whatever he meant, it didn't sound flattering. Good grief, you'd think a snake had slithered into his hand! Christie reached behind her neck, gathered her hair with a decisive gesture and brought it all tumbling over one shoulder.

Matt watched her, rubbing his jaw thoughtfully. "Maybe your father's right," he said. "You seem to need someone to look after you."

It was as if he'd picked up the glass from the table and flung cold water in Christie's face. "You know my father?" she asked Matt indignantly. She could trace most of the pain in her life straight back to her father, Christopher Daniels the Third. For such a long time she'd tried to live up to his expectations, never quite succeeding. But she was free of his dominance at last. She didn't need him or any other man to look after her!

Matt gave an impatient shrug, as if he didn't like explaining himself. "I'm his new business partner."

"I see," Christie said slowly. "You're the person who took my place at Daniels, Peters and Bainbridge. Only now it's Daniels, Peters, Bainbridge and Gallagher.''

"That's the idea. But everything's gone to hell with the business and pretty soon there won't be anything left of it—all because of you, Christie Daniels.'' Matt looked her over with open disapproval.

"What are you talking about?'' she demanded. "My father's one of the most successful brokers on Wall Street. Surely he's all right—nothing has happened to him?'' A stab of fear went through her, a reminder of those childhood years when her father had meant everything to her. She was bitterly disillusioned with him now, but still she wished him no harm.

"You'd know what was going on if you answered your father's phone calls, or read his letters instead of sending them back unopened.'' Matt changed position restlessly, the old sofa springs creaking under his weight. He was a large, solid man, but no extra flesh was wasted on his powerful frame. He looked like a prospector who'd come down from the hills to outfit himself at the local country store. Certainly he didn't look like a New York City stockbroker...a man cut from the very same cloth as her father. Christie felt betrayed, as if Matt had entered her house under false pretenses.

She clenched her hands in her lap. "My relationship with my father isn't any of your concern,'' she declared.

"Unfortunately it *is* my concern.'' Matt leaned toward her. The expression on his face was ominous, reminding Christie of a grizzly bear she'd once seen at Yellowstone Park. "Do you think I wanted to traipse all the way out here to find you? The answer is no. But you're messing with my career, so I don't have any choice in the matter."

"I don't know what you're talking about," she protested. "I haven't had anything at all to do with my father's business for the last four months. How could I possibly affect your career?"

Matt uttered an oath under his breath. He stood up and went over to his suitcase, unzipping a pouch along one side of it. Taking out a manila folder, he brought it over to Christie and thrust it under her nose. "Read," he commanded.

Anger boiled up inside of her. She'd had enough of domineering men to last her several lifetimes! But she needed to know what on earth Matt was talking about. Opening the folder, she saw that it contained some legal documents as well as an envelope with her name scrawled across it. Immediately she recognized her father's bold handwriting.

Christie stared down at the envelope. It was made of heavy, expensive parchment; Christopher Daniels the Third used nothing but the best quality for every detail of his life. He was a perfectionist who demanded the same perfection in others. Christie's hand hovered over the envelope. During the past few months she'd battled with guilt and sorrow because of his estrangement from her father. And yet it had been such a relief to be away from him, no longer under his domination. Surely her anger toward him was justified after all the years he'd tried to control her every decision. He had no right to intrude on her life again!

Christie glanced up at Matt, who had gone to stand in front of the fireplace. He was scowling at her col-

lection of porcelain cats that adorned the mantelpiece. She ripped open the envelope. The sooner she
knew what was going on here, the better. Quickly she
scanned the letter, written on the same heavy parchment as the envelope.

My Dear Mary Christine

I am badly hurt that you've refused all communication with me. I see no alternative but to
send Matthew as my emissary.

That last day you hurled some harsh accusa-
tions at me but you gave me no chance to respond, to defend myself. All my life I've worked
and struggled for one thing only—to leave a wor-
thy inheritance for you. That's all Daniels, Peters and Bainbridge has ever meant to me. Very
well, I admit that I "engineered" the engagement between you and Oren Peters, as you so
bluntly put it. But was I wrong? Oren is a decent, ambitious young man, and the firm is his
heritage as well as yours. His father was my closest friend, much more than a mere business as-
sociate. Why shouldn't both our children join
together and continue our legacy? You seemed to
care genuinely for Oren yourself, until you discovered my "complicity."

Of course, none of this matters anymore. You
have rejected your heritage and, therefore, Daniels, Peters and Bainbridge can no longer have
meaning for me. Mary Christine, I'm dissolving
the company after thirty years of building it up.
Without you here, my heart simply isn't in my
work anymore. Matthew will give you the papers

you need to sign so that we can proceed with the dissolution. You're still a major stockholder and I can't go through with this unless you give your approval. Ironic, isn't it? You finally have the upper hand with me. I suppose that's what you wanted all along.

> I remain ever,
> Your father

Christie read the letter twice, and then she laughed out loud in disbelief. "He's surpassed himself," she exclaimed. "Threatening to give up the company! He'd never go through with it—he'd rather chop off all his toes. But this is a masterful attempt to make me feel guilty so I'll go back to New York—absolutely masterful." For a moment she experienced sincere admiration for her father's scheme, and then she threw his letter down with a gesture of contempt. She was furious at him for concocting this plot to manipulate her. But even more than that, she was disgusted with herself. Blast it all, she was actually starting to feel guilty again—which was exactly what her father wanted.

Matt had swiveled around toward her. "I don't think you understand," he said, a steeliness in his voice. "Your father's completely serious about dissolving his business because of this sentimental hogwash. Somehow you've got to straighten it out with him before he does something stupid. I promised to bring you those papers, but I have no intention of letting you sign them."

"Seems we're in perfect agreement. I have no intention of signing them, either." She pushed away the manila folder.

"You have to do more than that," Matt persisted. "You have to resolve things with your father. It doesn't matter how you do it—call him on the phone, or better yet fly back to New York with me. You're the only person who can convince him to change his mind. The sooner you get started, the better."

Christie was incensed by his blatant interference. She glared at him. "I'm not going to let you or my father manipulate me," she declared. "Besides, if you're really worried about the company, you and Oren Peters can buy out my father. Terence Bainbridge is about to retire, so you won't be able to count on him, but you and Oren would probably make a nice pair," she observed scornfully.

"That would be a good joke, all right, me going into business with your lightweight ex-boyfriend."

"There's nothing lightweight about Oren," she objected. "He's just as domineering and pigheaded as my father." She gazed pointedly at Matt. "My father surrounds himself with men like that. *You* seem to be no exception."

He ignored this insult, picking up one of her porcelain cats, the one with bluebells painted on its tail. He examined it with a critical expression as he spoke. "Even if I wanted to buy out your father, I don't have that kind of money." His mouth twisted into a slight grimace. "My last partner got mixed up in some insider trading and destroyed our entire firm. I've had to start all over again—and now I find myself in the middle of another fiasco. This time it's an absurd, crackbrained family argument. Hell, nothing in my life makes sense right now!'' He brought down the porcelain cat with such a loud "clack" that Christie winced. By some miracle it didn't shatter into pieces. It just lay there curled on the mantelpiece, smiling smugly to itself.

Christie gave Matt a cool perusal. "You're blaming me for all the problems in your life. That hardly seems fair."

He began pacing around, nudging aside a wicker chair to give himself more room. "I blame all the corruption and insider trading in the stock market. I blame my partner for destroying my business and my faith in friendship. I blame your father for behaving like a sentimental old fool—and, yes, I blame you for running away from New York and leaving behind a catastrophe for someone like me to clean up." He stopped and glared at a tall, spindly curio cabinet that blocked his way. "Why the devil do you have so much furniture?" he demanded cantankerously. "This place is like an antique store gone berserk."

"I like collecting antiques," Christie asserted. "I never had time for that in New York. I never had time for *anything* there." She glanced around, enjoying the clutter that surrounded her—a scarred rolltop desk hunched in one corner like a beast nursing its wounds, an old-fashioned steam radiator she'd found at a secondhand store down in Santa Fe, an ornate Victorian plant pedestal carved with hieroglyphics. So far she'd had a great deal of fun discovering furniture in Egyptian Revival, Renaissance Revival, Rococo Revival, Colonial and Gothic and Japanese Revival.

She turned back to Matt, wishing she could make him see how much this new life meant to her. It brimmed over with surprises and pleasures every day. But Matt Gallagher was from her father's world and probably couldn't understand how small, simple things brought her joy. She'd have to try a different line of defense for herself.

"Listen, Matt," she began, "I didn't just run away. The stress had been getting to me for a long time." She shook her head ruefully. "When you're a stockbroker, the only thing that matters is pushing your commissions higher and higher—driving up your numbers until they're better than last week or the day before. I was starting to wake up with hives every morning. It got so bad I had to wear turtlenecks to work to cover all the red blotches." Christie shuddered at the memory. "I was living my father's dream, not my own—that was the main problem," she went on. "And then my engagement to Oren exploded sky-high. I found out that my father arranged the whole thing—he practically bribed Oren to propose to me! That was the last straw. It was bad enough having my father run my life, but he went too far when he contrived a marriage for me. I had to leave after that— don't you see?"

"No matter what happened, you should have stayed in New York," Matt insisted. "You should have resolved your problems instead of running away from them."

He was infuriating. Matt Gallagher made her feel as if she'd been a coward, but she'd had to flee New York for her own survival. "I'm not going to fall for another one of my father's schemes," she stated flatly. "You can tell him that for me."

"I won't be a go-between for you and your father," Matt warned. "That won't solve anything. You've got to deal with him directly and stop this craziness of his. I'm not going to stand by and watch another company destroyed around me. You can count on that."

The blood burned in Christie's face. "You're wasting your time!" she exclaimed. "As far as I'm concerned, Christopher Daniels the Third can do whatever he damn well pleases."

Matt faced her, his hands jammed into the pockets of his jeans. He looked dangerous, like a hell-bent lumberjack. "No matter what it takes, I'll make you see reason, Christie."

"I won't be dictated to by any man, Matt Gallagher. Especially not by you!"

He smiled for the first time—a deceptively engaging smile. "We'll see about that, Christie," he said softly. "We'll see."

CHAPTER TWO

CHRISTIE FOUGHT her way up from the depths of the sagging old sofa. But she was still unsteady after nearly choking to death, and a wave of faintness swept over her. She swayed and Matt rushed to grab hold of her. He seemed to be making a habit of coming to her rescue. His grip was sure and firm yet surprisingly gentle. There was a smattering of freckles across the skin of his arm. She felt an urge to run her finger over them and a confusing warmth spread through her.

"Are you all right?" Matt asked in a concerned voice.

"I'm okay—really I am," Christie said, pulling away from him. She found his gentleness disturbing. "Well, then," she declared, "since you're determined to stay in Red River, the Blue Spruce Inn on Main Street probably has a vacancy. I'm sure you'll be very comfortable there."

"You're not going to get rid of me that easily," he said in a grim voice. "I'm staying right here."

"Forget it!"

"I have a reservation, don't I?"

"Technically, yes . . ." she admitted.

"Then you can't refuse my business. I'm a paying guest, like anyone else."

Christie gazed at him quizzically. She was torn. Deep down she realized she was attracted to Matt Gallagher and actually wanted him to stay. She didn't like the thought of him walking out the door and out of her life. But if she was smart, she'd boot him from the house right now, before her emotions got carried away. Matt had been sent here by her father—he was another high-powered stockbroker who threatened her independence. She couldn't afford to be attracted to him.

Yet surely Christie was strong enough to withstand his appeal. And Matt would only be in Red River a few days, anyway. Why not let him stay? "I'm a businesswoman," she said after a brief moment, "and I suppose it would be foolish to turn away a paying customer. Just don't expect any special treatment because you work for my father."

"That's fine with me," he agreed.

"Darn right it's fine."

"That's what I said, didn't I? It's fine!"

They stared at each other, seeming to have reached an impasse. It was Christie who finally spoke. "I'll take you to your room now and you can get settled in," she said matter-of-factly. "You can fill out a registration card later." Without waiting for a response, she led the way out of the parlor toward the stairway.

Matt picked up his suitcase and followed her. She'd only gone up a few steps when he grasped her arm again. "Slow down," he warned. "You'd better take it easy for a while."

She didn't want to be this close to him. His touch had too much effect on her, as if it reached right through her skin to the sensitive ends of her nerves.

But it was true that she still felt shaken. She allowed Matt to support her arm all the way up to the third-floor landing. Turning down the hallway, she led him to the corner bedroom.

She opened the door with a flourish. "Well, this is it," she proclaimed. Antiques sprouted gloriously in the room. There were two bureaus with mirrors, a rocking chair and an armchair, a side chair and a slipper chair, several glass-fronted bookcases, a rustic pine desk and a miniature harpsichord in perfect playing condition. In the midst of all this a king-size bed guarded its space like a fortress under siege.

"It's cozy in here, don't you think?" Christie asked, sliding her way between one of the bureaus and the imitation-bamboo rocker. Matt stood in the doorway, surveying the room as if it might be booby-trapped. At last he came in, depositing his suitcase on the bed. He reached down to test the mattress, giving Christie an acrid look at the same time.

"I knew you'd be happy with this room," she remarked, propping her arms along the top of the art nouveau side chair. Christie liked bizarre and unusual chairs; the back of this one was carved in a dramatic pattern of wisteria vines, which made it quite uncomfortable for sitting.

"Look, Matt," she said in a conversational voice, "as long as you're going to be in Red River you might as well enjoy yourself. There's plenty to do here. Fishing, rafting, hiking..."

He glanced at her sardonically. "I won't have time for any of that. I'll be flying back to New York on Monday, and you'll be coming with me."

Christie frowned at him. "I'm never going back to New York. I won't give up the new life I've started."

He unbuckled his suitcase and flung open the lid. "No one's asking you to perform any grandiose sacrifices, Christie. All you have to do is go to New York and make your father behave rationally. Then you can fly right back to this paradise of yours, out here in the middle of nowhere."

Christie leaned forward so intently, she almost sent the chair over backward. "If I go to New York, he'll find a way to keep me there. That's the whole point—he's trying to play on my guilt, my emotions. He's always been superb at that."

Matt shrugged. "So maybe you'll end up working in his company again. It's not such a bad life, being a stockbroker and living in New York City."

Christie shook her head. "There's just too much pressure. Doesn't it ever get to you? I mean—look at yourself! You're all tense and stirred up, like a volcano that can't decide whether or not to erupt. How can you live like that?"

He scowled into his suitcase. "Sure, the pressure gets to me," he conceded irritably. "I'd be crazy if it didn't. Hell, it gets to me all the time! But I can't just walk away from a career after devoting fifteen years of my life to it. I believe in sticking to a commitment, seeing it through even when things get bad—not running away from my responsibilities the way you did."

"Sometimes a commitment has to change," she argued hotly. "For way too long I tried to fulfill an obligation to my father. But I can't sacrifice my own happiness to please him. My commitment to myself is more important."

Matt gave her another sour look, but didn't offer a rebuttal. Christie felt triumphant for having scored the winning point. She went to sit on the bed, jouncing up and down a little on the mattress. It was a good, firm one; Matt shouldn't have any trouble sleeping on it. She envisioned his large, powerful body sprawled out in restless sleep...

Christie swallowed hard, bringing her imagination back into line. She watched as Matt tossed shirts out of his suitcase. They were all encased in plastic wrappers, as if he had walked into a store and ordered "ten casual shirts to go."

"Why did I bring all this junk?" he grumbled, unrolling an impressively long pair of yellow tube socks. He made it sound like his clothes had jumped into the suitcase of their own volition, without any approval from him.

Christie peered into the suitcase herself. She saw a flannel jacket in green-and-blue plaid and a pair of navy-blue corduroy pants. Neither item looked as if it had been worn.

"Excellent choices," Christie pronounced, fingering the soft flannel of the jacket. "But did you bring along any shorts? And how about a basic pair of sneakers?" She leaned over so she could get a good look at the shoes Matt was wearing right now. They were heavy-duty hiking boots, so new they didn't bear even one scuff mark. "Well, those are pretty decent," she said approvingly. "You seem to be all set for the mountains. I think there's real hope for you."

"You're a very nosy person."

"Yes, I am," Christie admitted, completely unabashed. She straightened up, bringing her hair forward again so she could twine it into a loose braid. "I'm terribly nosy—and friendly, too. Those are the things that made me a passable broker. I was always interested in my clients because they were people, not because I wanted their commissions. They seemed to like that. Can you figure it out? I was a stockbroker who deep down hated trading stocks."

Matt leaned against one of the bureaus. He folded his arms and studied Christie with a clinical sort of interest. "Your father says you were a very successful broker—not just a passable one."

At these words, Christie's hands rested motionless on her hair. "How strange that he never said as much to *me*," she remarked bitterly. "He made it clear I was always falling further and further behind his expectations."

Matt continued to study her as if she were a puzzle in need of solving. "Maybe you should just tell your father you need more feedback," he suggested. "More appreciation."

"And you think that will settle all the problems between us?" she scoffed. "It's not that simple, Matt. I want respect as well as appreciation from my father. I want him to accept that I have a right to achieve my own goals—not follow the ones *he's* set for me." She stood up and navigated a path among the jumble of antiques until she reached the window. Just across the road a grassy ski slope rose majestically, a brilliant emerald green in the late afternoon light. The pine trees that grew thick on either side of the ski run were a darker green, the color of deep jade. As always, this view gave Christie a sense of peace and well-being.

"I've found something special in Red River," she said firmly. "My aunt brought me here for a wonderful vacation when I was fourteen. It was such a magical summer, and deep inside I always kept the dream of returning here. Now I have! I've chosen my own kind of success, instead of giving in and accepting my father's choices. Do you realize this is the first time in my life I've actually done that? It wasn't easy and I'm proud of myself."

"Congratulations," Matt said without any conviction. He went on unpacking his suitcase, muttering to himself under his breath. From what she could hear, he was complaining in equal parts about his confounded clothes and Christie's extreme foolhardiness.

She watched as a pair of gray sweatpants and a ragged brown sweatshirt flew through the air and landed in a heap on the bed. "It looks like you've actually worn those," she noted with interest. "Workout clothes—you run in them, that's my guess. Am I right?"

"As a matter of fact, yes." He sounded reluctant to speak, as if she'd discovered something too personal about him.

"It's good that you exercise, especially living under all that tension the way you do. But how about your diet?" she asked accusingly. "Do you eat properly or do you just guzzle soft drinks and coffee all day? Of course, you have all those lunches and dinners with clients, but they're not very healthy. You could end up with a stomach full of ulcers, you know."

He didn't seem inclined to elaborate on his eating habits. "Ulcers," he echoed. "That reminds me, I'm hungry. Where would I find a good restaurant around here?''

Christie stepped away from the window. She gazed at Matt's russet hair and strong, rugged features. He was much too attractive. Physically he looked as if he would fit right into this mountain setting. But it was clear from his harassed expression that he was completely out of his element. Christie experienced an unexpected surge of empathy. And she felt that she still owed him something for saving her life. ''You don't have to go out for dinner,'' she told him. ''You're welcome to eat right here, with me. I could have something ready in no time.''

A line etched itself into his forehead as he frowned. He didn't look excited at the thought of dining with her. ''I wouldn't want any 'special treatment,''' he said dryly.

''Suit yourself.'' Christie marched to the closet, stubbing her toe against a chair leg on the way.

''You're a walking disaster area. You ought to come equipped with warning signs.''

''I didn't start having accidents until *you* came along,'' she contended. Christie took two clean towels from the closet shelf and plunked them in Matt's hands. ''The bathroom is down the hall,'' she instructed him. ''No one else is staying on this floor right now, so you'll have it all to yourself.'' She walked to the door, making it safely through the maze of antiques. Pausing, she glanced back at Matt. ''The Miner's Café down the street serves a mean fish steak,'' she said. ''But if you decide to join me downstairs for a meal . . . just consider it a gesture of gratitude for saving my life. I don't usually serve dinner to my guests," she added sternly, "but just this once I'm willing to make an exception."

Christie went out, leaving him to make his own decision. It would be perfectly all right if he didn't join her. No longer did she require male companionship in her life.

Back in the parlor Christie glanced ruefully at the dressmaker's form that lay sprawled on the floor. She set it to rights. Now it stood with an offended air, like an imperious lady who couldn't believe she'd been subjected to such indignities.

"Sorry, Old Grace," Christie murmured. She smoothed out a fold of the material, no longer in the mood to design a dress.

Her gaze was caught by a flash of white on the coffee table. Christie picked up the button that had caused her so much trouble. It lay innocently in her palm, and she curled her fingers over it. The button seemed to represent the bond she felt with Matt. But Matt Gallagher belonged to a world she'd left far behind. Perhaps he *had* acted quickly and expertly to save her life, but he would have done the same for anyone. It was pretty embarrassing actually—coughing up a button in such an inelegant manner. That wasn't the way she liked to introduce herself to people. And yet, in spite of all this, Christie felt as if something unique and earth-shattering had transpired.

"Oh, damn!" she confided to Old Grace. "I really don't need these kinds of feelings, even if he *did* save my life. So why am I hoping he'll come down for dinner, after all?"

Grace apparently had no answers. But Christie herself was beginning to suspect what was going on here. Most likely she was suffering from the maiden-in-distress/hero-to-the-rescue syndrome. In the grip of this malady, a woman would feel intense gratitude toward her rescuer. Such gratitude could easily spark a few romantic fantasies.

Christie's own experience had taught her that far too many emotions were mistaken for romantic love. She seriously doubted that such a thing as romantic love even existed. The warmth she felt toward Matt was simply that...basic human warmth and gratitude, with a couple of hormones thrown in for good measure.

She dropped the button into her cigar box and snapped down the lid. No man was going to intrude on her new life—certainly not Matt Gallagher. No matter how grateful she might be and no matter how attracted she was to him, he was a member of the enemy camp. She would not allow herself to forget that.

Feeling more in control of her emotions, Christie strode into the kitchen. This was one of her favorite rooms in the house. It was large and drafty, yet somehow homey at the same time. Long ago someone had painted a fanciful border of birds and flowers along the ceiling. The artwork was crude and the once-bright colors were faded now, but Christie liked to imagine that any moment those improbable robins and canaries would start chirping at her.

She surveyed the big, ugly stove but refused to be daunted by it. Cooking was another new skill she felt determined to master. In New York she'd eaten out all the time. At noon it had been her habit to grab a cup of minestrone from the soup cart outside the building, and a banana or apple from the fruit vendor at the corner. She'd gulp down her food on the steps of Federal Hall and then hurry right back to work. But that sort of thing was no longer acceptable to her. She cherished visions of herself orchestrating homey, soul-satisfying meals. Already she was making great progress in this direction. And tonight, just in case Matt Gallagher did join her, she was going to prepare a stunning dinner.

It wasn't that Christie wanted to impress him, or prove that she possessed domestic skills. Good grief, of course not! A woman only used such ploys when she was out to capture herself a man. That was the last thing Christie intended. It was simply a matter of pride. As long as she was going to cook dinner, it should be the best meal possible—even if she'd be the only one eating it. Forget Matt Gallagher!

The ancient refrigerator hummed and whirred in its mysterious way, and Christie started rummaging through it. Soon she had slices of eggplant frying in olive oil and tomato sauce simmering in another pan. She turned on the oven and began heating the whole-wheat rolls she'd baked yesterday. The sounds in the kitchen harmonized in a comforting medley of sizzling and bubbling. An aroma of basil and oregano wafted through the air. She grated a hunk of cheese at the counter, savoring the cool, mellow light of evening. The mound on the cutting board in front of her grew and grew, lovely curls of cheese falling from the grater...

She was so engrossed that she didn't hear Matt push his way through the swinging door behind her. He cleared his throat, and she twisted around, putting a hand to her neck. She could feel the pulse beating there.

"I didn't mean to startle you," he said hastily.

She gave him a wry smile. "Don't worry. This time I don't have anything in my mouth." They stood gazing at each other for an awkward moment. Christie wrapped her hands in the dish towel she'd tucked into the waistband of her skirt.

"Well," Matt said. "I thought I'd take you up on that supper of yours."

She felt inordinately pleased, and started bustling around the stove. "Just have a seat at the table over there," she said. "I'll have this put together in a flash."

He pulled out a chair at the scarred oak table and watched as she went on working. Much too self-conscious, Christie dropped her spatula in the tomato sauce, splashing little red flecks all over her T-shirt. She dabbed at the spots with a paper towel, but that only smeared them more. Christie berated herself for making such a foolish impression. Then she stood at the counter with her back to Matt, vigorously chopping up a bell pepper. She reminded herself she didn't need to impress him. Since she was no longer looking for any type of relationship with a man, she could afford to relax and just be herself.

Feeling relieved, Christie was beginning to move in a competent rhythm—reaching into the cupboard for plates and bowls, juggling three different pans on the stove, thumping a head of lettuce on the counter to loosen the core. She was conscious of Matt still watching her movements, but she no longer worried about what he thought of her. It gave her a welcome sense of freedom. After a short while she brought two heaping plates of eggplant Parmesan to the table, with a bottle of wine and a bowl of pepper-and-cucumber salad. She smoothed a napkin into the bread basket and arranged the hot rolls invitingly inside. Christie believed that small details were essential to a good meal: a fresh bar of butter displayed on a china plate, currant jelly spooned into a glass bowl, cloth napkins instead of paper ones. She sat down across from Matt and surveyed her table with contentment. Steam rose from the plate in front of her, and she dug into her eggplant. She was ravenous after her unsettling afternoon.

Neither she nor Matt spoke. Matt ate with concentration, rather like a judge at a baking contest. Then he glanced up. "This is delicious," he said with an air of surprise. "I'm used to eating restaurant food all the time. I'd almost forgotten what a home-cooked meal tastes like."

Christie smiled, warmed by his compliment. "I'm glad you agree with me—this is a much better life-style than your own."

He speared a leaf of lettuce. "Let's not start making global statements here. I said that I liked your cooking, that's all."

"Thank you," she answered with gratification, wrapping some melted cheese around her fork. "So, Matt, where are you from? Are you a native New Yorker?"

"I grew up in Brooklyn, but I've lived in Manhattan for years."

"Until I moved here, I'd lived in Manhattan all my life," she told him. "When I was growing up I shuttled between my father's apartment on Park Avenue and my mother's apartment on Central Park West."

"That's right, your parents are divorced. So are mine...seems we have a few things in common, at least on the surface." He rubbed his jaw, not looking particularly thrilled with the idea he had just presented.

"How old were you when it happened?" Christie asked.

"What?" he said distractedly. "Oh—my parents' divorce. I was thirteen."

"I was almost that age myself when it happened to me. I was twelve. It was an awful experience—my parents got into a real power struggle over me. But they ended up with joint custody." Christie gave a smile tinged with bitterness. That custody battle had been an act of defiance for her mother against Christopher Daniels the Third. It hadn't represented any real interest in parenting. After it was all over, Juliet Daniels had reverted to her usual impatience with being a mother. Immersing herself in her avocation of world traveler, she'd seemed relieved to have Christie's life dominated so completely by an autocratic father.

Matt drank some wine. "It was a pretty rough experience for me, too," he said grudgingly. "I lived with my mother for a while, until she decided I was too wild for her. Then I lived with my father until *he* decided I was too wild. I finally moved out on my own when I was seventeen."

Christie grinned. "I'm trying to picture you as a wild teenager. It's difficult because now you seem so..." She searched for the right words. "So steady and dedicated to your work."

Matt broke open a roll and spread it lavishly with butter. "Are you saying that I'm a staid, dull person?" he asked dryly.

Her eyes roved other him; with his vivid, reddish-gold coloring there was nothing dull about him. "Staid isn't the right word, either," she mused. "The way you act, you make me think of a stick of dynamite about to explode. No, I wouldn't call you staid."

"That's a relief to hear," he said in a sardonic voice.

"Actually I think it's good to be dedicated to something, as long as it makes you feel happy. But I can't help wondering, Matt . . . *are* you happy?"

He pursued a cherry tomato around his plate, finally pronging it on his fork. Then he chomped down on it. "Of course I'm happy," he said crankily.

Christie wanted to discuss this subject some more; it promised to be intriguing. Matt seemed perpetually out of sorts, as if the circumstances of his life would no longer obey his bidding and he didn't know what to do about it. Exactly what was his concept of happiness? She started to ask him, but he interrupted her.

"This is an old house," he remarked. "Tell me about it."

Christie sipped her wine. Matt didn't sound genuinely interested in her house. She suspected he just didn't want to talk about himself anymore.

"Well, I was looking for a place that would lend itself to a bed and breakfast," she told him. "I already knew that Red River could easily support a small, hotel-type operation." She realized she was speaking as Mary Christine Daniels, the businesswoman, an effortless habit after her years in the New York financial district. But she hadn't told Matt about the spirit, the soul of her enterprise. She propped her elbows on the table and gazed at him earnestly. "The first time I saw this house, I wasn't at all sure it would be right for a bed and breakfast. It has eaves hanging down so far it looks like it forgot to cut its hair. And the wraparound front porch just doesn't know when to quit! But the house and I belong together somehow. Together we're going to sink or swim at this new life. Does that make any sense?"

"No," Matt answered after a moment. "So far I've heard you talk about making decisions because of 'magic' and 'dreams,' that sort of thing. I don't know how wise you're being."

"Maybe I'm not wise at all," Christie admitted. "But you know something, Matt? For the first time in my life I'm truly, completely happy."

He didn't offer her any more arguments, but he regarded her intently as he finished eating. Christie began to feel a little unnerved. What was he thinking? She tried to look back at him with calmness, but the intensity of his gaze made her heartbeat quicken treacherously. His eyes were like dark topaz. Suddenly Christie felt the way she had the first time she'd gone white-water rafting—exhilarated, frightened, swirling into the unknown. She held on to the edge of the table. The pine trees outside the window blocked the waning sun, and twilight deepened in the room. Matt's face was cast in shadow, making him seem more enigmatic than before. Tension thrummed between them. He reached across the table, and for a breathless moment she thought he was going to touch her. Instead he took her plate and stacked it with his own. He stood up and carried the plates to the sink. Christie watched him, unwillingly drawn by everything he did. He was a man of natural yet restrained gallantry. He placed the china plates in the sink with care, obviously realizing they were important to her.

Christie rose from her chair and randomly grabbed the bowl of jelly. She held on to it, not quite sure what she was going to do next, for Matt had come back to stand in front of her. She stared at the rich brown plaid of his shirt.

"Christie," he murmured experimentally, as if he had just discovered something new about her name and wanted to test the way it sounded on his tongue. He moved a step closer to her. She grasped the jelly bowl with both hands, holding it in front of her as a defense. But that didn't stop Matt from stepping even closer.

"Christie," he murmured again. It was a soft but inexorable command and she raised her eyes to his. Now her pulse had slowed to a thick, languorous beat of expectancy. She stood motionless in the hushed twilight, all her senses stilled and waiting. Then, very slowly, Matt bent his head and kissed her.

CHAPTER THREE

IT WAS A GENTLE KISS, like the touch of a silken whisper. Matt's lips brushed over Christie's softly, without demanding any response from her. Yet she did respond, her mouth pliant under his. Warm sensation flooded through her, as if Matt were a source of heat and light. His hands reached up to cup her face, caressing her as gently as his lips. His thumb stroked her cheek, tantalizing her with more of this tender delight. Christie sighed against his mouth and felt him smile even as he kissed her. Then he stepped back.

For a moment she kept her eyes closed, feeling oddly bereft. Gradually she became aware of the jelly bowl she was clutching. She opened her eyes and set it back on the table with a little clatter.

Matt's features were completely masked now by the velvet shadows of dusk, but somehow she knew that a smile still curved his lips.

"Thanks for dinner, Christie," he said, a husky laughter in his voice. He went out through the swinging door of the kitchen. Suddenly he seemed to be in a very good mood.

Christie stood where he'd left her, wanting to make a vigorous protest of some sort. But she didn't know what her complaint would be. Was she upset because

Matt had kissed her in the first place—or because he had stopped kissing her?

"I don't believe this!" she said to herself. She strode over to the wall and flipped on the light switch. The glare from the overhead bulb was too bright, too garish. She blinked like someone waking from a luxurious dream. The taste of Matt still lingered on her mouth, like wine....

"No!" Christie exclaimed. She plunked herself down at the table again, rubbing her temples as if to erase the memory of Matt's kiss. But the method didn't seem to be working. Something inside her had kindled at Matt's brief, elusive touch, something she'd never experienced before.

She didn't understand it. Oren had never made her feel this way, as if golden sunshine had sparked a flame deep inside her.

Christie drew a shaky breath. She didn't want a romantic involvement, especially not with a man like Matt Gallagher. She refused to tolerate any more overbearing stockbrokers! And yet she couldn't deny the new emotions stirring inside her just from that one touch of his lips.

"Blast you, Matt Gallagher," she said, thumping her hand down on the table for emphasis. "Just . . . blast you!"

EARLY NEXT MORNING eight little boys and girls swarmed through Christie's house, yelling and brandishing plywood swords. Christie leaned over the stair banister, trying to establish order.

"Stephanie!" she called in a reasonable tone. "Give Jason's sword back to him so you can both go home.

And don't forget, you're supposed to be a medieval lady, not a medieval knight. Get into your character! You want our pageant to be a resounding success, don't you?''

Stephanie wasn't listening. She had straddled Jason and was skewering him with the sword. He delivered an impressive death scene, arms and legs sprawled out and twitching violently. But the next moment he wormed his way out of her clutches and ran whooping down the hallway. Stephanie raced after him and they both catapulted out onto the front porch.

Christie descended the stairs and hurried to the back of the house, searching for more errant knights as she went. She stopped in the doorway of the breakfast room, dismayed at the sight that greeted her. Plates of half-eaten waffles were strewn across the table, and there was a puddle of maple syrup on the floor. It seemed her knights in shining armor had turned into an invading horde, leaving destruction in their wake.

Mr. and Mrs. Fanshaw, Christie's other two guests at the moment, were already in the room and surveying the mess.

"We came down for breakfast," Mr. Fanshaw said nervously, "and we found *this*."

"We also heard and saw children," Mrs. Fanshaw added. "Several of them. Miss Daniels, you never said anything about children being on the premises." She held on to her husband as if she'd discovered the presence of outer-space aliens in the house.

Christie smiled brightly. "It's only a temporary circumstance, I assure you. I can explain all about it—"

"No, thank you," Mr. Fanshaw interrupted. "We'll eat breakfast out this morning." He hauled his wife away, both of them glancing around in alarm as they made their escape.

Christie groaned. She took some napkins and bent down to mop the floor. Her hair fell forward and the ends dangled in the syrup. Just as she was wondering what could happen next, Matt strode into the room with a baleful expression on his face. A Siamese cat stalked behind him, tail waving high and blue eyes very round and guileless. Christie sat down on the floor and tried to wipe the maple syrup out of her hair.

"Good morning, Matt," she said. "I see you ran into Vincent."

Matt glared at the cat. "I woke up and found the darn thing chewing on my toes. It's been following me around ever since."

"Well," Christie said, "you must have good toes."

He gave her an acid look. "And then there was the screeching."

Christie glanced at Vincent in concern, watching him lap up the maple syrup. "I've never heard him screech before. Yowl, maybe. But he seems fine now."

"It wasn't the cat making all that noise," Matt said irritably. "It was a child wearing two towels stapled together. He said his name was Sir Dunsmore and he was looking for dragons."

Christie gazed at Matt's jean-clad legs from her vantage point on the floor. The denim was beginning to look a little more relaxed as it conformed to the muscular lines of his body. The man had great legs.

She scrambled to her feet, brushing off her own jeans. Today she was wearing a long-sleeved miner's undershirt in bright red, and her belt with the over-size silver buckle shaped like a bucking horse. She hooked her thumbs through her belt loops, watching as Vincent strolled over and rubbed his whiskers happily against Matt's leg.

"Can't you control this animal?" Matt demanded.

She lifted her shoulders. "Vincent is always curious about new guests. But he's discriminating, too. He seems to like you, and that's quite an honor."

"I hate cats," Matt stated bluntly.

Christie gazed at him in disapproval. "No wonder you have ulcers. You don't know how to relax and enjoy the right things in life. I mean, you can't even appreciate a good cat when you see one."

"I don't have any ulcers. Would you stop trying to analyze my stomach?" He poked at a limp piece of waffle that looked as if it had been flung across the room like a Frisbee. Meanwhile Vincent plopped down and stuck all four of his black paws in the air. It would have taken a hardened soul indeed not to reach down and rub the furry white stomach thus exposed. Matt, however, seemed completely unmoved. After a moment Vincent rolled himself right-side up again and began showing interest in the table of food. He crouched down into position for a spring, but Christie faced him squarely.

"Don't even think about it, Vincent," she warned. "I've had enough sabotage with my waffles already."

He tried to stare her down, but Christie remained adamant. Looking affronted, Vincent twitched his tail and bounded out of the room.

Christie turned back to Matt, and then found she couldn't look away from him. She liked the way his hair curled over his forehead, as if in rebellion at brush or comb. Something tightened inside Christie and she remembered how it felt to kiss him. She bit down hard on her lip, trying to fight his appeal. She fortified herself with the knowledge that he hated cats. How could she ever be seriously interested in a cat-hater?

She went to the big mahogany sideboard and found some waffles that hadn't been desecrated. She brought them to the table for Matt and herself. "Maybe all the knights have gone home by now," she remarked. "I don't hear any more strange sounds—do you?"

Matt sat down and poured a generous dollop of syrup on his waffles. His fingers came away stickily from the syrup pitcher and he frowned down at it. "I even hate to ask why Sir Dunsmore and his cohorts were filling the bathtub with water and laundry soap."

"Oh, no!" Christie exclaimed in horror. She started bolting for the door, but Matt's voice stopped her.

"Don't worry," he said. "I drained the tub and suggested that everyone under five feet tall should leave the house. You have a few suds floating around, that's all."

Christie slid onto a chair across from him, feeling relieved. "I think the children's pageant is going to work out just fine in the end. I'm co-chairman of the Red River Medieval Fair Days. We have some wonderful things planned. Madrigal singers, dancing, food booths—and of course the pageant. We're building a special stage for it."

Matt looked baffled. "How the heck did you get involved in all that? You've only been here a few months."

"I'm already part of the community," Christie said proudly. "It was Evelyn Tucker who got me involved in Medieval Fair Days. She's a member of my book discussion group that meets on Thursday nights, and of course we're both members of the Volunteer Fire Brigade."

Humor glinted in Matt's eyes. "What else do you do in your spare time?" he asked.

Christie picked up the honey jar shaped like a Japanese pagoda and held it high above her plate of waffles. She let the honey trickle down in a long, continuous bead as she contemplated her response. "I play on the town softball team, I'm a volunteer at the library, I'm a member of the fund-raising committee for the new museum...let's see, what else?" She glanced down at the big round pin on her shirt that urged Join the Red River Ramblers. "Oh, yes. I've just organized the Ramblers. That's a hiking club for people over sixty years old. Pretty good idea, don't you think? I even got Beth Larson to join, and she's seventy-three."

Matt began chuckling as she spoke. It was the deep, rich sound of subterranean laughter that hadn't worked its way to the surface yet.

"What's so funny?" she demanded.

His face was solemn now, but laughter still shimmered in his eyes. "You may have left New York City behind, but you brought the rat race right along with you. Your schedule sounds even worse than mine."

"It's not the same thing at all," she protested. "I used to have endless meetings with clients and I spent most of my life glued to the phone! I participate in much more fulfilling activities now—"

"Right. You go to committee and club meetings. That's a lot different than client meetings."

"Well, it is," she insisted. "The goals I have now make sense. I'm achieving a whole new kind of success, the kind that can be measured in human terms instead of dollar signs!"

Matt didn't seem impressed and went on eating. "Lord, you sound just like your father," he said. "Always talking about goals, achievement and success."

Christie felt stung by his words. She didn't want to be like her father—not anymore. Turning, she stared out the French windows at the row of hollyhocks rising tall along the back fence. In New York she'd never had a garden, just a few sickly geraniums in pots. Everything about her life had changed!

"Seems like I touched a nerve," Matt commented. "What did I say that upset you so much?"

Christie went on gazing out the window. "You don't understand," she said after a long moment. "When I was born, I was supposed to be a boy, Christopher Daniels the Fourth. I committed the sin of turning out to be Mary Christine Daniels, instead...but I tried to make it up to my father. I played soccer and baseball in school, and one year I even tried out for the football team." She gave a mirthless smile. "The coach said I would've made a great running back, but even my father objected to the idea of all those hefty high-school boys tackling me."

Matt pushed his plate away so he could rest his arms on the table. One of his elbows landed right in a puddle of syrup. He grimaced, but went on studying Christie.

There was a big vase of zinnias in the center of the table. She pulled it toward her and began rearranging the flowers with a vengeance. "You know what it's like trying to please my father, Matt? I went to college and majored in economics because that was what he wanted me to do. I struggled to graduate in three years instead of four, just so he'd be proud of me. And all he could say was that my grade average should've been higher." Christie shoved a yellow zinnia into the vase with such force she scraped off some of its leaves.

Matt pried his elbow out of the syrup. "Okay, so your father doesn't exactly pour on the praise. But he's like that with everyone. Heck, he's like that with me. Come to think of it, he never said anything about those two new clients I landed last week. But I don't let things like that bother me—why should you? Just go back to New York and straighten things out with him. Then I can get on with my life and so can you, damn it."

"You just won't quit, will you? I already told you—no way am I going back to New York!" She jumped up and started piling dishes on top of each other. Then she pushed her way through the swinging door into the kitchen. She cleaned off the plates furiously and put them in the sink, hoping that Matt would just leave her alone. But when she tried to go back to the breakfast room for more dirty dishes, she found the door blocked. She pushed against it yet it still wouldn't budge.

"Hey, what's going on?" she asked grouchily.

"Let me through," came Matt's voice. He pushed at the door from the other side, but Christie held firm to her own position. She pressed her hands against the door, leaning her weight forward.

"Matt, go out and do some sightseeing," she suggested. "It'll be good for you to breathe some fresh air and clear that city smog out of your brain."

"I think I'm going to drop the syrup," his voice answered.

Christie stepped back quickly and allowed Matt to come charging through. He was balancing the rest of the plates, with the syrup pitcher dangling precariously from one finger. He managed to deposit everything safely on the counter. Grabbing the dish sponge, he started washing the plates already in the sink.

"I can take care of this," she declared, elbowing him aside. "Just leave, Matt!"

"I thought women liked men who did domestic chores," he remarked, holding the sponge out to his side where her groping fingers couldn't reach it.

"You're not earning any points with me." Christie ducked around him and dived for the sponge. He tossed it easily into his other hand, thwarting her. She bumped against him, taking in his scent of fresh pine after-shave. He smelled as good as a forest breeze in the New Mexico mountains. When he grinned at her, his eyes were full of their own golden-brown light. Christie backed away from him, deciding that retreat was the wisest course of action.

Matt squirted half the bottle of dish-washing liquid onto his sponge. He seemed to be enjoying himself, humming tunelessly under his breath. Christie watched the muscles of his back move under his cotton shirt as he worked at the sink. Wrenching her gaze away from him, she marched to the counter and started scraping the rest of the plates clean.

"You know, both you and your father could use a good kick in the rear," Matt said. "I listen to him talk, and then I listen to you. I feel like I'm getting two halves of the same story, but they don't match each other."

Christie paused as she wiped off the top of the waffle iron. "Exactly how much has my father told you?" she demanded. "He's not usually talkative about family matters."

"He talks plenty to me. Maybe he's never praised you directly, Christie, but with me he can't seem to say enough good things about you. That should count for something. He keeps telling me how wonderful you are—that you're warm, smart, witty and beautiful." Matt offered the catalog of her virtues in a business-like manner, as if listing the Dow Jones averages for the day. Christie wasn't carried away by this dazzling description of herself. A horrible realization was dawning on her, and she crumpled the paper towel she'd been using.

"He's doing it again," she said, her voice shaking with anger. "Once wasn't enough for him. He's doing it all over again!"

Matt turned from the sink, eyeing her with curiosity. "What are you talking about, Christie?"

She drew a deep breath. "I already told you how my father tried to set me up with Oren Peters. That didn't go as he planned, so now he has another plot. He's trying to set me up with *you*." She jabbed an incriminating finger toward Matt.

He laughed, his expression incredulous. "You're really paranoid, Christie. You make your father sound like some sort of crazed marriage broker."

"Maybe he's missed his calling," she snapped. She folded her arms against her body as she confronted Matt. "It all adds up, if you'd just look at the evidence. My father telling you all those glorious things about me, then sending you here to lure me back to New York. He could've just as well sent Terence Bainbridge, who's like my own grandfather. But no, he chose you for the mission. That's very significant. And then there's the way you kissed me last night!"

Matt wiped his soapy hands on a dish towel. "What does our kiss have to do with anything?" he asked, his brow furrowing.

"You must have known all along what my father was up to," she accused recklessly. "It would suit your purposes, wouldn't it? If I fell in love with you, think how much easier it would be to get me back to New York. I'd go to work for my father again, he wouldn't sell the business and all your problems would be neatly solved."

She saw instantly that she'd gone too far. The look on Matt's face was thunderous, his eyes turning as hard as agate. But when he spoke, his voice was surprisingly controlled and tinged with only a hint of mockery.

"You're really amazing, Christie. You've just taken a nice, innocent kiss and turned it into something warped. You can't see that your bitterness about your father is distorting everything you think. Lord, I feel sorry for you." He threw down the dish towel in a gesture of disgust and walked to the door. He pushed at it with such force that it continued to swing on its hinges a long time after he was gone.

Christie hugged her arms even more tightly against her body. She felt empty inside, as if she'd forfeited a valuable possession. The sweet memory of Matt's kiss . . . yes, it was tainted now by her own suspicions. Oren had courted her for the promise of more power in the company. But was she right to suspect Matt of a similar crime?

Christie took a deep, shaky breath. All her instincts told her that Matt Gallagher was a man of integrity. She didn't really believe he was like Oren Peters. But even if Matt hadn't conspired in the scheme, Christie felt sure her father was trying to engineer another romance for her. She knew him too well; it was exactly the sort of move he would make, a calculated attempt to keep his power over her.

She went to the sink and twisted the tap. Hot water gushed over the sudsy plates, some of it spraying up to scald her fingers. Oh, her father was brilliant! After all those years he knew exactly what sort of man would attract her, and he couldn't have picked a better choice than Matt Gallagher. She made a strangled sound that was half laugh, half sob and turned the water on even harder.

Lisa Barrera came wandering into the kitchen. As usual, Lisa's head was buried deep in a book, her dark curls bobbing forward into her face. Without glancing up, she skirted the counter, sidestepped Christie at the sink, pulled out a chair and sank down gracefully at the table.

"Good morning," she murmured, turning a page. Lisa never looked where she was going, and yet not once had Christie ever seen her stumble or bump into anything. Lisa was a high-school student who had worked part-time at the bed and breakfast since its grand opening.

"There was a gorgeous male standing in the hall when I came in," she said, turning another page. "He looked slightly discombobulated, like he'd wandered into the house by mistake. But he went up the stairs, so I suppose he belongs here. He has the most unusual shade of rust-brown hair. Not quite red, but almost."

Christie started rinsing the plates, splashing even more hot water on herself. "He's tolerably goodlooking," she allowed. "But his hair *is* actually red. It's dark, of course, but definitely still red."

"I can't agree with you," Lisa said, propping her chin in her hand and leaning even closer to her book. "He has brown hair, with undertones of red. And 'gorgeous' is the only word to describe him. 'Goodlooking' is too mild a term, and so is 'handsome.' 'Comely' is not only outdated, but in this case an inappropriate modifier—"

"Lisa," Christie protested, "enough!" It was impressive how much sensory data Lisa managed to absorb, even with her head stuck in a book. She probably knew exactly how many freckles were scattered across the bridge of Matt Gallagher's nose.

Christie didn't want to think about Matt's freckles. She turned off the water. "Lisa, do me a favor," she said urgently. "Take over for the rest of the day. I have to get out of here, that's all. I'm going up into the mountains."

"No problem." Lisa turned another page calmly. Christie wished she could share some of Lisa's placidity. Just knowing Matt was in the same house filled her with a frantic sort of anxiety. Surely up in the peacefulness and solitude of the mountains she'd be able to sort out her emotions. She yanked open the refrigerator door and grabbed some hard-boiled eggs. Next she pulled out a jar of homemade mayonnaise, and soon had some egg salad piled onto slices of her cracked-wheat bread. She wrapped up the sandwiches and dragged her ice chest from one of the pantry shelves.

"Lisa, please run down to Carl's for a bag of ice and a couple of lime sodas. And if you see the aforementioned gorgeous male anywhere, don't tell him what my plans are. I just want to slip out of here without having to talk to him."

This, finally, was enough to bring Lisa out of her book. She glanced up for the first time, her dark eyes blinking with interest. "There's something going on between the two of you," she deduced. "I wondered why you were so charged with excitement, Chris. You'll note that I used a term that brings electricity to mind. You're rushing around, crackling with emotional static—"

"Lisa," Christie said firmly, throwing some fruit into the ice chest, "just go down to Carl's."

Lisa closed her book with obvious reluctance, but accomplished the errand with her usual efficiency. Only a short while later Christie had the ice chest loaded in her old Land Rover. She clambered into the driver's seat, eager to make her escape.

"Running away again?" Matt's deep voice inquired at the open window.

Christie gripped the steering wheel, staring straight ahead. "I'm not running away, damn it. I'm going about my own business."

"Maybe so. But it seems to me you have a habit of running away when things get bad." Matt propped an elbow in her window frame and leaned casually against the Land Rover.

Christie's hands tightened on the steering wheel until her knuckles turned white. She twisted her head to glare at Matt. He was wearing a Boston Red Sox hat so new that it hadn't yet conformed to the shape of his head. It perched awkwardly on top of him, like a bird unsure of its roost. For some reason Christie's resentment toward him began to deflate. She tried to recapture it.

"No matter what you think about me, Matt Gallagher, I'm going to spend the day enjoying myself—on my own. I've had enough of you badgering me."

"Your friend Lisa says you're going for a mountain drive and you'd be glad to have me come along."

"You were misinformed." Christie made a mental note to initiate a serious discussion with Lisa about the importance of loyalty to one's employer.

"We still have a lot to talk over, Christie. This seems like a perfect opportunity." The next moment he'd gone around to the passenger side and climbed in beside her. He stretched his long legs out comfortably. "I'm ready whenever you are."

Christie wanted to howl in frustration. Matt was her adversary, sent directly from her father. He'd been poking and prodding at her relentlessly, trying to wear down her resistance. But his presence alone was enough to weaken her defenses—just to have him sitting here beside her, masculine and vibrant.

She drummed her fingers against the steering wheel. Matt infuriated her, but he also made the blood thrill warmly in her veins. Christie looked over at him and saw the engaging grin on his face. She tried to calculate how long a stick she would need to pry Matt Gallagher from the Land Rover.

"You said I needed to go do some sightseeing," he reminded her. "Here's my chance."

"Oh, what the heck," she gave in crabbily. Without saying another word, Christie turned the key in the ignition and revved the engine. She didn't look at Matt. But a moment later the Land Rover clattered down the gravel drive and headed with both of them toward the mountains.

CHAPTER FOUR

THE LAND ROVER JOUNCED over a narrow dirt road that wound its way higher and higher into the forest. Spruce and pine trees loomed overhead, casting mysterious, deep green shadows. Aspens stood out in contrast, their slender, ivory-white trunks rising like flagpoles. Christie expertly skirted a boulder that had tumbled into the middle of the road, the steering wheel twisting under her hands. Sometimes the Rover behaved like a stubborn, high-spirited mule, and had to be shown who was boss. She gave the wheel another good crank, using such force that Matt lurched sideways. He anchored his arm more firmly in the window.

"You should be a New York taxicab driver," he observed. "You'd be great at the job."

"No more city streets for me," Christie declared, "under any circumstances. All those traffic jams, and drivers snarling at each other. No, thank you! I learned to drive on country roads, when I was in college and finally away from the city for a while. That set the tone for me. Someday I want to compete in one of those rally races they have down in Baja California—nothing but me and my car for miles and miles of desert." She took the Rover jostling over the rut-

ted road, and Matt's body bounced in a corresponding rhythm. He pushed up the brim of his hat.

"I see you're already practicing for the race," he
remarked, gripping the top of the window frame to
keep from flying out of his seat.

Christie paid no attention to his sarcasm as she
pressed down on the accelerator to send the Rover
surging forward. Pebbles churned under the wheels
and sprayed out to the sides. A breeze whipped Christie's hair back in a tangled stream. She felt suddenly
lighthearted and carefree, as if she were a falcon soar-
ing on the mountain wind. She hoped it was only the
loveliness of the day—and not Matt's nearness—that
was making her experience these sensations.

He shook his head as she exuberantly dodged another boulder in the road. "I'm not too sure about the
way you drive," he commented, "but this vehicle of
yours is really something. It's built like a tank."

Christie put her hand on the gearshift knob and felt
the good, strong thrum of the engine vibrating into her
fingers. She smiled. "I never owned any kind of car in
New York. But here you can't survive without one—
forget taxicabs and subways! So I told myself I'd buy
a sports car, the way I'd always dreamed. Then one
day I saw this old Land Rover sitting under a pine tree
in someone's front yard, with a raggedy For Sale sign
taped to the windshield. There was grass growing up
around the tires, and it looked like it hadn't been
moved in years. All my common sense told me I'd be
foolish to buy it . . . so I kept going to the dealerships
in Santa Fe, looking for a sports car. But I couldn't
forget this old thing, no matter how hard I tried. It just

wasn't ready to be put out to pasture yet." She reached forward and patted the dashboard.

"Let me guess," Matt said. "There was just something 'magical' about this old Land Rover."

"Why, how did you know? That's exactly right! It had a lucky horseshoe fastened onto the front grill, and that's why I ended up buying it."

"You actually bought a car because it came with a horseshoe?"

"Well, after all," she said defensively, "the owner told me the shoe once belonged to a mare named Primrose."

"What does that have to do with anything?" Matt demanded.

"Primrose was an animal with high standards of excellence. She would only eat candy bars if they were made of both chocolate *and* caramel."

Matt rubbed his square, pugnacious jaw. "Trying to follow your logic, Christie, is like trying to figure out what makes the stock market go up and down."

Christie settled back against the cracked upholstery of her seat, shifting down into first gear as the road took a sharp rise. "Oh, everyone's got a system for figuring out the market," she said with a grin. "And everybody thinks everybody else's system is wrong. I bet Oren is still scurrying around the office, waving those mysterious charts of his and arguing with himself about up ticks versus down ticks."

"That's Oren, all right," Matt agreed wryly. "Every day he's convinced he's on the verge of a major breakthrough that will turn him and all his customers into millionaires. The secret is somewhere in his charts, he says. He pores over those damn things like an astrologer searching for signs of the future.''

Christie and Matt didn't speak for several moments. Matt seemed lost in his own thoughts, his fingers tapping an impatient tattoo on his knee. Christie felt a tension she couldn't define. She frowned as she gazed through the dusty windshield.

''Christie, were you in love with Oren Peters?'' Matt asked abruptly, breaking the silence. He sounded gruff. She was startled by his question, but found that she didn't want him to have any misunderstandings on the subject of Oren.

''No, I never loved him,'' she said. ''I *thought* I did for a little while—Oren knows how to be charming when he puts his mind to it. But I was just letting myself get swept away by my father, as usual. He kept telling me how happy he was about our engagement.'' Christie glanced sharply at Matt. ''That sort of thing will never happen to me again, I promise you!''

Matt scowled over at her. ''Do you honestly think I'm part of some deranged plot with your father? Good Lord, the last thing I need is to have you fall in love with me, Christie. For that matter, the last thing I need is to fall in love with *you*.'' His tone was blunt and unequivocal. At least he couldn't be accused of flattery, Christie thought dourly.

''All right, so I don't think you'd connive with my father in his matchmaking schemes. But you were sent here by him, and that's enough of a strike against you. You're on his side.''

''Damn it, I'm not taking sides, can't you see that? I'm just trying to straighten out my own life.''

Christie decided that Matt Gallagher was a very contrary sort of person. He made her feel contrary herself, and thoroughly unsettled. One minute she wanted to run her fingers through his hair to see if it felt as silky as it looked; the next minute she simply wanted to slap him over the head with his baseball cap.

The road narrowed until it was barely more than a track. The trees were so close now that their branches scratched against the sides of the Rover and poked their way through the windows like grasping fingers. Christie pushed on another mile or so and then stopped. Shutting off the engine, she swung open the door and slid to the ground. Her muscles were cramped and it felt good to stretch. After a moment she pulled a map out of her back pocket, spreading it flat on the hood of the Rover so she could study it.

Matt was tramping around, twigs crackling under his hiking boots, but he came to look over her shoulder at the crude map.

"What the devil is that?" he asked.

"Exactly what it looks like. I want to check out some property. That's why I'm up here."

Matt peered closer. "'Big Shelby's Gold Mine,'" he read from the scrawled handwriting. Then he laughed. "You've got to be kidding. You're looking for a gold mine?"

His derisive tone rankled Christie. Also, she found it difficult to concentrate with him standing right behind her like this. His arm brushed against hers, a contact that seemed intimate even though she knew it was accidental.

She cleared her throat forcefully. "I'm not looking for just *any* gold mine," she told him. "I've already traveled to a lot of the old, abandoned mines in these mountains, and none of them have met my qualifications. I'm looking for something..." she hesitated, then finished her sentence. "I'm looking for something magical, and I don't care what you think about that, Matt Gallagher." She refolded the map and tucked it back into her pocket. As she turned to face him, her chin tilted defiantly.

He gazed down at her, his eyes on her mouth. She moistened her lips, realizing that he was still standing very close. The expression on his face was unreadable, his eyes shadowed by the brim of his hat. But he bent his head toward her in a way that seemed wholly natural. Just as naturally Christie lifted her own head a bit more, no longer in defiance but to facilitate the meeting of their lips.

He kissed her matter-of-factly, his mouth cool and firm. Christie leaned toward him, her hands splayed across his chest. Even when their lips broke apart she remained supported against him, breathing unevenly. His own hands loosely clasped her waist.

"Treasure maps and gold mines..." he murmured. "You're as bad as Oren, chasing those fantasies of his. But at least your treasure map is more interesting than his graphs and charts."

"I'm not like Oren in the least," Christie returned. "All he wants is a lot of money and power." She stared at her hands on the crisp blue cotton of Matt's shirt. Even spread out like this, her fingers couldn't span the breadth of his chest. His body seemed as strong and solid as the tree trunks rising up around her.

"And what do you want, Christie?" he asked softly. "What hidden treasure are you hoping to find?" His hands were warm and steady on her waist.

Christie breathed in a scent of pine and didn't know if it came from the forest around her, or from Matt. She leaned just a little closer, needing to explain her feelings so he'd understand them. "I came to Red River to find something I lost a long time ago," she said in a low voice. "That summer I came here with my aunt . . . everything was so wonderful. Aunt Sarah was my best friend, someone who accepted me exactly the way I was. She fell in love while we were out here, with a man who seemed perfect for her. Somehow they both managed it so I didn't feel left out. The three of us went hiking and camping together, looking for old gold mines. It was like having a real family for once."

Matt studied her with a critical expression. "I get it. You're trying to recreate that summer, aren't you? Hunting for gold mines, that sort of thing. And since your aunt found a man in Red River, you're probably looking for one here yourself. Hmmph," he finished on a note of sour disapproval.

Christie blushed angrily. She didn't like Matt thinking he could dissect her life so neatly. And how could he hold her like this without showing any reaction at all? His chest rose and fell evenly under her hands, while her own heart was pounding out of tempo just at his touch. She pulled away from him, freeing herself.

"I'm not naive, the way you make me sound," she declared. "Yes, I did come back to Red River because of that one summer. I knew I could be happy here. And, yes—I'm rediscovering the pleasure of exploring for old mines. But you're dead wrong about one thing, Matt Gallagher! I'm not looking for any man at all.'' She strode away from him, to the other side of the Land Rover.

Matt strolled around to the front grill and examined Primrose's lucky horseshoe, still fastened there with bits of rusty wire. "Might as well admit it, Christie. You're too damn romantic about life. Otherwise you would've thrown away this horseshoe a long time ago. You'll probably fall for some jerk of a guy out here just because he'll know all the right things to say to you—things about magic and the rest of that nonsense you believe in." Matt sounded almost jealous. And he scowled off into the distance, as if he expected some mythical cowboy to gallop up this very minute and start sweet-talking away at Christie.

She reached down and grabbed a stick, snapping it in two. "I'm a realist," she said fiercely. "Maybe that summer I believed in romance. I was fourteen, and Aunt Sarah seemed so happy with the love she'd found. But you know what? They got married and everything changed. They live in Wisconsin now, bickering and fighting so much I can hardly bear to visit them." She tossed away the two pieces of stick. "I saw what happened to Aunt Sarah, I saw what happened to my own parents. And the travesty with Oren didn't exactly show me the secret of true love!"

Matt looked her over with a skeptical expression. "You sure seem fired up for someone who doesn't care about love."

"Well, what about *you?*" she challenged. "You know, maybe you're not such a cynic, either. Maybe there's some woman in New York who makes you do all kinds of crazy things in spite of yourself."

"Hell, no," he said, looking disgruntled. And that was all he had to offer. Christie kicked the right-front tire of the Land Rover. She was absurdly happy that Matt didn't seem to be involved with a woman. It took effort to remind herself that this subject shouldn't be any concern of hers.

She went to pull open the back door of the Rover and hauled out her ice chest. "I'm hungry," she announced. "It's lunchtime." She paid no attention to the fact that noon was still some hours away. Being around Matt seemed to disturb all her normal eating habits.

He took the ice chest from her and set it under a tree. Together they settled down next to it. Christie passed Matt a sandwich and a lime soda.

"If I'd known you were coming with me, I would've made a lot bigger lunch," she said. Christie was developing serious urges to prepare extravagant, gourmet meals for Matt. This was most disturbing, but still she wanted to ply him with heaps of her very own spaghetti a la Gorgonzola, any number of cheese blintzes and thick slices of her superdeluxe carrot cake. What was happening to her?

Matt polished off his sandwich and nodded in appreciation. "You're a darn good cook. Even your egg salad tastes better than anyone else's." He settled back against the trunk of the pine, stretching out his long legs and pulling down the brim of his hat. "This is all right," he murmured, giving an expansive yawn. "This isn't bad at all...."

Christie couldn't see his eyes under the brim of his hat; it was only after a few moments of listening to his steady breathing that she realized he was fast asleep. She sat cross-legged on the damp ground of the forest, eating her sandwich and watching Matt.

His hands rested on his stomach, balancing between them the bottle of lime soda. His mouth had opened slightly, and a gentle snore issued from it. He looked so at ease, so relaxed, as if all the tension had flowed out of him. Christie wished she could put her head in his lap and stretch her own legs out. That sounded like a very agreeable thing to do.

She gripped her hands on her knees to keep herself from crawling over and nestling up against Matt. But she went on gazing at him. The sinews of his arms were lean yet well developed; he probably worked out at a Manhattan gym somewhere, when his busy schedule gave him the chance. All the lines of his body were drawn with strength and boldness, but here and there Christie discerned whimsical details about him—angles that were unexpectedly softened. His earlobes, for instance, looked vulnerable as they poked out from under his hat. And there was something about his elbows...they stuck out awkwardly from his shirtsleeves, as if they didn't know quite what to do with themselves away from the confines of a suit jacket.

Christie wanted to lift off his hat and kiss him. Matt Gallagher made her feel the same way she did whenever there was chocolate fudge in the house. She kept nibbling on the fudge, taking just one more taste even though she knew she'd already eaten far too much. With Matt she craved one more glance from his hazel eyes, one more caress from his gentle hands. He would be leaving on Monday. Could it really hurt to give in and savor one little kiss....

She dug her nails into her palms until she felt pain. No, she would *not* give in. Matt was far more hazardous to her health than an entire pan of chocolate fudge!

He stirred in his sleep, mumbling something under his breath that sounded like "sell, damn it, sell." As he shifted position, his almost-full bottle of lime soda took a dangerous tilt to the right. It was anchored precariously by his slack fingers, but any moment it threatened to go toppling over. Christie leaned forward, glad to have something to concentrate on besides Matt. She watched the bottle as it listed sideways a bit, and then just a bit more.

Christie scrambled toward Matt on her knees, catching hold of the bottle just before it capsized. Matt came awake with a start, struggling upright.

"What the devil!" he exclaimed, knocking off his hat with a flailing arm. The arm almost swatted Christie and she ducked. But she was still leaning over Matt on her knees, her gaze centered on his mouth as she clutched the soda bottle. He had such an expressive mouth, wide and mobile. Right now it was twisted, denoting some sort of perturbation, yet even so it looked appealing. If Christie were to bend over just another inch or two, a kiss would be inevitable...

She resisted the temptation valiantly, jerking herself away from him. She landed on her seat with an ungainly thump, sloshing lime soda on her jeans.

Matt stared at her. "Why did you let me fall asleep?" he demanded.

"You seemed like you needed a good nap."

He dug into his pocket, took out his watch and frowned at it. "Good Lord, it's not even ten-thirty in the morning. I've never taken a nap at this time. In fact, I've never taken a nap at all!"

"There's always a first time for everything," Christie pointed out.

"I really must be slipping," he muttered, cramming the watch back into his pocket. "Being out here in the middle of the woods—that's the problem. Usually I spend Saturday at the office."

"That's truly pathetic. Think of everything you miss when you're shut away in that place, fifty stories above street level." Christie picked up Matt's baseball cap and started molding the brim into a better shape. "I mean, think about it, Matt. On Saturday everyone else is out having fun in Central Park, and you're sitting in a little office without any windows, studying economic reports."

"My office has plenty of windows," he said.

"Oh?" Christie paused. "You're not in my old office, the one squeezed in behind Terence's?"

"No, I have that big corner one. Used to be a conference room, I think."

Christie squashed the hat brim between her hands. Blast it, she'd always wanted that corner office, with windows along two whole walls so at least a person didn't feel trapped. Her father had insisted it remain a conference room. Why should Matt Gallagher be able to waltz into Daniels, et al. and get windows from her father just like that?

Her resentment flared. She didn't know if it was directed at her father, or Matt, or both of them put together. Why did she care what happened at Daniels, Peters, Bainbridge and Gallagher? She was well rid of the place!

Christie shoved the baseball cap at Matt. When he put it on his head, she saw that she'd been too vigorous with the brim, bending it so it looked oddly lopsided. She glared at Matt as if it was all his fault.

He pressed the cap further down on his head. "I didn't come up here to take naps and pass the time of day. We're going to talk about you coming back to New York on Monday, Christie. You don't have much time to get ready, and we need to rehearse what you'll tell your father."

"Rehearse?" she echoed in disbelief. "What are you supposed to be, my coach?"

"It's become obvious to me that you can't just walk into your father's office without some advance preparation. You're much too emotional about him—you need someone who can help you separate feelings from facts before you confront him."

Christie opened and closed her mouth like an enraged fish. "This is getting worse and worse," she exclaimed at last. "Forget it, Matt. I'm not going back to New York with you. But I'll tell you one thing. If and when I ever confront my father, you can be darn sure *you* won't be part of the deal." She grabbed the remains of their lunch and hauled the ice chest back to the Land Rover.

Matt followed her inexorably. "We have to talk about this, Christie—"

"No," she stated. "We don't have to talk about anything. I'm going to look for my gold mine right now. You can come with me, or stay here as you please." She took her hat from the back of the Rover. It was old-fashioned, made out of straw with an enormous, floppy brim. Whenever Christie wore it she felt like she'd traveled back in time to become a Victorian lady. Usually she enjoyed the sensation, imagining herself in a hoop skirt as well, but today she merely jammed the hat on her head and strode off through the trees. The hat's long blue ribbons waved out behind her.

Matt clumped along after her. "How can you tell where you're going?" he asked.

"I looked at the map, that's how."

"Doesn't seem good enough to me. We're not even following a path."

"Yes, we are," Christie asserted. "You just have to know how to see it."

"There isn't any path here."

"Yes, there is!"

"Where?"

Christie brought herself up short and Matt collided with her. His arms came around her as she was about to go toppling over. His hold on her was sure and strong—and just as beguiling as it had been yesterday, after he'd saved her life. She struggled away before she could succumb to his touch.

Reaching into her back pocket, she pulled out the map and slapped it into Matt's hand. "There. You read it and see for yourself."

He unfolded the wrinkled sheet of paper and frowned. "Looks like a three-year-old drew this," he complained. "How the heck can you tell anything from it?" He turned it upside down, studied it for a moment, and then turned it right side up again. "Where did you get this, anyway?"

She blew out her breath in exasperation and plucked the map from his hand. "If you must know, the real-estate woman gave it to me. It's a copy of the original map drawn by Big Shelby himself. He's the one who staked a claim to the mine back in the 1890s. Big Shelby really *was* big," she informed Matt. "He was so tall he used to smack his head something fearful going through the door of Flo Jackson's Gold Arrow Saloon. He never remembered to duck in time. But he was in love with Flo and he just couldn't stay away from her—"

"Christie, what does this have to do with the map?"

She thought about it for a minute. "Absolutely nothing," she decided. "But that's not the point."

"What *is* the point?" he asked, looking baffled.

"Beats me. You're the one who got this conversation all tied up in knots." She turned and strode off through the trees again. Matt followed, making several caustic remarks about a certain person who had lived in New York City all her life but now, by some lunatic stretch of the imagination, believed herself to be a wilderness scout.

Sunlight drifted down through the trees; birds twittered and argued with each other in the branches overhead. "I wonder if those are blue jays," Christie mused. "I won't really know until my first meeting with the Feathered Nest Bird-watchers' Club next week. Ever done any bird-watching, Matt?"

"I think I'm tracking a yellow-breasted cuckoo at this very moment," he remarked, greeting her frown with a withering smile.

It was a beautiful day and no matter what Matt said, she felt completely in her element tramping here in the forest. She settled into a brisk but easy pace, swinging her arms at her sides. As much by instinct as anything else, she followed Big Shelby's trail.

She and Matt walked for quite some time. The secret life of the forest went on all around them, heard in small, mysterious rustles and scurryings. After a while Christie glanced casually at her watch. According to her estimate, they should have reached the mine by now. Well, all right, maybe they should have reached it *long* before now. But there was no sense in admitting that to Matt. Trying to be as nonchalant as possible, she fished the map out of her pocket again and squinted at it.

"We're lost, Christie," Matt said. "We've been lost since the minute we left town."

"We've experienced a slight...misdirection, that's all. I'll have us back on track in no time." She kept her voice confident and peered more closely at the map. Then she glanced around. The pines and spruce trees crowded around her in confusion, like soldiers who had broken ranks. Darn it, she'd lost all sense of the trail.

"Face up to it, Christie. You're a city girl. You belong back in New York—not out here pretending to be Davy Crockett. The part just doesn't fit you."

All sorts of protests churned inside her. She wasn't playing a part—she *did* belong here! Blast it all, she wouldn't start questioning herself because of Matt. She had no reason to feel these niggling self-doubts, and she pushed them firmly out of her mind.

But one irrefutable fact remained. She was lost, all right . . . lost deep in the forest and deep in the mountains. With Matt Gallagher.

CHAPTER FIVE

CHRISTIE WALKED ahead a few yards and plunked herself down on a mossy tree stump. Matt came up next to her.

"Move over," he said.

"There isn't enough room for both of us," she answered grumpily. "You'll have to sit somewhere else."

But Matt wasn't giving her any choice; already he was sitting. She found herself nudged to the very edge of the stump, where she had to balance precariously. Matt's thigh was pressed against her own, and he spread out the map so they could both look at it.

"All right," he said, "we're going to handle this in a logical, rational manner. The map says we should be headed north. It seems to me north is that way." He stuck a thumb out to his left, as if he were trying to hitch a ride.

"Actually north is this way." Christie gestured ahead expansively.

"Lord, where's your sense of direction?"

"That has to be north," she insisted. "I mean, all you need to do is look at the slant of the sun and that tells you everything." She craned her neck back so she could give a practical demonstration of this scientific principle. She stared into the sky, but all she saw were evergreen branches rising above her in graceful tiers.

The sun's intentions were well hidden from her. "Anyway, that *is* how it works," she said defensively.

"I'll get us to this gold mine. Come on." He confiscated the map and went loping off.

"Wait," she called, running to catch up with him. "Moss! Look—it grows on the north side of trees. Or is it the south side?"

"It's my turn to lead the way. You can forget all your half-baked wilderness lore and just follow me."

Christie didn't like to be a follower. She far preferred to be a trailblazer instead, even if she didn't know exactly where she was going. But she trotted along behind Matt, trying to stay up with him and finding herself distracted by the flex and stretch of his leg muscles. As a result she kept smacking into branches and tripping over stones.

The clearing came suddenly and unexpectedly, the trees opening up onto a bright meadow of wildflowers. On the other side of the field a grove of aspens shimmered with light, as if it had captured the sun in its leaves. Christie stood very still, taking in the sight of a weathered old cabin surrounded by a tumbling fence and sheltered by the benign shade of the aspens. A prospect hole gouged the mountainside nearby, but after all these years of abandonment it didn't seem a desecration—merely a part of the landscape.

"This is it," Christie said in a whisper, as if to speak any louder would shatter the spell. She didn't know exactly how it happened, but she found her hand clasped in Matt's. Together they waded through the wildflowers, bees flicking around them in lazy protest.

Christie and Matt went to investigate the mine shaft first of all. It was buttressed by rotting timbers, and Christie thought of all the dreams moldering in that dark tunnel.

"Big Shelby never found much gold here," she said, poking her head cautiously inside while she held on to the crown of her hat. "I don't suppose many prospectors did. It's sad...so much of their work and energy wasted."

"I don't know," Matt said reflectively. He squatted to sift his hands through the dirt. "It probably wasn't such a bad life. If one claim didn't pan out, you could pack up your gear and move on to a new one. Wouldn't matter if you ever found gold. You'd be living an adventure."

Christie was surprised by his words, and the hint of longing she thought she heard in them. She backed away from the mine so she could regard him fully. "Prospecting doesn't seem like the kind of thing you'd endorse like that. It means leaving when things get bad, never committing yourself to one place—always looking for fortune somewhere new."

Matt straightened up, wiping his hands on his jeans. "I was just theorizing," he said. "Woolgathering... daydreaming. It sounds good, being a gold miner. Not having so many damn responsibilities, roughing it outdoors..." He shook his head. "But that's only a fantasy. Real life is never so simple." His face tightened in a mixture of pain and regret. Then he climbed down to the stream below, not looking at Christie.

She tied the ribbons of her hat under her chin and followed him. The water was clear and shallow, trickling over mineral-stained rocks. Christie sat down, a smooth boulder at her back, and began undoing the bright yellow laces of her high-top sneakers. She'd laced up her shoes good and tight this morning, so it took a little while to free herself of the sneakers. Next came her socks, vivid red to match the color of her shirt; Christie believed firmly in color coordination. Now at last she was able to roll up the legs of her jeans. Matt had been watching these activities of hers with a sour interest.

"Matt, what made you decide to become a stockbroker, of all things?" she asked. "Why not an airline pilot, or an archaeologist? Or a wildlife photographer. Anything with a little excitement."

He picked up two pebbles and rubbed them together, giving Christie a wry smile. "Obviously you never captured the excitement pulsing all along Wall Street," he said. "That's what drew me fifteen years ago—the sheer adventure of it, the action, the game. Playing the market with the chance for a fortune always just out of reach. Talk about prospecting—I felt like I was part of the biggest gold rush in history!"

Christie eyed him speculatively. "But you don't feel that way anymore, do you?" she prodded. "You talk about all that like it's in the past." Wiggling her toes, she plunged them into the cold stream. Her fuchsia toenails glimmered under the water.

Matt frowned at the pebbles in his hand, jiggling them like dice. "I was a lot younger back then. I was idealistic, too. Hell, I thought everybody would play the game fair. My partner was supposed to be someone I could trust, my best friend..." He gave an impatient shrug. "How old are you, Christie?" he asked abruptly.

"Twenty-seven."

"I remember being twenty-seven," he muttered. "But a few months ago I turned thirty-five..." He paused. "I'm sure you don't want to hear about all the confusion in my life," he went on, his voice gruff.

"Yes, I do," she said earnestly, submerging her feet all the way and pressing them against the bottom of the streambed. "I want to hear everything about it." She raised her head so she could see Matt from under the brim of her hat.

He stood a short distance away from her, gazing into the water. "I thought I'd resolved everything," he murmured. "What my partner did to me—I thought I'd put all that behind me. I joined your father's firm, and then..." His voice trailed off. After a moment Christie finished the sentence for him.

"Then you found out about me. I'm another big disruption in your life."

"That's right," he answered grimly. "It was only a few days after my birthday when your father started making noises about dissolving the company. So here I am...thirty-five years old, at the midpoint of my career—and my life feels like a jigsaw puzzle I can't fit back together anymore."

Christie leaned against the boulder, propping herself up with both palms flat against the ground. Sharp rocks prickled into her skin. Even though her feet were icy to the bone, she kept them planted in the water. "I just finished changing my entire life. Maybe you need to do the same thing," she suggested to Matt.

He tossed a pebble into the stream, his movements vibrating with pent-up energy. "You're asking something impossible. I can't change my life completely—and neither can you, Christie." His voice was blunt. "Sure, you've done some window-dressing to the outside, but underneath you're still chasing success exactly like your father. I see it in everything you say and do. You can't just relax and enjoy your life—it has to be full of goals and accomplishments. Look at all those clubs and committees you belong to. Bird-watching, hiking . . . libraries, museums, pageants, I don't know what else. Lord, you even said something about fire fighting. You think if one project is good, ten are better. That's straight from your father."

She struggled to her feet, splashing water around. "I won't be like him! He's never satisfied with anything—or anyone. He just keeps setting higher and higher standards that no one can possibly reach. He can't even reach them himself. I refuse to live like that!"

Matt tossed another pebble into the stream. Drops of water sprayed upward, glinting in the sun like crystal jewels. "You can argue with me all day long," he said. "You can tell me how you want things to be—but that won't change the way they really are. You're an ambitious, driven person, just like your father."

She plowed through the water to confront Matt, her frozen feet somehow carrying her along. "You're saying all this just to avoid the real problem," she exclaimed. "The fact is, Matt Gallagher, you can't face the truth about your *own* life. You won't accept that something about it needs to change. I'd say you need a pretty drastic change, as a matter of fact."

"The only thing *I* need is for you to come to New York and straighten out this mess with your father. Then everything will fall back into place."

Christie stood in front of him. Her feet had gone numb, but she didn't care. She pushed her hat off her head, and it dangled from the ribbons knotted at her throat. "You're just using me as an excuse, Matt. All the confusion you're feeling—that won't go away no matter what I resolve with my father." She stared at him defiantly from the middle of the stream. He scowled back at her, taking off his own hat and digging a hand into his hair until it was thoroughly rumpled. Then he turned away as if to dismiss her.

"I'm going to take a look around the cabin," he said, sounding cantankerous.

"I thought I'd take a look at it myself." Christie stalked out of the water, but couldn't manage any dignity—her legs felt like toothpicks stuck into blocks of ice. Matt was already at the cabin as she fumbled with her socks and sneakers. Her yellow laces trailing in the dirt, she wobbled up to join him.

The door was secured with a formidable padlock that strained at the rotting wood. Matt put a hand on the low-hanging lintel. "Big Shelby must have smacked his head on this thing a time or two," he said.

"The real-estate lady gave me a key. I have it here somewhere..." Christie burrowed a hand into her pocket and brought out her key ring that had a plump goldfish charm attached to it. The ring bristled with keys she'd accumulated over the years and she didn't remember what half of them were for anymore. Flipping through them, she had to try a lot of different ones on the padlock before she was finally able to unlock it. The door creaked open and she stepped cautiously into the darkness.

Matt had to stoop as he came through the doorway after her. They stood together for a moment, waiting for their eyes to adjust to the gloom. All the windows had been boarded up, but here and there a chink of light filtered in. Gradually Christie was able to pick out details—a rusty metal bedstead with no mattress, a rack of tools along one wall, a grimy calendar tacked up on another. She drifted over to the calendar, peering to read the date.

"July 1947," she murmured. "That was long after Big Shelby's time, but apparently this property has gone through quite a few hands. No one's ever gotten around to making it into a real summer retreat. You know, they're not asking a bad price for it."

Matt was rattling the tool rack. "How much acreage is involved?" he asked in a businesslike fashion.

"I'm not sure, but I know it includes that whole field outside."

Matt ducked through the doorway again and went to survey the meadow. Christie came to stand beside him, covertly watching his profile. The lines of his features jutted out stubbornly, but when he spoke she sensed in him a longing, a yearning that had gone unsatisfied.

"It looks like good land," he said. "So much space and openness out here—but the mountains rising up around you. And there...listen to the quiet."

She closed her eyes. She could hear the thrumming of some insect nearby, a breeze stirring its way through the aspens, the call of a bird. Yes, this was silence compared to the jangle and roar of New York City streets.

When Christie opened her eyes again, she was disconcerted to find Matt studying her intently. She flushed under his scrutiny, feeling as if he could see right inside her and, therefore, knew how attracted she was to him. But she was determined not to look away; that would reveal one more sign of the powerful effect he had on her. She returned Matt's gaze with a steady regard of her own.

At last he smiled faintly and made his way over to the fence. "The latch on the gate is broken," he observed, fiddling with it.

"Most of the fence itself is down, so it doesn't really matter." Christie motioned at the roughly hewn posts that had fallen to the ground. The gate looked absurd, standing there almost by itself, but Matt seemed fascinated with it.

"I can fix this latch," he said, bending over it. "That's the problem, right there. I'll have it working as good as new." He vanished into the cabin, reappearing a moment later with a hammer and a pair of pliers. "These tools are in great shape," he told Christie enthusiastically. "I haven't had my hand around a good hammer since shop class in high school. Of course, I got expelled the second week of class for something inventive I did with a lathe, but that's beside the point."

Christie watched with some trepidation as Matt attacked the gate latch, but he seemed to know what he was doing. Her feet were tingling with sensation now and she could finally walk with a little steadiness. She wandered off into the field, pulling her hat up onto her

head again. Lisa had been teaching her all about
wildflowers, and she tried to identify the brilliant
blooms spread out before her in the grass. The tall,
wavy ones colored orange-vermilion, surely those were
Indian paintbrush. The blue ones had to be lupine,
and the delicate white flowers were known as snow-
berry. Christie wanted to belong so completely here in
New Mexico. She wanted to learn everything, do
everything that would make her an integral part of this
landscape. And she wanted to do it all perfectly...

Christie sat down hard in a clump of grass, dismayed as she listened to her own thoughts. Instead of
simply enjoying the beauty of the wildflowers, she was
worrying about making herself an expert on them.
That made her seem exactly like her father—just as
Matt had pointed out.

Christie took a blade of grass and peeled it down the
middle. She felt shaken. All her life she'd tried to mold
herself into the image of her father. It had been a great
relief when she finally realized she was her own unique
person. But now, because of Matt, a new and very
unwelcome realization was coming to her. All those
years of emulation had taken their effect, after all.
She'd actually been successful at turning herself into
Christopher Daniels the Fourth.

Christie dipped her head and pressed her hands
against her face. No, it just couldn't be! She didn't
respect her father anymore...and if she was like him,
how could she respect herself? Confusion churned inside her.

"Hey, I fixed it," Matt called to her. "I fixed the
gate."

He sounded so pleased with himself. Christie slowly raised her head. He grinned and exhibited his handiwork, swinging the gate back and forth in its frame of decaying fence. The latch clicked into place, just as it should.

"That's wonderful," Christie said with no conviction. Matt didn't seem concerned about her lack of fervor. Now he was exploring around the side of the cabin, tugging at a weather-beaten tarp.

"Look at this," he said. "A woodpile. I always wanted a woodpile."

Christie went to lean against the gate, finding it surprisingly sturdy. That was good, because she needed to anchor herself to something solid. She watched as Matt hefted up a rusting ax. He balanced it in his hands, a look of admiration on his face as he examined it. Then he extracted a good-size log from the pile and set it on a tree stump nearby. He started chopping away with gusto.

He was awkward at first, but eventually he settled into a rhythm with the swing of the ax. He gave the task his total concentration, with sunlight streaming down on him through the aspen leaves and patches of sweat forming on his back and under his arms. After a time he paused and began undoing the buttons of his shirt. Christie's eyes lingered on the powerful muscles of his torso as he shrugged out of the shirt and tossed it on the ground. She contemplated the red-gold hair that curled over his chest. But he didn't seem aware of her frank inspection. Gripping the ax, he went to work again.

Christie's self-doubts and confusion were overtaken by the sheer enjoyment of watching Matt. She liked the contrasts she saw in him. His arms were a golden brown up to the shirtsleeve line, but then an opalescent white took over. It was intriguing to see his muscles bunch under that fair skin as he wielded the ax. Christie smiled to herself; Matt obviously worked out on a regular basis, but he wasn't vain enough to spend time roasting his body under a tanning lamp. There was something essentially rugged about him. Except for the pale shade of his skin, he might have passed for a frontiersman of the Old West. The coiled energy inside him seemed to have found an outlet now. He split open one log after another.

At last he threw down the ax, wiping his forehead with the back of his hand. He looked startled to find Christie watching him. After a moment he came to stand on the other side of the gate from her.

"Lord, that felt good," he said.

"Well...maybe you could stock a log or two in your office in New York. That would give you a handy way to vent your frustrations." Christie's gaze strayed down to Matt's navel. It was well shaped and surrounded by a downy swirl of russet hair. Christie sighed. She forced her eyes upward again, restraining an urge to reach out and touch his chest.

"Frustrations," he echoed. "I have plenty of those in New York, all right. You know what keeps eating at me the most? It's this damn insider trading that's going on all over the place. I thought I'd get away from it at your father's office, but I was dead wrong."

At these words, Christie's attention was no longer riveted on Matt's physique. "Wait a minute," she protested. "My father may be guilty of a lot of things, but insider trading isn't one of them. He's scrupulously honest when it comes to the stock market. He—''

''Hold on. I'm not accusing your father of anything. Believe me, I made darn sure I could trust him before I went to work with him. But don't you see what I'm talking about, Christie?'' Matt thumped his fist down on a fence post. ''Corruption is everywhere in the market, like bad fumes seeping under the door. You can't get away from it—too many people are trading on inside information. The market should be about gamesmanship, testing your wit and skill. Instead it's a damn contest to see who can cheat the most and rake in the most money without getting caught!''

The passion in Matt's voice drew Christie, but he was reminding her of the life she'd left behind. She retreated from the gate, reluctant to be swept up in a discussion about Wall Street and all its problems. She hurried back into the field of wildflowers. To her frustration, Matt swung himself easily over the bars of the tumbled-down fence and pursued her.

''You know what the root of the problem is?'' he demanded excitedly. ''I'll tell you what it is—the very definition of insider trading. Go ahead, Christie, define insider trading for me.''

''I feel like I'm back in one of my business classes,'' she grumbled. ''But I'm looking for flowers right now, Matt. I'd really like to find some cow parsnip, if you don't mind.''

He wouldn't leave her alone. He kept right along beside her as she searched through the grass for clusters of white parsnip blooms. ''Come on, Christie. Give me the definition.''

"Oh, good grief," she said straightening up. "Insider trading is anytime you profit in the market from information you're not supposed to have. It's as simple as that."

"Aha! But how do you define information you're not supposed to have?"

She blew out her breath in exasperation, but found his intensity beginning to take hold of her. "All right," she said, "let's take a hypothetical case. Suppose your uncle is head of a big fast-food chain. You're his favorite nephew because you're the only one in the family who'll eat all those greasy hamburgers and french fries of his." Christie shuddered. "Anyway, this uncle trusts you, so he tells you that he's going to make a takeover bid on Company XYZ, another restaurant chain. Once his bid goes public, he'll be offering a very handsome price for XYZ's stock so that all the shareholders will sell to him. There! That's a prime example of insider information. Your uncle told you all this in strictest confidence, Matt," she said earnestly, caught up in her story. "Sure, you can sneak out right now and secretly buy stock in XYZ, then make a killing when the price shoots sky-high. But your uncle is bound to find out you took advantage of his trust—especially when the Securities and Exchange Commission comes knocking at your door. Say goodbye to all those hamburgers and french fries. Not that they were healthy for you, anyway—you'd be much better off eating some of my soybean meat loaf."

Matt sat down in the grass, looking rather dazed. "I was trying to make a point," he said. "Wasn't I?"

"Yes, you were." Christie now felt ready to encourage him in this conversation, and settled down beside him. "Maybe it would help if I invented another uncle for you."

"Please don't. Okay, you've given me a classic example of insider information that would be illegal to use. But turn it around a little. What if I just *think* my uncle's going to take over XYZ? Using all my intuition and my knowledge about him, I come to that conclusion. What then? Is it wrong for me to buy up some options in XYZ and then make a fortune when my uncle announces the bid?"

Christie wrinkled her nose. "All right, insider trading is hard to pin down exactly. There's an awfully fine line between what's legal and what isn't."

"Right!" Matt said triumphantly. He leaned toward her. "That's the whole problem, right there. No one really agrees on an exact definition. The rules are vague, so they're easy to get around. And people think it's all right to play dirty as long as you don't get caught."

"Yes... I suppose that's true," she said distractedly. She was examining Matt's eyelashes. They were long and thick, a darker shade of red-brown than his hair. No man should be allowed to have such superb lashes.

"Why are you squinting at me like that?" he demanded. "Do you have something in your eye?"

"Um...no." She drew back from him hastily. "You were talking about fine lines and all, Matt."

"Right—take my partner as an example. For years he prided himself on being a market insider, just skirting the right side of the law. It didn't take much of a step for him to start trading on illegal information."

"You're right," Christie decided. "It's like everybody's breathing fumes and they go haywire. I'm just glad I'm away from it all—and that I can laugh at it now."

"I can't laugh," Matt said grimly. "I want to do something about the greed, the craziness! At least point it out to all those gullible investors."

Christie stared at him. "Write about it, Matt. Write about your experiences with the stock market. That's what you need to do. Newspaper and magazine articles, maybe. Or go all the way and write a book!" Now she was the one filled with excitement and intensity. What a great inspiration she'd just had. Already she could see Matt's book with his photograph on the back cover, piles and piles of copies displayed on racks in the stores.

He stared back at her. "What the devil are you talking about? I haven't written anything since all those confounded college theme papers."

"Oh." This revelation brought Christie down to earth again, but she still liked her idea. "Maybe you should keep a journal, Matt. That would be a good place to start. I hear it's an excellent catharsis for the emotions."

"Good Lord," was his only reply. He didn't sound too encouraging, but Christie wasn't easily dissuaded once she got hold of an idea.

"I know a good title for your book," she said. "You could call it 'My Life Off the Wall.' You know, a sort of pun on 'Wall Street.' I like it, don't you?"

He looked her over as if she'd lost all her marbles. She lifted her shoulders.

"All right, so maybe you could come up with a better title," she conceded. "But no matter what, I think you should write down some of your feelings, Matt. I really do. It would do you good."

"Hmmph," he uttered in a skeptical tone. Still frowning, he watched a small green bug crawl painstakingly across the back of his hand. It bounced up and down with an odd gait, as if walking on springs. After a moment it spread out a minute pair of iridescent wings and went flitting away. Matt followed the meandering course of its flight, and then he turned to Christie again. "Don't you have to get back to Red River?" he asked, his voice constrained now. "You must have at least one or two committee meetings waiting for you."

Unwillingly she glanced down at her watch. "Well, yes, the museum fund-raising board is having a special session today," she admitted. "I promised to attend."

"We might as well get going, then. There's nothing to keep us here."

"No...there's not." But even as Christie spoke, she knew that she wanted to spend the whole rest of the day here with Matt, arguing with him, looking at him—just being with him in a special place that seemed all their own.

It was much too dangerous for her to feel this connection with Matt, lulled into it by the fragrance of the wildflowers and the lazy humming of the bees. She scrambled to her feet, trying to break the spell woven around them.

"Yes, we'd better go," she said. "Before it's too late...we'd just better go!"

CHAPTER SIX

CHRISTIE and Matt walked slowly back to the cabin. Matt picked up his shirt and slipped it on; then he covered the woodpile with the tarp. He didn't seem in any great hurry to leave, even though he'd been the first to suggest it. Christie bent to tie up her shoelaces all the way, finding the need to delay their departure. Just as Matt was about to put on his baseball cap, she grabbed it from him.

"Wait—I never did get the brim right," she told him. She worked at it for a long moment, then handed it over. "Try that."

He pressed the cap down on his head. It seemed to belong there now, and the brim was angled just right. Matt was starting to settle into his country clothes. His jeans were smeared with dirt here and there, and his shirt wrinkled just the right amount. He looked as if he belonged in the New Mexico mountains, not stuck away in a New York City skyscraper.

"Christie," he said, his face serious as if he were about to reveal something important.

"Yes?" She secured the cabin padlock, feeling unaccountably nervous.

"Today, spending time with you here..." He didn't seem to know how to finish the sentence. "Look," he began again, "I'd like the name of the real-estate agent that told you about this place."

Christie hesitated, stuffing her big ring of keys back into her pocket. "Surely you're not thinking about buying it, are you, Matt?"

"It's not a bad piece of land. It would make a pretty good investment," he remarked.

His cool, businesslike words sparked anger inside Christie. She stood protectively in front of the cabin. "An investment!" she exclaimed. "Is that all you see here? Don't you care about the beauty, the peacefulness? All you want to do is make a fast buck—you don't give a hoot about anything else!"

"That's how you want to see me, Christie. It's not the way I really am," he warned.

"Then why would you buy this beautiful piece of land simply as an investment? That's like trading stocks. Never hanging on to anything for its own sake, always having to make money from it."

"Give me a chance, will you? I wasn't thinking of turning a profit on this place. There are all kinds of investments, you know." He paced back and forth, his hands jammed into his pockets. "The problem is . . . I've never purchased anything tangible for myself. I deal in money, and most of the time it's money I can't see or touch—just electronic numbers flashing on a computer screen. I don't own anything meaningful, not one thing! I rent an apartment, I lease a car now and then . . . but I don't have a single patch of dirt I can dig a spade into and call my own."

Christie leaned back against the rough wood of the cabin wall. "Suppose you bought this place, Matt. It's not going to do you much good when you're two thousand miles away in New York. You're not exactly being logical."

"There's nothing logical about the way I feel right now. And it's all your fault," he complained, narrowing his eyes at Christie.

"Don't blame your problems on me again. I didn't ask you to come along today—you practically forced your way into the car."

"I thought I could talk some sense into you. Instead I feel like my brain is turning into cottage cheese."

"Why don't you buy yourself a little farm in Connecticut or Rhode Island?" she asked.

He stopped pacing. "For some deranged reason I like this particular field—this cabin, these mountains. But the location is all wrong. This place should be half an hour outside New York City."

"Well, thank goodness it's not. It belongs right here in New Mexico. And I'm not giving you the name of the real-estate lady because *I'm* going to buy this land. It's just what I've been looking for."

Matt rubbed his neck. "You already own a house in Red River. Why do you need anything else?"

"I told you, I was looking for a gold mine with special magic. And now I've found it."

"You're being even more illogical than I am," he grumbled.

"Maybe—maybe not. But I want this land," she said stubbornly. She straightened up and faced him. "Go back to New York, Matt. Buy yourself one of those fancy apartments across from Central Park. That should be enough greenery to keep you satisfied. Maybe you look like a mountain man, but you don't belong here—not in your heart.''

Matt smiled. "Are you sure *you* belong here, Christie? Are you positive about that?''

His challenge pierced through her defenses, and self-doubt nagged at her again. She could no longer deny that she was like her father—driven, ambitious, always reaching for new goals. But the ability to strive and achieve seemed useless in this woodland setting. An inner tranquility was needed instead, the art of simply letting go and enjoying one's surroundings. Christie longed to master this art—and there was the irony. She was setting another goal for herself, striving yet again.

"No matter what, I *do* belong here!'' she declared, fighting her own fears as well as Matt's skepticism. Then she swiveled away from him and marched through the field of wildflowers.

He caught up to her on the other side of the meadow as she stopped to look back. She wanted to make a picture in her mind: the old cabin huddled behind its sagging fence, the aspen grove radiating with sunlight, the flowers with their deep hues of vermilion and sky blue.

It was all so lovely—but that wasn't the reason Christie had found something special here. This place was magical because she had shared it with Matt. Oh, blast! He was intruding on every part of her life, touching every emotion. Turning, Christie plunged through the trees of the forest.

"You're going the wrong way again,'' Matt said behind her. She clenched her fists, but allowed him to lead the way. He took an unerring course that ended

up right at the Land Rover. Christie didn't understand it. What did city-bred Matt Gallagher know
about wilderness tracking?

He ran his hand along the side of the Rover. "This
is one heck of a wagon. I'd sure like to try it out."

"Would you, now." Christie ignored his broad hint
and climbed into the driver's seat. She put her key into
the ignition, only to find Matt poking his head
through the window.

"After tomorrow it's back to taxicabs and crowded
streets for me," he said. "I might never have a chance
like this again." He grinned at her hopefully, looking
like a kid who'd just gotten hold of his first bicycle.

"Oh, good grief." Christie scrambled over to the
passenger's side. Matt swung himself in, a gratified
expression on his face as he handled the steering wheel
and the gearshift knob. Then he buckled his seat belt
and started the engine.

"You know, your key ring is way too heavy," he
told her. "Having this much weight hang from the ignition switch could do some damage."

"I'll take that under advisement." Christie yanked
her own seat belt into place, provoked by Matt's interference. Next thing she knew, he'd be wanting to
run her bed and breakfast. Her mood wasn't helped
any by the way he expertly turned the Land Rover
around on the narrow road. It had taken Christie a
long time to adjust to the heavy-duty feel of the vehicle. Matt, however, seemed right at home from the
beginning, shifting gears with ease at all the right moments. His left arm hung casually out the window and
he grinned all the way down to Red River. Glancing
over at him, Christie was struck by the sheer happi-

ness on his face. No worries or problems seemed to plague him now. Something constricted inside her; she liked Matt when he was carefree and contented. Oddly enough, she liked him just as much when he was all riled up. Christie wondered how it would be to share Matt's good times and bad times. He was probably impossibly cranky whenever he had a cold or the flu. On the other hand, she suspected he'd be a lot of fun some winter night snowed in with her, nothing to do but play card games and snuggle in front of the fireplace...

Goodness, what was she thinking? In another minute she'd have them hobbling around with matching canes after spending a cozy lifetime together! Nothing could be more ludicrous. On Monday he'd be leaving Red River and she'd never see him again. That was the way it had to be. She couldn't let herself forget that he was her father's emissary. Christie forced herself to stare straight out the windshield, both hands gripping the sides of her seat with determination.

Matt pulled smoothly into the driveway of her house, parking just beyond the sign that announced in swirling script Christie's Bed and Breakfast. She'd had the house repainted in a shade of hyacinth blue so it would match the color of her sign. As always she experienced a warm sense of homecoming here. This was exactly the kind of house she'd have loved as a child, with its dormer windows jutting from the attic and its front yard rambling down at a slope. It had been her haven these past few months, guests wandering in and out of it but not leaving an imprint...until Matt came along. His vibrancy would leave its essence; Christie was all too sure of that.

She slid out of her seat. "I have to get ready for that meeting," she said crisply. "See you around, Matt."

"Hey, don't forget your keys." He tossed them to her and watched as she caught them neatly in midair. "Great catch," he said. "I bet you're a pretty decent player on that softball team of yours."

She considered this statement. All her life she'd been good at smacking a ball with a bat and sprinting for home plate. Physically she was a strong, capable person—surely, then, she had what it took emotionally to withstand the appeal of Matt Gallagher. That was a comforting thought.

Feeling a welcome confidence in herself, Christie strode up to the front door and pulled it open. Then she glanced back over her shoulder. "Look at it this way," she said with spirit. "You'd have to be a darn good pitcher to strike me out, Matt. Just remember that!"

THE SKY HAD DARKENED to a deep cobalt that evening as Christie sat cross-legged on the parlor floor, the account books for the bed and breakfast strewn around her. She punched numbers forcefully into her calculator, substracting expenses from income. More than anything she was trying not to think about Matt. He'd been gone when she returned from her meeting and she hadn't seen him the whole rest of the day. Only Mr. and Mrs. Fanshaw had made a brief appearance to check out and pay their bill, peering around anxiously as if expecting a swarm of children to descend on them at any moment.

Now the big, old house was especially quiet, the silence disturbed only by the faint sounds of Lisa working in the utility room. What was keeping Matt out so long, blast it? Maybe he'd gone to the Miner's Café and met a pretty girl. Maybe the two of them were down at Hilda's Bar and Grill this very minute, dancing the Western two-step.

"Fine, Matt Gallagher," she snapped, with no one to listen. "That's just fine with me." She hit the wrong button on her calculator, gave herself the square root of her plumbing bill, and had to start all over again.

Lisa drifted by the parlor door. "I folded the last batch of linens," she said. "See you tomorrow, Chris. If you're wondering about the gorgeous male, he was mumbling something about fishing rods when he went out this afternoon."

"I wasn't wondering about him in the least," Christie defended herself, but Lisa was already gone. The house settled into a more pervasive silence than ever and Christie felt an unexpected loneliness. Before Matt had barreled into her life yesterday, she hadn't been lonely in the slightest. How could one person make so much difference? She glared at her calculator, which was a relic from her days as a stockbroker. Pushing it aside, she started adding up figures the good, old-fashioned way—using a pencil, a piece of paper and her brain.

There was a fearful rattle at the front door, and a moment later Matt came charging into the parlor. Christie stared at him. Several fishing rods sprouted from his hands at odd angles, a green tackle box was flung helter-skelter across his shoulder along with a wicker basket, a net dangled from his waist and a muddy pair of black wading boots engulfed most of his legs. He was wearing a khaki vest that bulged with all sorts of pockets and he'd exchanged his Red Sox baseball cap for a hat that had fishhooks dangling from the brim. His eyes were glazed over in a most alarming fashion. Christie recognized all the symptoms of a man who had walked innocently into a store, asked for one fishing rod and somehow ended up buying out the entire place.

He frowned at Christie, the hooks on his hat bobbing up and down a little. "Do you have any worms?" he demanded.

She nibbled on her pencil eraser. "Sorry, Matt," she said solemnly. "I'm fresh out."

"Damn, I need worms!" he muttered. He clattered and clanked his way out of the room. Christie listened to his progress; it sounded as if three elephants were crashing their way up the stairs. She felt immensely cheerful all of a sudden. Smiling to herself, she bent over her figures again.

"Eeeaaagh!" came a desperate cry from somewhere on the top floor. It was a horrible sound, full of agony. Christie jumped to her feet and took the stairs at a run.

"Hold on, I'm coming!" she called out. She reached the third-floor landing and rushed around its far corner, following the muddy tracks of Matt's wading boots. He was standing in the middle of the hallway, apparently intact. But he was holding his fishing net straight out in front of him. The net squirmed frantically, four black paws poking out of it and thrashing the air. A pair of blue eyes stared through the mesh in outrage. Matt looked triumphant.

"First thing I've caught all day," he announced. "What do you know about that?"

Christie took the net from him and set it on the ground. Both she and Matt backed away from it cautiously, as if it were a bomb about to explode. For a moment no sound or movement came from the depths of the net. Then, suddenly, a Siamese cat shot straight up into the air. A second later it went streaking down the hallway.

"I always thought Gomez would know how to move fast if he ever had any incentive," Christie remarked.

Matt glanced at her suspiciously. "I thought you said his name was Vincent."

"Gomez is Vincent's brother," she explained. "It's no good having just one cat, you know. It's too bad you don't believe in cats at all. You don't know what you're missing."

Matt grumbled something under his breath; it sounded like "crazy as loons." He creaked into his room with all his paraphernalia, Christie following close on his heels. He waved the fishing rods dangerously, trying to find a place to set them down among all the antiques. Christie took the rods before he could do any serious damage; she propped them next to the ornate Victorian bureau that, mirror and all, rose eight feet into the air. She supposed it *was* a bit crowded in here, but she couldn't bear to eliminate even one piece of furniture. Running a hand over the marble slab of the bureau, she watched as Matt sat down stiffly on the edge of his bed. He started to lean forward, then stopped himself with a groan. After a moment he tried bending over again, and the next utterance he gave was truly disturbing. He sounded like a frog with hiccups.

"Christie," he said reluctantly. "I can't seem to reach my feet."

He didn't need to say anything more. She knelt before him and obligingly pulled off his long wading boots, one after the other. She noted that Matt had large, solid feet, with high arches that added a certain grace. Christie liked a foot with a high arch.

He took off his hat and groaned again as he slid out of his vest. Christie stood up and helped ease his shirt away as well. The back of his neck was inflamed to a bright red, and his shoulders were only slightly less vivid.

"With a sunburn like that, no wonder you can't move," she told him. "You look like a half-boiled lobster. Don't go anywhere—I'll be right back." She hurried down to her bathroom on the second floor, grabbed a bottle of lotion and then jogged back up the stairs to Matt. Scooting onto the bed, she balanced herself on her knees behind him.

"What are you planning to do back there?" he asked. "I don't trust you." He tried twisting around, then winced and faced forward again.

"Relax," she commanded, squirting a generous amount of lotion into her palm. "This stuff is truly amazing. It'll take the sting out of anything. In fact, one time Vincent singed his hair when he jumped on top of the stove, and—"

"Please, spare me the details," Matt interrupted her.

Christie shrugged and began rubbing the lotion onto his neck with light, deft strokes. "Maybe you shouldn't have gone fishing on top of all that wood chopping you did today."

"You're not the best person to lecture on the subject of moderation," he said dryly. "But you have to understand, Christie. Today...I discovered something special."

He sounded solemn and intense. Christie's hands moved down to rotate over his shoulders. "Well, go ahead," she prodded. "Tell me about it."

"Trout," he proclaimed, his voice excited now. "In the end, that's what life is all about. Casting your line into some deep, blue-green water and waiting for that one fish. No hurry, no bustle around you...just waiting for trout."

Christie squirted some of the lotion on his back. Listening to Matt, she felt a sharp stab of envy. He'd been in Red River barely twenty-four hours, and yet already he seemed at home here in a way she herself hadn't yet conquered. Maybe it was because he *wasn't* trying to conquer anything. He seemed perfectly able to relax and enjoy the moment. Why couldn't she do the same? She never seemed content to savor what was actually going on around her. Instead she was always thinking ahead to the accomplishment of one more goal or project.

"I wish you'd been there with me, Christie," he went on. "I was at a beautiful lake, not very far out of town—and people tell me there are lakes and streams all over these mountains!" He flicked his wrist experimentally, as if he were still holding a rod. "There's an art to casting a fishing line," he murmured. "A real art..."

Then he held both hands out in front of him. "This is my career," he said, folding the fingers of his right hand onto his palm. "And this is trout." Now he

curled his left hand into a fist. After a moment he
sighed heavily. "I have two completely different elements here. I can't mix them together, not if I'm going
to go after any one thing wholeheartedly."

"There you have it," Christie affirmed. She peered
over his shoulder and pointed at his left fist. "Choose
that one. Quit your job with my father. Quit the stock
market altogether, the way I did!"

"I can't. I've devoted fifteen years to Wall Street—
fifteen good, long years of my life. I'm not about to
turn around and declare all that a waste. Not even for
the biggest, juiciest trout this side of the Mississippi."
With that he lapsed into silence, morosely scratching
a mosquito bite on his arm.

Matt Gallagher was a stubborn man. Christie gazed
at the back of his head, where a tuft of his hair stood
out in a bellicose manner. Oh, blast, there was something much too attractive about the deep russet color
of his hair. The motion of her fingers on his skin
slowed until it was almost a caress. Her heart seemed
to pulse in her throat as she touched him. The two of
them were enveloped in the mellow glow of the bed-
side lamp, lost in their own private and intimate world.

Slowly Christie raised her eyes to the bureau across
the room, knowing somehow that Matt was looking at
her reflection in the mirror. Without any volition of
her own, her gaze locked with his.

His eyes had darkened to a deep, smoky amber, the
expression in them betraying unmistakable desire.
Christie had sensed longing in him today—but nothing like the yearning now directed entirely at her. She
backed away from him on the bed, dropping her hands

from his shoulders as if his sunburn had heated right through to her own skin.

He swiveled around awkwardly, catching hold of her waist. Off balance, she went tumbling over on the mattress, taking Matt with her. They sprawled in an ungainly heap, the patchwork quilt rumpled beneath them. Matt's face was only a breath away from hers. He gave a wry grimace.

"Lord, even my lips hurt," he confessed.

She couldn't possibly resist him anymore. Lying close to him like this, her body felt as warm and heavy and sweet as if she'd been drinking mulled cider. "I'll be gentle," she whispered, then leaned forward and covered his mouth ever so lightly with her own.

At first the kiss took her skimming over the surface of pleasure. Then Matt deepened the contact between them, his arms tightening around her and molding her to his bare chest. She brought her hands up to his shoulders, clinging to him as her senses began whirling out of control.

Matt gave a low moan, and Christie gradually realized she was digging her fingers into his sunburned flesh. She loosened her hold.

"Sorry," she murmured against his lips. "Did I hurt you?"

"Pain never felt so good," he murmured back. "Christie, something is happening between us. You realize that, don't you?"

"Something . . . that's not supposed to happen."

"But it *is* happening. We can't deny that." He kissed the corner of her mouth, tantalizing her.

"No, we can't . . ." She twined her fingers through his hair, relishing the clean, silky feel of it. He captured her mouth fully now, his own hands losing themselves in the masses of her hair. He tasted of salt and sunshine. "Oh, Matt," she whispered shakily after a long moment, gazing down at him. "What are we going to do about this?"

"Maybe we'll just see what happens," he said in a husky voice. "You're the one who likes taking new directions, aren't you?"

She trailed a finger across his cheek, over the red-gold shadow where he shaved. "Yes," she murmured. "But if we want to see where we're headed . . . you'll have to stay in Red River at least a little while longer, Matt."

His lips found an exquisitely sensitive spot right below her ear. "Lovely Christie . . . come back to New York with me."

She stiffened against him, bracing herself with her palms on the mattress. "You know I can't do that. My life is here now—I can't risk losing what I've started to build!"

"And my life is in New York," he said quietly. His hands moved along the tense muscles of her back, as if to make her body pliable to him. She stiffened all the more.

"If only you wouldn't be so pigheaded, Matt. You know that you need a change—at least a vacation. Why not spend a few weeks here? That's all I'm asking."

"You know how clients feel about their brokers being unavailable for even a day or two. No, Christie, you're the one who needs to come to New York."

She went on gazing down into his hazel eyes, trying not to listen to him—trying to convince him he should

stay in Red River. "Trout, Matt," she said persuasively. Trout..." Then she couldn't say anything because he was kissing her again with a wild tenderness,
framing her face in his hands. The uncertain future
faded away as if it would never exist. For once she
lived fully in the present, caring only for this moment
of wonder in Matt's arms.

Music began to play in her head, the distant jin-
gling of chimes. What an effect this man had on her!
Only gradually did Christie realize she'd just heard the
sound of the bell at the registration counter downstairs. She dragged her mouth away from Matt's.

"Oh, blast...I have to go answer that," she said
distractedly.

"Ignore it. Whoever it is will go away sooner or
later." Already he was drawing her back toward him.
But the bell sounded again, faint yet persistent.
Christie rolled away from Matt, scrambling over to the
edge of the bed.

"It must be a guest," she said, trying to smooth out
the tangle of her hair. "I have to go, Matt."

"Christie—"

She didn't stay to listen. Weaving her way among
the antiques, she hurried from the room and went
down the two flights of stairs. It seemed best to put
some distance between herself and Matt until she
could think more clearly. She still didn't know whether
to be relieved or disappointed at this interruption.

At the registration counter she found two elderly
women waiting for her.

"We'd like a room for the night," one of them said
to Christie. "Unless you're contagious, my dear. You
look quite flushed, and I do hope you're not coming

down with a cold. Adeline is very susceptible to summer colds.''

"Abigail, you're the one always catching cold," protested the other woman. ''Don't try to fob your weak constitution off on *me*.'' Then she looked Christie up and down with a practiced eye. ''Young lady, you do appear to be positively feverish. I shall prepare one of my remedies for you, that's what I'll do. I'm famous for my remedies.''

Christie smiled weakly and pushed a registration card over the counter toward Abigail and Adeline. She hoped that somewhere, indeed, there was a cure for the malady that ailed her…the malady known as Matt Gallagher.

CHAPTER SEVEN

CHRISTIE JOGGED up and down on her exercise trampoline in the parlor, feeling her stomach slosh in a most disconcerting fashion. This morning at breakfast Abigail and Adeline had insisted she drink one of their mysterious concoctions—something they called a "tisane." It had been a cloudy brown liquid, with some sort of hairy root lurking at the bottom of the cup. So far this medicine had produced no encouraging results; Christie was still groggy after a restless night filled with dreams about Matt.

He hadn't come down to breakfast yet, and her nerves were strained just listening for the sound of his tread on the stairway. Why couldn't she stop thinking about him? It seemed obvious there could be no meeting ground between them. Her heart told her to stay in Red River, and his head obliged him to go on grinding away in New York. But it wasn't merely a matter of geography. Matt Gallagher believed in a way of life that had almost destroyed her. She couldn't risk going anywhere near that life again!

Christie jogged despondently, trying to exercise Matt out of her soul. She gazed down at her cat Vincent, who was sharing the trampoline with her. Somehow his head remained perfectly motionless, but his body bobbed up and down rhythmically, as if attached to a spring. His round blue eyes held a wise, contemplative expression.

A rustling noise came from the stairway. Christie jogged with a little more enthusiasm, Vincent also bouncing along at a livelier pace. But it wasn't Matt coming down to the parlor. Instead Gomez leaped into the room, chasing a crumpled piece of paper.

"Oh, what a lunkhead!" Christie exclaimed. "Sorry, Gomez, I didn't mean you," she added. "I was referring strictly to myself. A woman ought to have more resistance when it comes to a man's freckles."

Gomez rolled over on the floor, batting the piece of paper with his two front paws. Christie jumped off the trampoline and blotted her face with a towel. However, she hadn't managed to work up much of a sweat and the towel wasn't really necessary. She threw it aside in disgust; Matt Gallagher was interfering with just about every gland in her body. Stooping, she snatched the crumpled paper away from the cat. He glowered at her in protest, but she ignored him. She plopped herself down on the sofa and absentmindedly smoothed out the sheet of paper. Both sides were crammed with tightly packed scribbling, edge to edge. The writing had been accomplished with a leaky pen, at least judging by the splotches of ink. It didn't look like easy reading, but Christie settled back and started deciphering words.

She read the page through once. Then she sat up straight and read it two more times, her excitement growing. Finally she struggled up from the cavernous sofa and headed for the kitchen, still grasping the sheet of paper. She knew exactly what she was going to do now.

Ten minutes later Christie stood outside Matt's room on the third floor. Balancing a breakfast tray rather precariously, she rapped on the door. No answer came, but Christie wasn't daunted. She knocked again, just to give fair warning, then twisted the knob and sailed into the room.

"What in tarnation?" Matt growled from the pine desk in the corner. The floor around him was littered with wadded sheets of paper, and the top of the desk was strewn with its own disarray of papers—most of them crumpled up as well. Matt himself looked like something one of the cats had coughed up on the sofa: his shirt rumpled, clumps of his hair standing on end, his eyes bleary and red-rimmed.

"Goodness," Christie remarked, setting her tray down on one of the bureaus. She glanced at the bed, where the sheets hadn't been turned down at all. "Didn't you get any sleep last night?" she asked in consternation.

Matt ignored her question, hunching protectively over the chaos on the desk. "What are you doing here?" he grumbled.

"Well, I do run a bed and breakfast, you know. Looks like you haven't used the bed recently, and you didn't come down for breakfast. Somehow I have to make sure you get your money's worth in this place." She leaned over her tray, taking in a good whiff of the violets she'd arranged in a vase for him. Only a few details remained to be completed. She spooned grape jelly onto two slices of rye toast, stirred fresh peach slices into a dish of vanilla yogurt and arranged a spoon invitingly in a bowl of honey granola. Matt looked so exhausted he probably needed all the help he could get.

"Eat," she commanded, maneuvering one of the chairs in front of the bureau. After a moment's hesitation he came over and obliged her by devouring the toast. Once started with her food he kept right on going. Christie watched in approval from her perch on the windowsill. She waited until Matt seemed replete, and then she whipped the wrinkled sheet of paper from the pocket of her shorts. She waved it in the air.

"This is promising stuff, Matt," she announced. "Very promising. I especially liked these windmill things you drew around the edge." She pointed to the imaginative doodles.

"Where did you get that?" Matt reached her in two strides, not paying any attention when he knocked his shin against the Morris chair. He seized the paper away from her. "Good Lord, I didn't intend this for public consumption. It's nothing but drivel."

"Matt, you really are a good writer," she declared. She left the window and established herself in a chair behind his desk, smoothing out more sheets of paper. "Your writing has fire. I thought I was sick and tired of the stock market. But when I read what you had to say about it...you pulled me back to Wall Street, even against my will. I felt the frenzied kind of excitement one finds there...you captured it for me, Matt."

"Hogwash," he muttered, crunching the paper in his fist and prowling his way back to the desk. He stared down at it broodingly, then glanced at Christie.

"Did I convince you about the really important idea?" he asked. "You know—that genuine competition has to be brought into the market. Trading stocks should be a grand sort of game, with rules of fair play for everyone—government regulators, investors, brokers. That's my theme, Christie. That's what I want to get across! Did you see it?" He gesticulated as he spoke, energy radiating from him in spite of his tired eyes and rumpled clothes.

"Yes, Matt," she answered softly. "I saw it—and you convinced me just fine. The stock market means a lot to you, doesn't it? It's not just a job for you—the way it was for me."

"It's in my blood, Christie. I see the abuses, the corruption, and I itch to do something about it. The market is a game as fascinating as any other—football, baseball, you name it. But you have to play it right."

Christie didn't say anything for a long while. She was beginning to understand Matt a lot better now. No wonder he didn't want to leave New York, even for a few weeks. The stock market was like a heartbeat to him, vital and compelling. His writing had shown her that. But still she wanted to protest.

"Blast it all, Matt," she said, gazing up at him. "What about fishing, and having a piece of land where you can dig with a spade?"

He slumped down on the bed, leaning forward and pushing both hands through his hair. "I can't have everything, Christie. I'll always have a choice to make. If I pick one thing, I'll have to give up something else."

"I have everything," she said stubbornly. "Right here in Red River...everything I've ever wanted."

Matt lifted his head. "Maybe the difficult choices are still ahead of you."

She stood up abruptly, pushing her chair back. She didn't want to think about making painful choices. She'd worked so hard to create a new life for herself.

"I know one thing for certain, Matt. You shouldn't stop writing, now that you've started. You're going to have something publishable on your hands."

He gave a harsh, skeptical laugh. "I'm not going to kid myself about that. I was just trying to sort out my thoughts a little. Besides, I'll go back to New York and I won't have any time to write."

"So you'll make another one of your dreary choices. That's not the way things should be, Matt. It just isn't!"

"Show me another way," he said, yawning wearily. "Mix all the problems in my life together—the stock market, trout, you, gold mines, this damn fool writing you got me started on...mix it all up and make it fit together with any kind of sense. Then I'll believe you."

Christie didn't know how to feel about being included on his list of problems. She'd rated third place, after all, coming in behind the category of fish. But it gave her an oddly warm feeling to know she was disrupting Matt's life...perhaps as much as he was disrupting hers.

"Oh, get some sleep," she said gruffly, coming over to the bed and prodding him with a finger. It didn't take much pressure at all to have him lying flat on his back. She pulled the quilt over him.

"Lord, you look good in that T-shirt thing you're wearing," he murmured. "Want to hop in and join me?"

She pulled at the straps of her sleeveless leotard top and backed away from the bed. "Um...my new guests said they could teach me how to grow my own herb garden today. I'd better go get started on some marjoram and wort's root."

"Too bad. I was hoping we could pick up where we left off last night."

Christie swallowed hard. Matt seemed more irresistible than ever when he was tousled and unshaven like this, his head poking out from the quilt. She wavered in an agony of indecision. She longed to be close to him, if only for a few moments, a few hours. But what price would her heart have to pay afterward? Maybe Matt was right, after all—life was only a series of difficult choices!

His eyelids drifted downward as she watched him, and sleep came to him as easily as it had yesterday in the woods. Christie smiled, feeling a mixture of relief and regret. She waited until she heard Matt's peaceful snoring, and then she slipped from the room.

LATER THAT DAY a cat tail paraded back and forth in front of the bathroom mirror. Christie's head weaved in its own side-to-side motion as she tried to dodge the tail and get a clear line of vision. More by instinct than anything else she dabbed on some mauve eyeshadow. At last Vincent curled up in the sink and she had an unobstructed view of herself.

She looked awful. The eyeshadow wouldn't do at all; she'd somehow contrived to put a purple blotch on each lid. Darn, why was she so nervous?

"It's only a date," she told Vincent. "Actually you couldn't even call it that much—not when I almost had to use physical force to convince Matt we were going square dancing together."

Vincent purred imperturbably from the sink. Christie sighed and smeared cold cream on her eyelids. Tonight was the last time she'd be with Matt. She wanted to do something reckless and daring with him, something they would both remember when it was all over and they took separate directions. She didn't know if a square dance qualified as either reckless or daring, but it was the best she could come up with on such short notice. The last time, the last time…those words kept repeating themselves in her head in a poignant refrain.

"He doesn't mean anything to me," she whispered. "We're not even friends. We don't belong together, and that's all there is to it."

Her voice didn't sound very convincing. Christie grabbed a tissue and rubbed the cold cream away. She managed to get some mascara onto her lashes, and then decided to quit working on her face. With the emotional tumult she felt right now, even blusher would be a dangerous proposition.

She hurried from the bathroom and went to her closet. Her clothes for tonight were already carefully chosen—her blouse of soft blue chambray, with an extravagant fringe dangling from the yoke, her denim skirt that hung in deep folds to midthigh, her boots of rich, burnished leather. Christie arrayed herself in this

outfit, then brushed her hair until it fell in one unfet-
tered ripple to her waist. The moment had come to go
round up Matt.

She found him waiting for her down in the parlor.
He made quite an impressive sight, and she leaned
against the doorjamb to admire him. His broad-
shouldered frame was well displayed in a Western-cut
shirt with pearl-tone snaps, and his jeans rode low on
his hips with the weight of an enormous silver belt
buckle shaped like a buffalo head. His feet looked
better than ever in tooled cowboy boots, but best of all
was his magnificent ten-gallon hat. Christie curled her
fingers inside the pockets of her skirt, knowing she'd
be attending the dance with the most handsome and
dashing man in town.

"Let me guess," she said musingly. "You went
down to Mary Bell's Western Gear and ordered one
square-dancing outfit, to go."

He took off his hat and stared into its depths as if
expecting to find a rattlesnake coiled there. "I don't
know what's happening to me," he muttered. "Things
are getting out of control."

Christie came over to him. Standing on tiptoe, she
replaced his hat firmly on his head. "Whatever's
happening to you, Matt...I like it. Just let it keep
happening."

His attention was fully concentrated on her now, his
eyes lingering appreciatively. "You're beautiful,
Christie," he stated. "Prettier than ever." He delivered this compliment in a businesslike tone, but
Christie found herself blushing.

"The two of us are going to make a spiffy pair tonight," she said, trying unsuccessfully to be flippant. "Shall we go?"

They walked to the front door, where Christie taped a handwritten sign. It read Gone Dancing.

"Who's going to mind the place while you're away—the cats?" Matt asked dryly.

"I'm leaving the door unlocked so my other two guests can come in and out whenever they wish." Christie was quite satisfied with this simple arrangement.

"But what about the potential customers you'll lose by going out tonight?"

"Well, I'll have to lose them, that's all. I could never ask Lisa to take over—she wants to go to the dance herself."

"And of course *you* have to go to the dance."

"Of course," she agreed. "Otherwise *you* wouldn't go, and just think what you'd be missing, Matt!"

"Yeah, it'd be a real shame," he said, with a visible lack of sincerity. "Hopping around on a dance floor like someone with a screw loose—how could I afford to give that up?"

"That's exactly what I told myself." Christie stopped to realign one of her potted geraniums along the edge of the porch.

"I've been noticing something," Matt remarked. "You don't seem overly devoted to this new business enterprise of yours. Seems like you're always flitting off somewhere else."

Christie straightened up, brushing dirt from her hands. "I never flit. I'm very devoted to what I'm doing here. But I've spent way too many years cooped up in an office. There's nothing wrong with a job that gives you a little freedom!''

"Hey, it's not just the fact that you're going off square dancing tonight. You're juggling ten or twenty different projects in your life. You can't do anything well when you operate that way—there's just too much going on. Your business is bound to suffer.''

It was disturbing how he could always make her question herself. But she needed to succeed at everything she attempted, especially her bed and breakfast. She couldn't bear to think she might be failing in any way.

"As a guest, do you have any complaints about the accommodations?'' she challenged.

"No, not exactly—''

"And the service? The food?''

"I'll eat your food anytime, Christie.''

"I rest my case, then.'' She headed down the driveway in the early evening light. "My business is prospering—everything about my life is prospering, in fact.''

"If you say so.'' Matt fell into step beside her. He moved with a rather bowlegged gait, obviously not used to his cowboy boots yet.

"You know, it's a good thing you're leaving tomorrow,'' she told him. "It really is. I think you and I grate on each other's nerves. Don't you agree?''

"Yes, but it's a fascinating sort of grating. Makes a person want to keep coming back for more.'' He clasped her hand companionably, swinging his arm with hers as they walked down the street. Somehow it felt so natural, so right to be with him like this. He started whistling an unrecognizable song. The poor

man had the worst sense of pitch she'd ever heard in a
human being.

"Why are you suddenly so happy?" she asked in a
grumpy voice, fighting her attraction to him.

"I don't know. I just am, that's all." He swung
Christie's arm in an exuberant arc and went on with
his atrocious whistling.

The evening was especially beautiful, with a sky of
amethyst blue and a fresh, cool breeze stirring the
mountain greenery. Hummingbirds darted about,
drawn by the feeders hanging from house porches.
They hovered to sip the sweet, wine-red liquid, then
darted away again.

"Listen, can you hear them?" Christie said, pulling Matt's hand to stop him from walking on.
"There—that's it!"

He listened, then shrugged. "I don't hear anything."

"It's the hummingbirds. They make a very soft
strumming on the air, a vibration that almost has its
own melody. There it is again." She saw the incom-
prehension on his face and shook her head. "Too bad
your ears can't pick it up. If you stayed in Red River
even a few more days you'd start to hear it, I can
promise you that. This is a town full of hummingbirds."

They strolled onward, and now Matt seemed re-
flective. "Look, Christie, in my more irrational moments I actually want to stay in Red River a week or
two. Hell, maybe even longer than that. But it's just
not possible. Both you and I are going back to New
York tomorrow."

"Oh, now don't start that again—"

"You might as well accept the inevitable, Christie. Everything's arranged. I even had an airline ticket issued in your name."

She pulled her hand away and stared at him in disbelief. "Matt Gallagher, you're a sneaky, underhanded—"

"Don't get all riled up. I made the plane reservation for you in New York, before I came out here."

"That's supposed to make me feel better about it? But I shouldn't be surprised by all this. It's exactly the kind of nefarious plot I'd expect from you. Too bad it's not going to work. You'll just have to cash that ticket in." Christie took a sharp right onto Main Street, striding ahead of Matt. She was grateful for the indignation coursing through her. It was a heartening, invigorating emotion, giving her fortitude against Matt. She badly needed that right now, as her body seemed to tremble at his nearness, like air throbbing to a hummingbird's wing.

Matt caught up to her, and he didn't talk about New York anymore. He didn't talk about anything, in fact, allowing a deceptively comfortable silence to settle around them. She was on her guard, knowing he might launch an offensive at any time. Well, she was ready for him—she could defend herself against Matt Gallagher!

Many of the buildings on Main Street were modeled in an alpine chalet style. The new Red River Cultural Center was one of these, with a steep, shingled roof and scalloped wood trim everywhere. Matt balked as Christie led him up to the door.

"Listen," he began, "there's something you should know. I'm not a very good dancer. Basically I have two left feet. Sometimes it feels like three left feet. What do you say we just call it a night—''

Christie grabbed hold of him and hauled him inside. She was glad to see there were several groups of dancers already forming on the polished ballroom floor; Matt wasn't going to have much time to think about this. Her hand gripped tightly around his, she dragged him toward Lisa and a skinny boy with frizzy blond hair.

''Hello, Lisa. Hello, Stan,'' she said brightly. ''We only need two more couples. Ah, here they come. Looks like we're all set!''

Matt's fingers were working energetically to free themselves. Just to be on the safe side Christie clamped both her hands around his wrist, turning herself into a human shackle. Lisa arched her dark, graceful eyebrows, but wisely refrained from saying anything.

On a nearby platform, the members of Jeb Randall's Mountain Boys Fiddling Band tuned up their instruments. The banjo player twanged a chord. Jeb himself anchored his fiddle between his shoulder and grizzled chin. He raised his bow and inclined the bald dome of his head. On cue the band let loose with a toe-tapping country tune.

''Now, gents, bow to your partners,'' Jeb sang into the microphone in his high, reedy voice. ''And, ladies, curtsy right back with a smile. Join hands, circle left, turn around in single file!''

The eight dancers in Christie's group marched obediently in a circle. At least, Christie hoped there were still eight dancers and not just seven. She twisted her head, making sure Matt was behind her. He was right on her heels, his expression mutinous.

"I feel like a damn fool," he complained loudly.

Christie gave him an encouraging smile. "You'll get into the spirit of this, I know you will. Just give it a chance." He didn't seem convinced by her words, but she felt she could trust him enough to face forward again.

Jeb went right on calling the square dance, never missing a stroke of his bow on the fiddle. "Say, folks, it's time to do-si-do that partner afore she roams. That's right, sashay round the little lady, allemande left and weave back home!"

Here the men were supposed to weave in the opposite direction from the women. Christie had to get Matt pointed the right way and then give him a push to start him moving. After that he did just fine, although he kept holding out his right hand when it should have been his left, and his left hand when it should have been his right. None of the other three female dancers seemed to mind his mistakes in the least. Lisa might as well have unfurled a banner that announced Gorgeous Male on Premises, and Suzanne Brock held on to his hand such a long time that the rest of the group almost came to a jumbled standstill.

Matt and Christie ended up back together somehow. "Isn't this fun?" she asked, rocking from one foot to the other in time to the music.

"It's about on the same level as getting your fingers stuck in a bowling ball," he answered.

Christie wanted to pursue this topic—bowling was one of her new pastimes. But according to Jeb, it was now time to "Swing your partner round and round, see what a pretty lady you've found!" Matt planted his hand on Christie's waist, looking beleaguered as she showed him how to keep his right foot pressed next to hers so they'd have a pivot as they swung.

"All right, I think I've got the hang of it," he said with grim concentration. "Hold on, we're going for a ride." Around and around he whirled Christie, until she had to lean back against the solid weight of his hand and laugh with the sheer exhilaration of being in his arms.

"You're good at this," she gasped. "Darn good!"

He didn't answer, just gazed into her uplifted face as the two of them went on spinning in their own private dance. Everything blurred around Christie, all colors and shapes—everything except for Matt. He was her focus, her center, his gold-brown eyes burning a clear, deep flame. She wanted to hold on to him like this forever and never let him go. Never...

But Jeb was calling the next step and Christie was forced to move unsteadily out of Matt's orbit. She found herself swinging in someone else's arms, but it wasn't the same. The magic existed only with Matt.

Sometime later the Mountain Boys Fiddling Band took a break, and a balladeer started crooning from the record player. Someone turned the lights down low; the squares of dancers broke up into slow-moving couples. Now Christie had Matt all to herself, lost in his embrace once again.

"Christie," he murmured against her hair, "any minute now I'm going to step on your toes. I thought I'd better give you fair warning."

She pressed her face against the hollow of his neck. "You're doing fine, Matt," she said dreamily. "Just keep shuffling."

He tightened his arms around her, bringing her closer. His lips brushed over her ear. "We have to talk about tomorrow," he said in a low voice. "It's going to come upon us whether we like it or not."

She drew back a little so she could look at him. "Please, Matt. Let's forget about it for tonight. We only have a little while longer to be with each other... to enjoy each other. Don't spoil that."

"We'll be together if you take that plane with me tomorrow. Christie, listen to me. Listen for once. I've watched you this weekend. I've studied your so-called 'new life.' And I can tell you without a doubt that you'll never have any peace of mind until you go back and face your father."

"Stop," Christie whispered. "I don't want to think about him. I only want it to be you and me tonight."

"Your father sent me out here to stop you from running away. Damn it, that's what I'm going to do. I won't let you evade me any longer."

"Right," she said bitterly. "How could I forget? You came to Red River on a mission. I'm a problem in your life, a mess that needs to be cleaned up. So all you see is Mary Christine Daniels, errant daughter of mighty Christopher the Third. But that's not me. That's not who I really am!" She pushed out of Matt's arms, no longer finding joy in them. Turning, she ran from the ballroom, out into the starlit night. Needing motion of any kind, she raced all the way up to the covered bridge over the river. Her breath coming in gasps, she leaned against the railing and stared down at the shimmer of water below. A moment later a board creaked behind her. She didn't have to turn around to know that it was Matt.

"Christie," he murmured. "I've learned who you are. A warm, beautiful woman. Vibrant, desirable, brimming with the unexpected. I see all of that. But I also see how uselessly you're fighting to get away from your father."

Her hand slid over the rail in a restless gesture. "You have simple answers for me, don't you, Matt? I'll go back to New York, I'll convince him not to dissolve the business. That will make me proud of myself, and it'll let you get on with your own life."

He came to stand beside her, his outline shadowy under the roof of the bridge. "I've told you before that I don't think anything is simple." A ruefulness crept into his voice. "You know, Christie, since meeting you the chaos in my life has multiplied exponentially. Where I'll go from here—hell, I don't know. The only thing that seems clear now is the fact that you need to confront your father...for your own sake, not mine."

"You still don't understand!" Christie gazed intently at Matt, trying to discern his features in the darkness. "That last day with my father—it was awful. I worked up all my courage to go into his office, and then I completely lost control. All the rage built up inside me came bursting out. I was like a two-year-old throwing a tantrum. I yelled at him, I screamed...and he just sat there. Calm and impervious to all my emotion. Smiling that superior little smile of his, as if he knew he was going to win in the end. So I ran away. Just like you said, Matt—I ran away. I didn't answer his phone calls or his letters because I was afraid he'd find a way to break me down, get to my weaknesses. And then he sent you.'' She stopped, her throat raw and hurting as if the words she'd spoken had carried their own corrosive.

Matt leaned on the railing next to her. "You're not a weak person. You're strong. You need to show that to your father—confront him as an adult this time. Until you really stand up to him, Christie, he'll have power over you. You'll never be able to break free...not even if you travel another two thousand miles to get away from him."

She closed her eyes, listening to the water flowing under the bridge. Painfully, reluctantly, she sensed the truth in Matt's words. She'd fled New York like a wounded, rebellious child—not like a free and confident adult. But returning there would mean testing her own strength against her father's. She was terrified of that.

"I can't do it," she said in a taut voice, turning away from Matt. She despised her own cowardice, but it overwhelmed her now. "I just can't do it," she repeated. "Tomorrow you're going back on that plane...and you're going alone."

CHAPTER EIGHT

CHRISTIE WATCHED from the parlor window as Matt loaded mysterious parcels into the trunk of his rental car. There were two long canisters, a large paper sack stapled at the top and bulging in the oddest way, three boxes tied up with string and a new cloth suitcase patterned in wild stripes. Last of all Matt tossed in the leather suitcase he'd brought to Red River on Friday afternoon. It was now early Monday morning.

Matt slammed down the trunk lid with an air of finality, and Christie stepped away from the window. Her eyes ached from lack of sleep; she'd been up most of the night, confronting her fears and doubts in the lonely darkness. The morning had finally washed over her with a cool, pale light, but it brought no ease to her inner turmoil—only the shaping of a difficult, complex decision.

Matt came to stand in the doorway of the parlor. "I suppose I'd better settle my bill," he said, his tone formal and restrained. "It's a long drive to Albuquerque and I don't want to miss my flight."

"I haven't written up your bill," Christie informed him. "I can't decide how much you should owe me."

Matt frowned, his hands jammed into the pockets of his corduroy pants. "Seems to me like it should be pretty straightforward. I'll pay the going rate, whatever that is.''

"Yes, but there ought to be a surcharge for guests who cause aggravation and no end of trouble. Plus, don't forget the sight-seeing tour of the mountains and the square dance!''

"I could assess a few taxes myself," he said. "What about the cat hair in my scrambled eggs this morning? And the fact that I can't think straight whenever you're around—that's worth a hefty penalty, right there.''

Christie drew a deep breath. "You shouldn't complain about me today, Matt. I'm doing exactly what you want me to do. You see—I've decided to go with you, after all.'' There, she'd said it—committed herself. No turning back now.

Matt gave a slow, surprised grin that transformed his face. A warmth radiated from him, a warmth that seemed meant just for her. "This is great, Christie. Trust me, you're making the right decision.''

"I wish I could be sure about that." She rubbed her temples wearily. "Matt, I tried not to listen to you last night. I was scared to listen. But I stewed about what you said for hours and hours!" Her mouth twisted. "Four in the morning, that's what my clock said when I finally admitted you were right. I've got to face my father again. Damn it, but that's what I have to do. I have to finish this up with him like an adult, not like some screaming kid.'' Christie moved around the room, straightening the shade on one of her brass lamps and opening the lid of the antique music box that didn't make music anymore. She wanted to draw comfort from all the details of her house. "I know I have to do it," she repeated. "But I've never won any sort of confrontation with him. What makes me think I can win this one? Somehow he'll get his clutches deeper into me than ever—I can feel it!"

"Start trusting yourself," Matt said quietly. He crossed the room and reached out a finger to tilt up her chin. "There, just look him straight in the eye like this and tell him who you are, what you want."

Matt's touch soothed away some of the dread that had lodged itself inside her. Now his finger brushed over her cheek.

"And think of it this way, Christie," he said, his voice growing husky. "You and I...we'll have at least a few more days together."

"I've already considered that," she admitted, resisting the urge to burrow into his arms. "Believe me, it only makes everything more complicated. Whatever it is that's happening between us—if I let it cloud my judgment, I'll never be able to resolve things with my father."

Matt's hands moved over her shoulders, lifting the heavy waves of her hair. "Your father doesn't have anything to do with you and me," he said softly. "Can't you see that?"

"I wish I could," she murmured. "I wish it could all be that simple." At last she succumbed to temptation and leaned her forehead against Matt's chest. Relying on him was far too easy, far too dangerous— especially with her independence at stake, the way it was now. But she allowed herself this brief moment to luxuriate in his strength.

Lisa wandered in from the kitchen, her dark curls bobbing forward as she bent her head over a notepad. She was jotting notes onto it in her careful, precise way. "Excuse me," she said without looking up. "I didn't mean to interrupt anything."

Christie withdrew from Matt's embrace. "It's all right, Lisa. We were just—just getting ready to leave."

Lisa raised one eyebrow expressively and went on writing. "Let's see, I'm supposed to call Mrs. Dorchester and tell her that you won't be at the library meeting this week. And I have all the phone numbers of the Red River Ramblers, so I can call and tell them tomorrow's hike is canceled. Anything else?"

Christie shook her head without speaking. She hauled her duffel bag from the sofa and swung the strap over her shoulder.

"Don't worry about anything while you're gone," Lisa told her. "My sister Jolene is going to sleep over here with me, and between the two of us we'll keep the bed and breakfast running just fine."

"I'm sure you will." On impulse Christie flung her arms around Lisa, almost knocking her over with the duffel bag. "You've been a good friend, Lisa," she said mournfully. "Darn good."

Lisa extracted herself from Christie's bear hug. "Don't get all mushy on me. You're only going away for a couple of days."

"That's right." Christie flashed a defiant glance at Matt. "I'll be back before the week is out. This is a temporary visit, nothing more."

"I never expected it to be anything else," Matt said with a frown. "But it's time to go, Christie." He led the way outside.

Once she was seated in Matt's rental sedan, Christie found that she had to poke her head out the win-

dow and give her old blue house a lingering appraisal.
It was a rambling, unwieldy place, but it was her home
now—and she was leaving it. Christie felt a sudden
sense of panic. If only she could live here a few more
months, a few more years, before facing her father
again! Surely that would make her stronger, more able
to resist him.

But Matt had started the engine, and the tires
crunched over the gravel of the driveway. Christie was
leaving Red River... retracing the same escape route
she'd traveled those four months ago.

NEW YORK JARRED Christie with its brash glitter and
noise. In New Mexico she was used to seeing the stars
at night, and hearing nothing but the rustle of wind in
the pine trees outside her window. Here the lights of
skyscrapers glimmered like some new constellation
crowding the sky, and car horns blared all along the
street in a discordant symphony. The taxicab that Matt
and Christie were in hauled full speed around a corner; the burly driver obviously had an aversion to using his brakes. But Christie didn't blame him—New
York was a city for acceleration, not deceleration. She
felt her own nervous system tensing up to shift into
high gear, just as in the old days. She was wide awake
in spite of her sleepless night and the long plane journey.

The taxi wheeled ebulliently around another corner, and the driver gave a belly laugh. Evidently he was
enjoying himself. With the wild motion Christie found
her nose pressed against Matt's shoulder. She in-
haled, his scent reminding her of pine woods. Then she
straightened up.

"Matt, I wish you'd stop being so mysterious about our destination. What address did you give the driver, anyway?"

"It's a surprise," he answered. "You wouldn't want me to ruin a surprise, would you?" His voice was injected with a false jocularity that Christie found very suspicious.

"It's late, and I just want to get over to my mother's apartment." Her mother was traveling, as usual, spending the summer with friends in Nova Scotia. Her vacant apartment on Central Park West was the perfect place for Christie to spend a few nights. But now the cab was rollicking along the haphazard streets of the Village, past a myriad of colorful shops and cafés. It turned onto a very familiar street and came to an abrupt, screeching halt, the cabdriver waiting until the last possible moment before condescending to brake. He chuckled as if he'd just invented a new amusement ride. Christie and Matt both lurched forward, then bounced back against the seat. When she was sufficiently recovered from the jolt, Christie peered out the window. The first thing she saw was a cluster of three skinny maple trees, all growing from one meager plot of dirt in the concrete. She knew these particular trees quite well; they never seemed to grow or change much, clumped together like gangly teenagers who refused to age.

"What's going on here?" Christie demanded. "I used to live in that apartment building."

Without ceremony Matt plunked some keys into her hand. "After you left New York, your father took over the lease on your apartment. He was convinced you'd be coming back, and he wanted you to have your own place waiting for you.''

Christie stumbled from the cab, not knowing whether to laugh or cry. Her father's audacity was impressive. It was monumental, in fact—the way he made assumptions about his ability to control her life. And here she was back in New York at her old apartment, so far operating exactly according to his plan.

Matt joined Christie on the sidewalk. He was balancing her duffel bag over one shoulder, looking like a sailor on shore leave. She glared at him in the light cast by an old-fashioned street lamp.

''You should've told me about this ploy of my father's,'' she declared. ''Instead you kept quiet about it all weekend. What else are you hiding from me, Matt?''

He rubbed the back of his neck with his free hand. ''Let's go up to your apartment and get this whole business out of the way,'' he muttered. He leaned down to talk to the cabdriver. ''I'll be back down in just a few minutes.''

''Hey, take your time,'' the brawny man answered with a good-natured wink. ''I'll be here with the meter running. But your young lady looks mighty hot tempered to me. You'd better have a good story to tell her.''

Christie flushed, personally inclined to show the cabdriver some of her alleged hot temper. He and Matt seemed to be conspiring in a provokingly male fashion. Already Matt was propelling her up the steps of the mellow old brownstone.

Deep-rooted habits took over. As Christie unlocked the door to the lobby, she gave the key a quick sideways twist because this bolt was prone to stick. She entered the dim hallway, lit by an ancient chandelier hanging in the shadows far above. As usual, half the bulbs were burned out.

Every step Christie took was so familiar to her. She'd lived in this building since graduating from college. She knew right where the carpet runner on the stairs had a hole that always caught dangerously at shoe heels; she knew that Mr. Bretton in Apartment 2B always stood behind his door with a tennis racket whenever he heard footsteps approaching, ready to whack potential burglars over the head. Christie herself had almost been whacked by that tennis racket a few times.

Now she and Matt stood in front of Apartment 2A. With practiced ease she went through the complicated process of unlocking all the bolts that armored the door. Stepping over the threshold of the apartment, she found the lights already on and shining a welcome.

"Home, sweet home," she said caustically. "Who would have thought—" She stopped dead, frozen in dismay. For there was her father, rising from the armchair in the small living room. Christopher Daniels the Third...in the flesh.

Somehow Christie made herself swivel back toward Matt. "How could you do this to me?" she hissed. "It's too soon—I'm not ready!"

Matt's face was impassive, as if he felt absolutely no need to explain himself. It was her father who took over, as suavely and expertly as always. Christie heard his quiet yet commanding voice speak behind her.

"You did an excellent job, Matthew, bringing my daughter back to me. I'm always grateful to a man who delivers."

Christie winced, hating the way he talked about her as if she were a package that had been lost in the mail until Matt came along. But Matt didn't answer her father, staring hard at Christie instead. What message was he trying to bore into her mind? She stiffened, rejecting his silent efforts at communication. He had betrayed her trust—leading her straight into this trap without offering any warning at all.

Matt finally gave a shrug and set down Christie's duffel bag, his gestures portraying a rough impatience. "Good night, Christopher," he said curtly. He glanced at Christie again. "Hang in there," he added in a low voice. Then he was gone, leaving her to face her father alone.

She closed the door and made a big production of shooting the bolts into place. But there was no way to avoid this late-night confrontation, no matter how unexpected or unfair it might be. Christopher Daniels the Third knew how to outwait any opponent. Christie leaned her forehead against the door for a moment, took a deep breath and turned around.

He was a man of only medium height, and his build was slight. Even so, Christopher Daniels conveyed an imposing presence whatever his setting. His hair was prematurely white, as pure in color as a fresh snowfall. Thick and glossy, it waved back from his forehead with its own restrained energy. He was dressed impeccably in a dark suit; understated, expensive elegance was his style. Christie had learned when she was a very small child never to climb into his lap and rumple his clothes—never to hug him or muss his hair.

Now he made no move to touch her or express affection. That was entirely predictable. He stood where he was, his blue eyes examining her with thoroughness.

"You look well, Mary Christine. It seems that living in New Mexico agrees with you."

"Yes, it does." As always when she confronted her father, her stomach tightened with the vague conviction that she'd done something wrong. These days she needed to tilt her head only a bit to look into his smooth, remarkably unlined face. Yet she remembered too well what it was like when her father had towered over her and she'd had to crane her head all the way back to get a good view of him. Now she was an adult, but he still seemed to occupy a great height.

She walked briskly into the living room, trying to establish a more equal contact with him. "The furniture is exactly the same," she observed. "That's amazing. I gave it all away to Mrs. Kirby downstairs. What did you do—buy it back from her?"

"I paid her a very decent price. Both of us came away pleased from the transaction."

Christie looked around at the remnants of her New York life: the boxy sofa upholstered in a bland beige, the flimsy rattan bookshelves, the red vinyl armchair that was so overstuffed it reminded her of a mutant mushroom. For such a long time she'd meant to throw everything out and redecorate with antiques. By moving to Red River she'd accomplished that goal. Yet now all her former bad taste was back in place in this apartment, haunting her once again. She had to laugh at the irony of it.

"Care to share the joke?" her father asked.

Christie hesitated, then shook her head. Christopher Daniels was not known for his sense of humor. She sat down in the puffy vinyl chair.

"Look, sir... Father," she began, never quite sure what to call him anymore. "I take it you've gone to all this effort so I'll feel at home. But New York isn't my home anymore. I think that's the first thing you should realize." She was proud of her calm, reasonable tone, and she was beginning to feel a little more in control of the situation.

"And about this whole thing with Matt Gallagher," she went on in a forceful voice. "I know what you're trying to do! You think I'll conveniently fall in love with him and move back here. Sorry I have to disappoint you. That just isn't going to happen." Christie shifted around in the bulbous red chair, unable to get comfortable. Anger, hurt and longing all mixed together inside her when she thought of Matt. But she couldn't let her father know how very close she *had* come to falling in love this time.

Christopher sat down on the sofa across from her, automatically straightening the creases in his pants. He perpetually used subtle little gestures like that—always adjusting his silk tie, pulling down an immaculate shirt cuff to just the right point on his wrist, realigning his gold watchband. But his movements weren't nervous, merely precise. Now he gazed steadily at Christie, one of his elbows resting on the sofa arm.

"Mary Christine, I'll be frank with you. When I first met Matthew, it occurred to me that you and he might be compatible. But I learned my lesson after I tried to push you into an engagement with Oren. I'll never try that again. Matthew was simply the best man for the job of bringing you back. He's someone I trust.''

Christie bit her lip. He sounded so emotionless, so logical, calling her a "job" to be accomplished. Matt could sound cool and emotionless, too, blast him! And tonight he'd shown himself to be completely on her father's side. The subject of Matt Gallagher was too painful to even think about, however. It made Christie want to yell at her father. And yelling at him again for any reason simply wasn't going to work; she had to remember that. She struggled to keep her tone as moderate as his.

"I only came back to New York for one reason—to clear up this nonsense about you dissolving the business.''

He realigned the maroon silk handkerchief protruding discreetly from his breast pocket. "I assure you, Mary Christine, I was very serious in my intent when I had those documents drafted for your signature. But now I hope another alternative is possible.'' He paused, apparently for dramatic effect. His drama was always understated, which somehow made it more potent than if he were to indulge in histrionics. Christie found herself sitting straighter, the vinyl cushions squeaking under her. She waited apprehensively for her father to go on.

"Mary Christine . . . I'm getting old.'' He held up a well-manicured hand to stave off her protest. "No, don't tell me that I'm only in my fifties, that I'm in perfect health or that I'll indubitably live to be ninety-five. All those facts are true, by the way—I intend to survive to a very ripe old age. And I'll survive better if I know you've taken your rightful place in the family business. Starting immediately, you will be instated as chairman of the board at Daniels, Peters, Bainbridge and Gallagher. You will be the majority stockholder... the head of the firm."

Christie stared at him in stunned disbelief. "That's *your* job, Dad. I mean, Father... sir."

He looked bemused. "You never called me 'Daddy,' the way most little girls do with their fathers. I wonder why that was?"

"'Daddy' is the kind of person who gives you piggyback rides and takes you sledding," she said distractedly.

An expression she couldn't read flickered over her father's dignified features. It was gone so quickly she couldn't identify it—but perhaps it had been actual regret.

"Mary Christine, I'll admit we haven't been relaxed together like some fathers and daughters. I'm trying to make that up to you now. Your main complaint about me seems to be that I'm manipulative and overbearing. But when I resign from the company and you take over, you'll be in complete charge of the business. You'll be on your own, with no interference from me."

"That business is your life, Dad, so what are you talking about? You can't just walk away from it, no matter what you say!"

He stood up, moving with the limberness of a man half his age. His trouser hems fell into perfect position over his polished shoes; his pants were never too

short or too long. He strolled thoughtfully across to
the window. "A boxer or a football player should always quit his sport while he's still on top, while he's
still a champion. That's the way I want it to be for me,
Mary Christine. I have other plans, other projects,
don't worry about that. But I'm going to leave the
stock market gracefully. And it was always my intention to pass the company on to you . . . my daughter,
my heir."

Christie followed him to the window. "You're talking garbage. I know you, you're indulging in another
one of your schemes. First of all, you wanted to leave
your company to a son—not a daughter. And in the
second place, you don't believe I really *could* take over
the company. You have absolutely no faith in my
competence." Her voice trembled with suppressed
anger. But this time she wasn't going to act like a kid,
she reminded herself fiercely. She stared out at the row
of buildings across the street.

Her father shifted position. For a moment it seemed
he would step closer, and he raised his hand as if to
touch her shoulder. But after a brief hesitation he
folded his arms and gazed straight out the window
himself.

"I believe I should clarify a few things," he said in
his even, expressionless voice. "It's true that I wanted
a son. I was disappointed when your mother and I
learned that her health wouldn't permit her to have
any more children. This may surprise you, Mary
Christine, but I wanted a houseful of children—boys
and girls both."

"Instead you ended up with just me," she said
woodenly, her own voice as controlled as his.

"Not 'just' you—it wasn't like that at all. Even when you were a baby I could see you were smarter, faster, better than any boy around. I've always been proud of you...I haven't expressed it very well, that's all. When you left for New Mexico—I thought I'd lost you. I want you back, Mary Christine. I don't know how else to say it."

She gripped the windowsill. This was the closest her father had ever come to showing any affection for her. It shook her. She'd spent so much of her life worshiping him, wanting his praise and love. Was he offering them to her at last? Or was this one more move in another of his complicated power games?

"It's very late," he said, glancing at his watch. "You need some rest, Mary Christine, and perhaps some food. You'll find your refrigerator well stocked, I believe. Think about what I've said—don't make any rash decisions. That's all I ask."

Christie didn't answer. He was being too darn reasonable...offering her too much, and then actually giving her time to think about it. Now he walked to the door. He used the unhurried gait that always took him quickly where he wanted to go. Christopher Daniels achieved a myriad of goals and activities without ever seeming to rush anywhere.

"Wait," she called after him. "Just tell me the truth about Matt. No matter what you say, I know you planned something for him and me. Damn it, you knew I'd be vulnerable to him!"

Christopher smiled faintly. "I'm being honest with you. As your father, of course I want you to end up with a good man. Someone like Matthew—perhaps even Matthew himself. But he has a strong will, and so do you, Mary Christine. I'd be foolish to think I could force either one of you into anything.'' With that he let himself out the door. Immediately the apartment seemed to shrink a little, as if diminished by his exit.

Christie stalked to the cramped little kitchen and pulled open the door of the fridge. It was crammed with all her favorite foods. Bagels from that wonderful bakery on Second Avenue, two bottles of sweet acidophilus milk, a jar of orange marmalade...and in the freezer, a carton of frozen chocolate-chip yogurt.

She was surprised her father knew so much about her tastes, and for a moment she was touched that he'd gone to all this trouble. Then she remembered what an observant man he was, always filing away little facts in his brain that might come in handy at a later date. He did that with everyone! And as far as going to any amount of trouble, his secretary had probably done all the shopping.

Christie slammed the refrigerator door shut. But already her stomach was rumbling in protest. Because of nervous strain, she hadn't eaten much all day. With a sigh of capitulation she opened the fridge again, taking out a bagel and the jar of marmalade.

There was nothing like a real New York City bagel. Christie ate it slowly, savoring every bite. And the entire time she felt like a traitor to herself. Somehow Red River seemed much too far away tonight.

CHAPTER NINE

THUMP THUMP THUMP! There it was again, a muffled banging sound. It had been going on for quite a while now and it simply wouldn't stop. Christie buried her head deeper under the pillow, scrunching her eyes tightly shut. All she wanted was to drift back into sleep, where no confusing problems awaited her. The morning was blessedly cool for a New York summer, and she was very warm and snug under her covers. She wanted to remain that way.

THUMP THUMP!

"Oh, rats!" Christie emerged blearily from the haven of her bed. She grabbed her robe and padded to the front door. Here was the source of all that obnoxious banging. "Who's there?" she demanded.

"It's me," came Matt's deep voice. "Let me in, will you? Some guy with a tennis racket keeps trying to attack me."

She scowled at the door. "Go away, Matt Gallagher. You're not my favorite person right now."

"We have to talk, Christie. Let me in there!"

She knew him well enough to realize that he wouldn't go away. He was stubborn, mule-headed and completely impossible. Mumbling in disgust, Christie went about the elaborate process of unlocking the door.

"What's taking you so long?" Matt's voice complained.

She yanked at a bolt, then went after another one. "In Red River half the time I leave my front door wide open. That's a much more rational way to live, you know." She undid the last of the locks.

Matt came charging into the apartment, fresh and vibrant this morning. He was wearing his navy corduroy pants again, and a shirt of blue-and-green plaid. His sleeves were rolled up and Christie could see the reddish-gold hair on his forearms. Oh, no. Next thing she knew she'd be exploring for freckles. She backed away from him, rubbing her eyes to bring herself fully awake.

"Those are great pajamas," Matt remarked.

Christie glanced down self-consciously at her thin cotton pajamas, decorated with a pattern of black Scotties in red bows. She drew her robe tight and cinched the belt. The robe was a bright, fire-engine red, exactly matching the bows on the Scotties.

Matt's eyes were a smoky amber. "Yes, those are some pajamas," he murmured, advancing toward her. "You look extra soft in them . . ."

Christie retreated into the kitchen, barricading herself behind the counter. "Don't start anything with me," she commanded. "I'm not in the mood, not after what you did to me last night."

He leaned in the doorway, his eyes lingering on her mouth. "For some reason you make me think of fresh blueberries," he said musingly. "That's right, blueberries fresh-picked and spilling out of a tin pail, just waiting to be tasted."

"Have this instead." Christie reached into a bowl on the counter and tossed him a peach, which he caught smartly in an overhand grip. He took a good bite out of it, juice trickling down his chin. Then he grinned at her.

"It's a great day, isn't it?" he asked.

"Just wonderful," she rejoined. "You and my father are probably conniving at something else behind my back. I can't wait to find out what's in store for me."

He came to sit on a stool at the other side of the counter, chomping another bite from the peach. "Look, I wasn't too happy last night about keeping you in the dark. But tell me this—would you have come up to your apartment if you'd known your father was here?"

"Absolutely not. But that doesn't justify what you did." She splashed milk into a bowl of puffed rice cereal, then ladled on some orange marmalade. Matt watched her closely.

"Good Lord, you're actually going to eat that glop you're concocting?"

"This was my favorite breakfast when I was six years old," she said gloomily. "My father remembered that, just like he remembered everything else." She waved her spoon around. "Look what he's done here! He thinks he's a genie or something, recreating my old life in every detail. He expects me to fall right back into it, as if I'd never left."

"At least he's not talking about dissolving the business anymore," Matt pointed out.

Christie glanced at him sharply. "You know all about it, don't you? How my father wants me to take over the firm, just like that. I suppose the two of you planned out this whole ridiculous plot, step by step.''

"It's not a plot—your father genuinely wants you to head up the business. But the first I heard about it was this morning, when he telephoned me at my place. He sounded pretty excited about his plan."

"He never sounds excited about anything," she said skeptically.

"Sure he does. You just have to know how to read his signals. When he talks slower and more calmly than usual, it means he's really busting with enthusiasm."

Christie munched her cereal, and an intriguing new thought occurred to her. "Matt, have you considered all the implications of this plan? I'd end up being your boss! I bet that thought doesn't thrill you too much. Admit it."

He studied his peach pit. "I could handle you. You'd find out right away that it's no good trying to manage me."

"Ha!" She dug her spoon down into her soggy cereal. "You've met your match in me," she said with relish. "I might like a chance to get you under my thumb and see you squirm, Matt Gallagher."

He reached over and took hold of her left hand, lightly caressing her fingers. "Hmm . . . you do have a lovely thumb, Christie. But you'd never be able to get me under it."

She snatched her hand away. "This is all idiotic talk, anyway. The idea of me running the firm is completely absurd."

"Why? Your father thinks you're capable of doing it. I agree with him, as a matter of fact—I'm convinced that if you ever devote yourself to one project, you'll succeed brilliantly at it.''

Christie smoothed back her tangled hair, baffled by all her conflicting emotions. In the last twenty-four hours she'd received some heady praise. First from her father and now from Matt, both of them talking seriously about her ability to head up one of Wall Street's most prestigious brokerage houses. It was hard not to be swayed by such extravagant appeals to her ego. At last she seemed to have her father's unqualified approval. And if she agreed to his plan, she'd be working every day with Matt. Oh, that was temptation, indeed...

She pushed away her bowl of cereal with an abrupt motion, sloshing milk onto the counter. ''I can't believe I'm actually considering any of this,'' she exclaimed. ''I'm letting it go to my head, that's what. Being a stockbroker gives me hives! You know, Matt, there may not be a lot of glory or a lot of money in running a bed and breakfast. But it's fun and it makes me feel good inside. That's the bottom line.''

Matt propped his elbows on the counter and leaned toward her. His golden-brown eyes were intense. ''Christie—if you come back to your father's company now, things will be different than they were before. Heck, it'll be *your* company this time. The more I think about the idea, the more I like it. You deserve an opportunity like this.''

''I'm trying to tell you I don't *want* the opportunity, no matter how great you think it is.''

''But what about the two of us, Christie? If you stay in New York, we'll have a chance at something together.'' His voice had dropped down to the huskiness she found much too compelling, and his hands reached to cup her face. She closed her eyes briefly.

"Matt...you knew I was only coming back to New York for a few days," she whispered. "That was the agreement all along."

"Things have changed. Your father's given you a new chance at your career. And, darn it all—I want *us* to have a chance." He brought her closer, but the counter was an obstacle between them. Christie ended up straining forward on the tips of her toes, bent over awkwardly with the belt of her robe dangling in her cereal bowl. She didn't mind, however, because her head was cradled against Matt's chest. She fingered the soft material of his shirt.

"You can't forget Red River any more than I can," she murmured. "If we had anything special, it happened there. Don't you see?"

"We can capture the specialness anywhere, Christie. Let me prove it to you. Spend the day with me—I already told your father I won't be in to work."

This last statement was enough to make her straighten up quickly, smacking Matt's jawbone with the top of her head.

"Ouch," he said. "Lord, you have a hard skull."

"I don't believe it!"

He rubbed his jaw, wiggling it from side to side as if to make sure it still worked. "It's true. You're amazingly solid under all that pretty hair. I feel like I just got butted by a goat."

She ignored these comments about the density of her skull. "You know what I meant—I can't believe you're actually taking another day off. This is truly an event! Is this the same person who told me he hadn't been on a vacation in fifteen years?''

He looked disgruntled. ''This doesn't mean I'm slipping or anything. After today—that's it. Back to work as usual.'' But he didn't sound overly fervent.

''The Red River effect is still holding,'' she said triumphantly. ''You have all the signs—inability to sit still in an office, fondness for corduroy pants, early-morning cheerfulness on a Tuesday.''

''You make it sound like I have some kind of disease,'' Matt objected.

''Well, maybe you do. Wait right here while I get ready. I think I *will* spend the day with you—just to find out how serious your case really is.'' Christie hurried into the bathroom, closed the door and cranked on the shower faucets. She felt lighthearted. It couldn't hurt to spend this one day with Matt in New York—just one day, nothing more. She slid out of her robe and pajamas, then stepped under the invigorating stream of the shower.

Christie began soaping in her usual brisk manner, but after a moment her hand paused on a sudsy shoulder. Taking a shower seemed very intimate in this small apartment, with Matt waiting out there on the other side of the door. Her skin was heating up in a most disturbing way, and she didn't think it was just the effect of the hot water.

Haphazardly she dumped some shampoo on her head, wishing she didn't have so much blasted hair. Today she washed and rinsed it in record time, hopping out of the shower with a sense of relief.

But her body was still flushed and tingling with an awareness of Matt's presence. She wrapped herself in a big, fuzzy towel, yet even that didn't help subdue her wayward physical reactions. Christie stared at her reflection in the fogged-up mirror. It was like gazing at herself through a mist, and she was unable to discern the expression in her own eyes. But she knew what she felt…a powerful, frightening yearning for Matt. And she knew what would happen if she deliberately opened that door right now and walked out to him.

Christie grabbed her comb and frantically started yanking it through the wet snarls of her hair. She was hurting her scalp, but she needed any sensation to counteract the pulse of longing inside her. This desire of hers wasn't merely physical, that was the most terrifying part. Her emotions for Matt were starting to run far too deep and intense. Where would they take her if she actually gave in to them?

A long moment later Christie opened the bathroom door and stepped out. She was wearing her robe with the belt firmly knotted, and clutching a towel to her body as if that would somehow protect her from her own feelings.

Matt was in the living room, his back turned to her. He was speaking on the telephone. "I tell you, Sawyer, that's a highly undervalued stock! We should be buying right now, not selling." His voice was impatient, but full of energy and life. Christie felt oddly deflated and relaxed her grip on the towel. While she'd been entertaining fantasies about Matt, he'd been getting caught up in the stock market once again. She watched him a moment longer; he gesticulated freely with one hand as he spoke, jabbing his finger into the air for emphasis. He seemed completely unaware of Christie's presence behind him, but even so her body still ached for his touch. She turned and hurried into her bedroom, closing the door between them.

Christie felt only a little more composed by the time she buttoned herself into the one dress she'd brought from Red River. It was a sleeveless cotton print scattered all over with whimsical flowers in shades of mulberry and plum. The waist was trimly fitted but the skirt swirled freely around her legs. She pulled her wet hair back into a ponytail and buckled on her sandals. Then she sailed out of the bedroom. Matt was off the phone by now. His hair looked dishevelled, as if he'd been poking his hands into it.

"Let's go," she said, trying to ignore the appreciative way he was studying her. Darn this dress—the neckline was much too low. She ought to have worn a turtleneck, anything to fortify herself after those disturbing desires in the shower.

"Christie," Matt said, but she just wanted to get out of the apartment. She prodded him downstairs and outside to the stoop of the building. Unfortunately Matt wasn't a person to give up easily.

"Christie," he began again. "You keep acting like you're afraid of what's happening between us."

She hugged her arms against her body and started walking down the street. She set a rapid pace, but Matt took one stride for every two of hers.

"Maybe you're afraid of it, too," she challenged. "Maybe you're just as scared as I am about where it could lead."

"Look, Christie, I'm willing to acknowledge right now that you make me feel . . . crazy. Unhinged. No other woman has ever done that to me. Sure, it's scary. But I want to find out what's next for us."

She turned the corner, still moving at a good clip. "I want to find out, too," she said. "But I'll tell you what's making *me* crazy, Matt. It's the way you act like it's all one and the same thing—me taking over my father's business, you and I having a relationship. A package deal, all neat and tidy! Why does it have to be like that?"

He took her elbow as they were jostled by other people on the crowded sidewalk. "You're wrong, I'm not looking for a package deal. Suppose you don't take your father up on his offer. You've had enough of the stock market—that's understandable. You tell him no thanks, and then you start up a bed and breakfast right here in Manhattan. It's a great idea, in fact. You'd have more business than you could handle. And it would just leave you and me. No more interference from your father." He smiled, as if he'd just solved everything about her life in the space of two minutes. Christie retreated to the doorway of a small jewelry shop, gazing at the window display of ceramic earrings.

"You just don't understand," she said to Matt. "All my life I've made choices to please a man—my father. If I start making choices simply to please *you,* it's the same thing all over again."

Matt stared at the jewelry display himself. "How can any rational woman dangle something like that from her earlobes?" he demanded, pointing at a pair of earrings that looked like giant, fluorescent pinwheels. Then he turned to Christie. "Seems to me I've offered you a pretty fair compromise here. Sure, you'd be moving back to New York, but you'd still have your choice of careers. I'd do everything I could to help you get set up. What's so bad about that?''

She blew out her breath explosively and started walking again. "For one thing, a bed and breakfast in Manhattan is the most absurd idea I've ever heard. I can just see myself with a few tiny rooms in a walk-up, putting out the welcome mat. In Red River I have a big house and garden. That's what I want to share with my guests—a real home.''

"No problem. Buy yourself a house someplace nearby, like Connecticut—''

"Stop," she ordered, planting herself in the middle of the sidewalk. "Matt, you're missing the whole point. I'm the one who decided to move to Red River. I'm the one who bought that old house and painted it exactly the right shade of blue. Those choices might seem insignificant to you, but to me they're everything. If I move to Connecticut—even if I find a great house, a perfect house, it's still *your* choice. Not mine!''

"Lord, you're the most stubborn woman I've ever met. How can any relationship exist without compromise?''

"You can't ask one person to do all the compromising," she stated flatly. "And that's exactly what you're doing, Matt. You're asking me to make all the changes. What are *you* willing to give up?''

He opened his mouth, then shut it without saying anything. He seemed to be stymied by her question. At the same time, he and Christie were now blocking the passage of an elderly woman who was walking an overweight dachshund. The dachshund sat down on Matt's foot, panting laboriously.

"Come along, Patty," said the woman, pulling on the dog's leash. "Just one more block—I promise that's all."

Patty vacated Matt's foot, standing up and wagging her tail. She burrowed a path between Christie and Matt, the old woman toddling along after her.

"Now, there's a relationship," Christie remarked, watching the two of them go down the sidewalk. Patty's long stomach rolled from side to side between her four stubby legs, but she moved with alacrity. "I mean, they're both getting exactly what they need from each other."

"Is that how you picture yourself in the future, Christie? Tucked away in Red River with your two cats for company... and no man to make unreasonable requests of you."

"There are worse fates," she said defiantly as she and Matt cut across the street. They walked together in tense silence, nothing resolved between them. Christie accelerated her pace, her damp ponytail flopping against her back in an energetic rhythm.

"Hey, what is this?" Matt asked. "Are you trying to run away from me? It won't do you any good. Damn it, we're going to spend the day together and you're going to have the most fun you've ever had."

She glanced over at him. "Be sure to tell me when the fun begins."

"It's starting right now. We're going to catch a bus, and then you'll see exactly what I'm talking about." There was a determined look on his face as he propelled Christie along.

A short time later they stood in a ticket line at Battery Park on the very tip of Manhattan. The early-morning coolness had burned off completely, and the sun bored down from the sky with implacable heat. Christie lifted her ponytail and flapped it around, trying unsuccessfully to fan herself. Damp patches of sweat had formed on the back of Matt's shirt and under his arms.

"I bet you haven't been to the Statue of Liberty since you were a kid," he said.

"Actually, no, I haven't—"

"You're going to enjoy this. Trust me, this is going to be the best day of your life."

A hot breeze rolled an empty soft drink can against Christie's foot. She nudged the can away with her toe and flapped her hair around some more, feeling rather like a horse swatting at flies with its tail.

"Are we having fun yet?" she asked.

Matt frowned at her. "As a matter of fact—yes, we are."

"Good. I wouldn't want to miss anything, you know."

"Just wait till this line finally starts moving. Then you'll see what fun is all about." Matt looked more grim and determined than ever.

The line *did* move...eventually. Matt purchased two tickets, waving them in triumph. He and Christie fought their way through the crowd to stand in another line, waiting to board a ferry. She wiped a trickle of perspiration away from her forehead.

"Are we still having fun?" she asked.

This time he didn't answer, only gave her a sour look. He bought two lime sodas from a soft-drink cart, and thrust one of them into her hand. She drank eagerly to soothe her parched throat. Lime soda...that was what she and Matt had shared up in the New Mexico forest. But it just didn't taste as good here in New York. She was glad of that, very glad.

"Matt," she began, "this idea of yours isn't working. You might as well accept it. You're having a lousy time! But you *did* enjoy yourself no end in Red River."

"I'm having a great time. And so are you. Just wait until we're on the ferry. Then you'll see. This'll be the best damn day you ever had in your life."

Sometime later Christie sank gratefully onto a bench on the top deck of the ferry. Her dress clung to her body, wilted by the heat. She stretched her legs, flexing her toes. Matt settled down beside her.

"All right, this is it," he said. He glanced around expectantly as the ferry moved out onto the water. A small boy of about eight or so sat down next to him.

"I'm going to be sick," the little boy announced in a calm, matter-of-fact voice. Matt straightened up, an uneasy expression on his face.

"Hey, kid—don't do it here. Where are your parents?"

"My mother's standing over by the rail. But she can't stop me from being sick. Nobody can."

Matt jiggled Christie's elbow. "Do something!" he hissed. "Lord, look at the kid."

Christie peered around Matt. The child did look rather green, but was still calm. She gave him a reassuring smile. "I think you'd better go to your mother," she said. "It will make you feel better."

"No, it won't." The little boy gazed back at her solemnly. "I'm going to be sick."

Matt grimaced. He was turning somewhat green himself. Christie reached over and patted the little boy on the shoulder.

"Now, listen here," she said in a tone of encouragement. "Nothing in life is inevitable. That's the first thing you have to learn. You're not going to be sick! Go stand there by your mom and take in some fresh air. You'll see that I'm right about this."

The boy was silent for a moment, as if giving her words some deep thought. But then he shrugged. "I'm still going to be sick," he said. The child stood up and went swaying toward his mother.

Matt rubbed his forehead. "I like kids a lot better when they're not about to upchuck on my shoes," he muttered. "All right, now we're getting somewhere. We're really going to have fun." But with every lurch of the boat his skin grew more pale. Christie suddenly felt guilty. He was trying so hard to have a good time, and she hadn't been cooperative in the least. It was time she relented, if only a bit. She pulled Matt to his feet.

"Come on, you need some fresh air yourself." She prodded him over to the side of the boat, making sure she kept him well away from that little boy. "Now, look at the view," she encouraged him. "It'll take your mind off the fact that . . . you're going to be sick."

Matt glared at her from his slumped position at the rail.

"Sorry," she said hastily. "But, really, look at the view."

The Manhattan skyline was gradually receding from them. Old and new skyscrapers balanced each other in graceful contrast. The modern towers rose up in a sheer, awesome simplicity of height, their starkness tempered by the more ornate stone and brick of the older buildings. Altogether it was a stunning sight—an island of skyscrapers, rising from the ocean.

Matt straightened up, apparently feeling better. "You're right," he said. "Look at that. There's no other city like it in the world. Think of what you've been giving up these past few months. Going to Broadway shows, eating at all the great sidewalk cafés, bicycling through Central Park."

Those were all attractions she'd been able to put firmly out of her mind . . . until now. Matt's voice was seductive as he listed the pleasures of living in New York City. She had to fight back.

"What about all the pollution?" she demanded. "Look at it right now—the sky is that awful charcoal brown instead of clear blue. What about the grime and soot you have to wipe off your face at the end of every day? And the traffic, the noise—"

"The polar bears at the Bronx Zoo," he murmured in her ear. "Radio City Music Hall and the Rockettes. The Coney Island boardwalk."

Darn him, he was really playing dirty now. Nostalgia swept over her, heightened by the tang of ocean air and the cries of sea gulls. She could almost taste a Coney Island hot dog. With an effort she turned away from Matt, but now she was faced with the majestic beauty of the Statue of Liberty. The statue was immense and imposing yet molded in such detail that the folds of her robes seemed fashioned from heavy cloth rather than from sheets of metal. And she raised her golden torch to the sky as a beacon to all the long-ago immigrants who had passed in weariness and bewilderment through Ellis Island. That beacon seemed a pledge to the future, as well as a memorial to the past. Christie had taken so much for granted when she lived here; now it all looked fresh and magical to her because she was seeing it with Matt.

When the ferry docked at Liberty Island and Matt was on solid ground again, he seemed filled with renewed energy and enthusiasm. He pulled Christie along. "I bet it's been years since you climbed all the way to the top of the statue, hasn't it?" he asked.

"Yes, but—"

"Aha, I knew it! Now you're really going to have fun."

Christie had always considered herself an athletic person, capable of any physical undertaking. But by the time she and Matt had toiled up the statue's pedestal, she was wheezing for breath. Stair climbing just wasn't one of her sports.

"I think that's good enough," she panted. "We can rest here on the balcony for a while, then hop on the elevator and go back down."

"No chance. We're going all the way to the top." Matt dragged her on to the next staircase.

"This is ridiculous," Christie told him as they wound their way upward. "Whatever you're trying to prove to me, it's not going to work. I'm not going to have some wonderful revelation that will convince me to stay in New York!"

Matt stopped abruptly, drawing her close to him. "Come on, admit it," he said persuasively. "You're having fun, aren't you?"

"No, I'm not," she muttered.

"I know you are. You'd rather be right here with me than anywhere else in the world. What will it hurt you to say it?" He was using unfair tactics, his hand moving in a caress over her bare shoulder. Christie stiffened, but it was no use fighting his appeal. Blast him, he was right! She was hot, tired and cranky, and a belligerent lady was trying to squeeze past them on the stairs. Yet in spite of all that, Christie wanted to be here with Matt Gallagher, inside the Statue of Liberty. She wanted to be with him no matter where he was.

She pulled away from him and went on climbing, right on the heels of the belligerent lady. But no matter how quickly she took the stairs ahead of Matt, she couldn't escape her fear... the terrible fear that already she was losing her Red River dreams.

CHAPTER TEN

MIDNIGHT GLITTERED outside on the streets of Manhattan, but the atmosphere in Rudy's Tavern was so dark and smoky that Christie could barely see Matt's face across from her. They were sitting in an intimate booth near the piano bar. Spotlighted at the piano was a thin woman of severe plainness. In a lush voice disconcertingly at odds with her appearance, she crooned out a 1940s ballad of unfulfilled love. The words were both melancholy and passionate, echoing Christie's mood. She turned her beer mug round and round in her hands. Nothing seemed capable of easing the dry ache in her throat. Every time she looked at Matt, the ache just got worse. She was grateful for the shadows that enveloped both of them now.

"Are you glad we spent the day together?" he murmured, setting down his own beer.

"Yes—no...oh, it turned out to be wonderful and you know it, Matt. But we've argued our problems back and forth for hours. Any solution for us seems farther away than ever."

"But it *was* a good day."

"It was...magical," Christie admitted reluctantly. After clambering all the way to the top of that darn statue and back down again, she and Matt had simply wandered through Manhattan together. They'd savored everything—eating pastry and sausage for lunch in Little Italy, browsing at all the secondhand shops on Canal Street, loitering on Seventh Avenue and consuming two cones apiece of Mike's Fat-Free Double-Chocolate-Fudge Frozen Yogurt. They hadn't done anything spectacular, but Christie knew she'd never forget a single detail of their day. Matt had been right after all when he had predicted how much fun they were going to have. She would always remember stopping with him to admire a tub of violets that brightened a drab fire escape, and she'd remember the way they'd perused an entire brick wall plastered with theater posters. Small things, poignant memories that would be imprinted on her mind forever...

But now the day was over. She and Matt were creating the last memory. Christie pressed her hands down on the nicked wooden table, wishing the lady at the piano would sing something more cheerful. Instead she launched into another ballad about impossible love.

"Christie, I'll tell you why none of your arguments hold up for me," Matt said, leaning toward her. "They're all based on some obscure defense of your principles. You refuse to set up a bed and breakfast in Connecticut because you think that'll threaten your freedom of choice. But in concrete, practical terms, what would you really be giving up? Answer me that."

Christie began shredding a paper napkin. "The freedom to make my own decisions is more than some obscure principle, Matt! It's the most precious thing I have right now, after all those years of being dominated by my father. I won't give it up easily. And don't you remember what you said when we were up at Big

Shelby's Gold Mine? I asked you why you couldn't buy some land close to New York. And you told me you didn't want just any piece of land. You wanted *that* piece. Well, I feel the same way about Red River. It's a special place...and it's my home now. Finding a real home isn't something a person should take for granted.''

Matt didn't seem to have any rebuttal to offer. Christie sensed that she should press her advantage. ''I've been thinking about something else,'' she went on. ''Let's suppose I do give in to you, and I buy myself a house in Connecticut. I change my whole life around for you—fine, wonderful. But that won't resolve the crisis you're going through on your own, Matt.''

''I never once said I was going through any damn crisis,'' he muttered.

''You don't have to say it. You're practically sprouting with frustration and discontentment. No matter how much you try to deny it, slaving day after day in the stock market isn't making you happy anymore. You're too disillusioned by all the sneaky insider trading, and people doing petty things to get around the rules. But some misguided sense of loyalty is keeping you stuck in the mire you detest!'' She wadded up all the shredded pieces of her napkin, invigorated by her own fervent words. And at last she seemed to be getting through to Matt, at least a little.

''Damn it, Christie.'' His voice was low and taut. ''All right, so a lot of things about the market are eating at my gut. They won't give me any peace.''

''So write about them,'' Christie persisted, trying to search out his expression in the murkiness of the tavern. "There are a lot of investors out there who'd appreciate any advice you could give them."

"Come on, Christie, who am I kidding here? I'm no writer. It takes a lot of audacity to sit down with a pen and a blank sheet of paper, and think you're going to create something halfway intelligible. I tried to do it last night, after I left your apartment and went to my place. I must have stared at that confounded piece of paper for three hours. I couldn't think of one single word that wasn't garbage." His voice was weighted with disgust.

Christie waved away a billow of cigarette smoke that intruded from the next booth. "Matt, congratulations. You've just had your first case of writer's block! Isn't that wonderful?"

"Sometimes I think you've really lost all your onions. This is one of those times."

"As a matter of fact, onions are very good for your health. Did you know that? And anyway, I think I know what your problem is. You need the right atmosphere for writing. In Red River you didn't have any trouble putting words down on paper. I mean, it all seems so clear now, doesn't it? You need to go back to New Mexico so you can write. There's no other solution!" Christie slapped her hand on the table in triumph. He couldn't argue with her this time. She'd completely won her case. Feeling jubilant, she clicked her mug against Matt's in a toast. Unfortunately, he didn't fall into the spirit of things and he left his beer sitting there on the table. Christie had to drink to his writing career on her own. "Here's to your brand-new future," she proclaimed. "Matthew Gallagher, market commentator. I love the sound of that. I think it's wonderful."

"Lord, you just don't seem to understand. I already have a career. I've devoted a lot of time and effort to it. And I'm good at it. Being a stockbroker is something I do well, Christie. I enjoy that feeling. I don't enjoy the way I feel when I sit down to write—incompetent, inept, inadequate. Am I finally getting through to you?"

"Yes, you are. Basically you're telling me that writing scares the heck out of you. Well, who wouldn't be scared? It's a totally new career, and it means starting from the beginning again. No accomplishments to back you up yet...just you and that blank piece of paper."

He laughed mirthlessly. "What do you know. Seems you do understand, Christie."

"Wait, I'm not finished," she told him. "Sure, I can sympathize with all your doubts and misgivings. But you can't let them stop you! You have what it takes to be a good writer. Maybe even a great one, as a matter of fact."

"When I was with you in Red River...I got swept away by certain things. Certain delusions. For a while there I actually pictured myself writing for a living, and fishing whenever the mood took me. What a fantasy!" He sounded both rueful and wistful. "But that's all over now," he went on after a pause, his voice turning somber. "I'm back in New York, dealing with real life again. That's the way it should be."

Christie wanted to reach over and shake Matt by the shoulders. She wanted to pull his ears, whack his head—do whatever it took to make him believe in his own dreams. Instead she kept her hands curled tightly in her lap, knowing how futile such efforts would be. Blast it, she couldn't seem to convince him of anything. He was just too darn obstinate.

The singer at the piano stood up to take a break, her austere black dress and dark hair blending into the shadows. Someone started the jukebox going, and another sad love song drifted onto the air. Christie had reached her limit—if she listened to any more sorrowful lyrics, she'd be sniffling in Matt's arms. She slid out of the booth.

"We're not doing each other any good," she declared. "Just take me back to the apartment, Matt, and we'll call it a night . . . a morning," she amended, realizing how long she and Matt had lingered together today. The trouble was, she wanted to go right on lingering with him.

Once they arrived at the apartment, Matt himself seemed reluctant to leave her. But he also seemed restless and keyed up. He prowled around the living room, stopping only to prod at miscellaneous items of furniture—an ugly steel magazine rack, a glass-topped cocktail table that had no charm whatsoever.

"This place doesn't look like you," he observed. "Not at all."

"Good," she said emphatically, glancing around. "I feel like a stranger here. I've outgrown this apartment. It's ironic . . . and a little sad. In his own peculiar way, I think my father sincerely wanted me to feel at home."

"You sound like you're not quite so angry at him anymore."

"Last night he really surprised me," she admitted. "He made a totally unexpected move."

"The next move is yours, Christie," Matt said abruptly. "It's not mine, or your father's. What are you going to do?"

"Why...I don't know," she answered, caught off balance by the directness of his question. "You've hardly given me any time to think today—"

"We've talked about your options." His voice was brusque. "Now it's up to you to choose one of them. You can accept your father's offer, or set up a bed and breakfast somewhere out here...or you can just fly back to New Mexico and be done with it. You wanted choices? You've got them, all right."

Anger flared through her. "You make them sound more like ultimatums than choices."

He came over and stared down at her. "We've talked it all out, Christie. Words won't solve what's between us. I've wanted you all day. Lord, I've wanted you since the first minute I saw you and you were choking on that damn button. Even then you were the most desirable woman I've ever known. Now it's time to do something besides talk."

His nearness made it difficult for her to think rationally, logically. She stepped back, but he caught hold of her wrist. His eyes were a dark, burning gold.

Her heart beat wildly, pulsing heat through her veins. But still she tried to tug away. "Matt, wait—"

His mouth descended on hers, silencing her protest. With masterful purpose his hands moved down her back, her hips, pressing her toward him. She held herself rigid, resisting the domination of his touch as long as she could. But it was her own desire that defeated her, her own need for Matt. Giving a low moan of capitulation she yielded to him, her lips growing compliant under his. And then she returned his kiss instead of merely receiving it, bold and eager with her own demands. When at last she broke away from him, her mouth was soft and bruised with passion.

But this was only a prelude. His hands still on her hips, Matt rotated Christie's body in a slow, sensual dance until she was leaning against the wall. He reached up to loosen the elastic band that held her hair captive, and now it tumbled over one of her shoulders in a wave of honeyed silk. Matt smoothed it aside and traced his finger above the low neckline of her dress. He was privateering her senses, stealing the last of her self-control. She trembled as he began unfastening the buttons along the front of her bodice.

"You're so beautiful," he murmured, his voice thick. He slipped the narrow straps of her dress down over her shoulders and bent to kiss the first gentle swell of her breasts.

She clung to him, her fingers weaving through his russet hair. But a remnant of self-preservation stirred inside her. With each caress of his hands, each touch of his lips he was possessing her, making her his. If she didn't fight this sweet domination, he would own her completely. "Matt...don't," she whispered, straining back against the wall.

He lifted his head. "Are you still afraid, Christie?" His voice was harsh now, uncompromising in its tone. "That's the real problem between us, isn't it? You're afraid to trust your own feelings. Goals, accomplishments...those you can handle. But not this.

You think that if you give in to your emotions, you might really end up compromising your principles.''

She twisted away from him, bringing the curtains of her hair protectively over her bare skin. ''You're distorting everything,'' she exclaimed hotly. ''You're the one who won't give in, Matt—not to anything. You refuse to listen to your own feelings, even when they tell you that your life is making you miserable and something has to change!''

''Maybe we're two of a kind,'' he said mockingly. ''Have you considered that? Both of us afraid to be swept away by our emotions…afraid of where they'll take us.''

Christie was silent, holding her arms crossed over her chest, averting her face. She didn't want to listen to him. After a moment he went to the door.

''The next move is still yours, Christie,'' he said. ''You can't get around that, no matter how hard you try. Your father has stated his case…and I've stated mine. Some points just aren't negotiable.'' He left her, pulling the door shut behind him with a forceful bang.

Christie yanked up the straps of her dress. Matt Gallagher was so blasted inflexible, intractable, infuriating! She wished she had something good and heavy to hurl at the door, but the only thing available was a peach she'd left out on the counter.

She sank onto a stool, pressing her hands against the flushed skin of her face. She still felt the effects of Matt's touch, as if she were suffering the aftershocks of an earthquake. She longed to feel nothing at all. And maybe that meant he was right…maybe she truly was afraid of her own emotions.

She grabbed the peach, turned and threw it straight at the door. It landed with a "splat" right in the center panel, then fell soggily to the floor.

Christie didn't feel better in the least.

THE SKYSCRAPERS of New York's financial district loomed over Christie, shutting out the early-morning light. She walked along quickly through this unnatural gloom, reaching the steps of Federal Hall where she'd gulped countless lunches. Now she could sit down here for once without having to rush frantically. She stretched out her legs, but such leisure in this place was an odd sensation. For a moment she had the urge to jump up and hurry off to generate some more commissions for her father—but only for a moment. How things had changed for her!

Down and across from the steps was the stately facade of the New York Stock Exchange. But Christie didn't need to see it; she could close her eyes and capture an image of its classical pillars jutting high above her. She knew that her own personal vision of the Stock Exchange dated all the way back to a time when she was three or four years old, and her father had brought her here to impress her future calling upon her mind. He had succeeded admirably in his intent—as a kid she'd experienced nightmares about those pillars coming to life and chasing her like lumbering giants.

Christie leaned forward and wrapped her arms around her knees. Last night she hadn't had to worry about nightmares or dreams of any kind. She'd barely slept at all after her searing confrontation with Matt. His words had haunted her, as well as his kisses. He demanded that she make a decision, and of course a decision was inevitable. But none of her choices seemed clear. Alone in the apartment, she'd examined every alternative over and over again. Not one of them produced a sensation of peace or well-being. Instead she was lost in a turmoil of conflicting desires and longings.

A rumpled young man climbed the steps, his jacket identifying him as a floor trader on the Stock Exchange. His pockets bristled with pencils and his tie hung askew even though his frenetic workday had yet to begin. He sat near her with a doughnut in his hand, pulling on some earphones and retreating into his own private world. His face had a closed-in look, betraying no emotion. Christie glanced away, realizing she'd violated the New York rule about not staring at other people. But the man's shuttered expression seemed out of place to her—the stock market, after all, was driven primarily by human emotion. Why did so many people try to put up a cool front? Her father was like that; even when he made a killing in the market he would betray no more than a small, pleased smile. He seemed to think that expressing his feelings would make him too vulnerable. Had she herself inherited that tendency from him? She'd always thought herself so open, so unlike her father in that way... but apparently Matt didn't agree with her. According to him, she was afraid of her own emotions.

She stood up swiftly, brushing off her cotton twill pants. Less than a week ago she'd felt carefree, enjoying her new existence in Red River. Then Matt Gallagher had charged into her life and shaken everything up. Because of him, she'd started to question all her motivations, all her actions. Worst of all, Christie couldn't stop hankering for him—not even for one second!

She walked down Wall Street and entered a building graced with the elaborate stonework of an earlier generation. She took an elevator up to one of the highest floors. When she stepped out into the lobby of Daniels, Peters et al., her feet were cushioned by a carpet of deep, luxuriant pile. All the paintings on the walls were originals, scenes of New York City executed by well-known and respected artists. Every detail here reflected her father's taste; only furnishings of the highest quality were allowed and they had to be subdued, as well. The plushness of the carpet was, therefore, modulated by a discreet, gray-green color that always reminded Christie of seaweed.

It was so early that only a few of the more dedicated brokers were at their desks in the big room—also known as "the sweatshop." Already they were hunched over their telephones, the receivers clenched against their ears while they tapped madly at their computer keyboards. Not one of them even glanced up at Christie. Well, she knew what it was like. She'd spent her own apprenticeship grueling away in that room before graduating to her own small, private office.

She went down the hall and opened a door of dark, richly grained wood. After a moment's hesitation she stepped over the threshold, into her father's personal domain.

She'd rarely been in his office alone before and she found herself treading almost on tiptoe. She approached his huge mahogany desk and cautiously lowered herself into the leather chair behind it. Christie felt engulfed by the massive dimensions of the chair, yet her father always looked larger than life when he was sitting here. Did he really believe she could take over for him after he'd ruled the company with such an imposing dictatorship?

The surface of his desk was polished to a sheen; there were only a few neat stacks of paper on it, along with several copies of financial magazines. Christopher Daniels led an extremely busy but also highly organized life. It wasn't that he had to scramble for commissions like the other brokers in his firm; his own group of clients was limited and very select. Yet he never allowed himself the luxury of spare time. He continued to play the market with intense seriousness, as if confronting some colossal chess opponent.

Christie was surprised at how comfortable she found her father's chair. She leaned back in it and propped her feet on the desk. She smiled, because she couldn't imagine Christopher Daniels ever relaxing enough to put his feet up anywhere. He didn't know what he was missing. But the sensation of power creeping over her . . . surely he'd experienced *that*. He thrived on wielding power.

Being in control of the firm was a very tempting idea. Christie flexed her toes in her sandals and relished the thought of instigating some new policies. First of all, the brokers in the sweatshop room would receive higher bonuses for demonstrating initiative. Day-care facilities would be arranged in the building. Everyone would actually be required to go home for dinner on Thanksgiving Day—

Her reverie was interrupted as the office door opened on noiseless hinges. Matt and her father came into the room, side by side. Christie's toes stopped wiggling. Suddenly her bright, cherry-red toenail polish seemed a little too blatant. She straightened hastily, her feet swinging down onto the floor.

"Um, good morning... Sir. Father. Dad."

"Mary Christine, I didn't expect you so soon this morning. I'm glad to see you." Her father quickly disguised any surprise at finding his sanctuary invaded.

"Hello, Christie." Matt sounded casual—almost cheerful, in fact. She felt two conflicting urges. One was to snap a rubber band at him. The other was to jump up and kiss him. Neither one of these impulses seemed appropriate with her father around.

The two men made a striking image together. Today Matt was wearing a business suit in a light brown, tweedish material that made his coloring look more striking than ever. The trousers and jacket were expertly tailored, but nonetheless Christie preferred him in cowboy boots and jeans. She glanced from Matt to her father and then back again, taking in a noteworthy fact. Usually her father's presence was enough to make any other man fade into the background. This wasn't so with Matt. He stood beside Christopher Daniels with an easy confidence, nothing subservient in his manner. He was the one taking over the room this time.

"Mary Christine, I see that you're trying out your new chair. How does it feel?" asked her father with a joviality she'd never heard from him before.

She stood up, no longer comfortable behind this desk. "Come on, Dad, it's still your chair. It doesn't fit me. I was daydreaming in it a little, that's all."

"You can order yourself another chair, one more suited to you," he said seriously. He often missed the emotional nuances in a personal conversation like this, and Christie was compelled to elaborate her meaning.

"I'm not going to take over your job, so I won't need any chair at all. I've thought about it, Dad, I really have. I've tried to put myself in your place, to see what I'd do if I was in charge here."

"Taking command comes naturally to you," Christopher said with a nod of approval. "That's what I raised you for, Mary Christine. You'll come to see that I'm right."

A familiar exasperation welled up inside Christie. As usual, her father wasn't listening to her. He was still determined to bend her to his will, no matter how much she might object.

Matt wore a thoughtful expression. "Obviously the two of you have some things to talk over," he said. "I'll leave you alone to do that."

"No, Matthew—please wait," Christopher asked. "I believe you can help me convince Mary Christine to see reason."

Matt hesitated, but then he shrugged. He positioned himself against a bookshelf a few feet from the desk. Christie was aware of his gaze as she faced her father. She was trembling, but she forced herself to speak in a quiet voice.

"Dad, it's time for you to listen to me. Really listen. It means a lot to me that you'd ask me to take over the business. That's the first thing I want you to know. Before now...well, I never believed you had much confidence in me. Sure, you always talked about handing over the business someday. But it seemed like a vague promise that would never really happen. I thought it was just another ploy to keep me slaving away as a stockbroker." She stopped, wanting to make sure that she was choosing the right words. But it was impossible to tell if she was getting through to her father. He pursed his lips slightly and settled down in one of the chrome-and-leather chairs across from the desk. Automatically Christie sat down again herself, landing with a bounce in the immense executive chair. People were always rising and sitting a beat behind Christopher Daniels, trying to match their actions to his. It was an annoying habit that she herself couldn't seem to break.

Matt, however, remained standing, quite independent. He gazed at a potted rubber tree as if wondering how a tropical plant like that could survive in a Wall Street skyscraper. Perhaps only Christie knew that all the beautiful, healthy plants in her father's office were fakes—unlike the paintings. Artwork, after all, didn't have to be watered and nourished every day, and he could, therefore, allow it to be genuine.

"Mary Christine, I'm glad you realize how much I want you to take your rightful place in the business," he said now. "You're my daughter—you're a Daniels. For those reasons alone I've always had confidence in you. But I've done more than trust in the excellence of my own gene pool. I tested your abilities when you were working for me. You proved yourself capable of handling anything I set before you."

Christie found it unsettling to hear herself described as a "gene pool"; it made her feel as if all sorts of bizarre little creatures might be swimming around inside her. But praise from her father had been so limited that she wasn't about to question it today.

"Thank you, Dad. It makes me happy to hear you say all this. I mean—I've always wanted your approval. And at last you're telling me I have it. That's really something!"

"I don't see the problem, then," he returned. "I'll assign my shares over to you and you'll become chairman of the board. Chairperson, I should say. You'll be one of the most powerful women in New York City."

Power...there were so many meanings to the word. The greatest power of all was to choose her own way in life. That was something she could never forget. She lifted a paperweight in both hands, a shining globe of silver that reflected the morning sunlight.

"Dad—maybe with a lot of work I'd make a decent administrator of this company. I'd probably make some changes that would be good for employee morale. That would be my strong point...but no matter how I look at things, the bottom line is still there and I can't ignore it. I don't *want* to be a stockbroker. That's it, pure and simple." Very carefully she set the silver paperweight back on its stack of neat papers. Then she stood up and came around the desk. She looked down at her father.

"The stock market is your dream, not mine. I know you want to share it with me—but that's just not possible. I can't pretend anymore to be someone I'm not. And I don't believe you really want to leave this company of yours. You were trying to find any way you could to get me back...but it would hurt you too deeply to give up the business. I saw the expression on your face when you found me sitting in your chair just now. You felt . . . invaded.''

There was the barest flicker of emotion in her father's blue eyes; then it was gone. He adjusted the crease of one of his pant legs. ''I assure you, I'm perfectly capable of walking away from this office without a backward glance.''

Christie smiled a little. ''Oh, I believe that. You really would walk away without a glance, even if you were all torn up inside. Someday, Dad, you and I are going to be able to talk about our feelings for each other. Not today . . . it's too soon, and we're too much alike in a lot of ways.'' She glanced over at Matt as she spoke. ''That's something I've learned in the past few days. And you know what? I'm glad I've inherited so much of your ambition and drive. Maybe I go overboard sometimes—well, a lot of times. But I still think you've given me a lot of good qualities. That's your legacy to me. That's my inheritance.'' She took a deep breath and walked to the door. ''Goodbye, Dad. Start enjoying your own business instead of worrying about who you're going to leave it to.''

He stood up. ''Mary Christine, you're not going away again, are you?'' he asked in a tone of disbelief. Perhaps he still hadn't listened to a word she'd said. It hurt, knowing he needed to hold on to her . . . knowing she couldn't let him hold on. He was losing her in ways he couldn't yet accept. But one thing was certain. Christopher Daniels wouldn't appreciate anyone's pity, least of all her own.

''Goodbye, Dad,'' she repeated softly, and then she left him.

She was striding down Wall Street again by the time Matt caught up with her. He moved into step beside her.

"Christie, you should be proud of yourself! You were finally able to stand up to your father. I think you really made him see how you feel."

"I'm not sure about that. But you shouldn't have to worry about him dissolving the company, or doing anything crazy like that." She kept her tone brisk, even though her throat was tightening with an unspoken yearning for Matt.

He grasped hold of her arm so she couldn't go on walking. "We have to talk about you and me now. Don't try to run away from me, Christie."

She reached out a hand and steadied herself against a wall of cool, dove-gray stone. There were no brash colors along this street, only muted shades. Christie had never truly belonged here; she craved brightness in her life. But she wondered if she'd ever find brightness anywhere after what she had to say to Matt.

"I'm not running away from you," she began stiffly. "It's not like that. I realized something, up there in my father's office. You and I—we've been trying to force each other to be a certain way, just as my father's always tried to mold *me*. But we have to stop! We'll end up hating each other if we keep on like this. Whatever decisions you make about your life, I want you to make them on your own. No interference from me—that's the only answer." Tears prickled behind her eyelids, but somehow she kept her voice rigid and strong. "I'm leaving you, Matt. I'm going back to Red River."

CHAPTER ELEVEN

TWENTY green corduroy dragons were lined up on Christie's sofa. They all had red felt scales poking up along their backs, black buttons for eyes and foam stuffing that made them look very well fed. Several of them suffered from lopsided stitching, but just about the time Christie had started sewing dragon number ten, she'd gotten the hang of things. Altogether, she was proud of her efforts as a seamstress. So why wasn't she happy, blast it all?

She stabbed her needle into dragon number twenty-one. It was a beautiful summer morning, and she was preparing for the inauguration of Red River Medieval Fair Days. Vincent and Gomez lay peacefully on the Persian rug beside her, curled around each other in half-moon shapes. Christie was doing exactly what she wanted, where she wanted, and with the two cats of her choice. Everything was perfect, damn it. Perfect!

Lisa wandered past the door, her head buried in a huge, seven-hundred-page novel. It was a wonder how she managed to hoist the thing around with such ease. "Still pining after the gorgeous male, Chris?" she asked from the depths of the book.

"I wish you wouldn't keep saying things like that," Christie said irritably, yanking at a snarl of green thread. "I already told you, Matt Gallagher is part of my past. If he hasn't even bothered to mail me a post-card all these weeks, why on earth should I pine for him? Good grief! He knows why I can't contact *him*. It's my code of noninterference. He doesn't have to honor the same code! Not really. He knows my tele-phone number. Just one lousy phone call would be enough—''

The phone jangled from the hall, and Christie nearly stitched her fingers together. She scrambled from her chair, tripped over the cats, pushed Lisa aside and grabbed the receiver.

''Hello?'' she gasped.

''Good morning, Mary Christine.'' It was her father's moderate, cultivated voice greeting her from the other end of the wire. At first Christie felt a lurch of disappointment inside her, then a wariness. Was her father calling to instigate another one of his plots? She hadn't heard from him since leaving New York, and perhaps he'd been busy scheming—perhaps he still didn't believe what she'd told him that day.

''It's good to hear from you,'' she said despond-ently, watching as Lisa drifted into the kitchen. ''How are you doing?''

''Fine, thank you.'' He paused. ''How are you?''

''Just fine, thank you.'' She chewed on a strand of hair.

''I hope your bed and breakfast is doing well.''

She sighed. ''Yes, actually it is. I'm running full occupancy most of the time now, but my overhead is still low.''

''That's good. Very good. Of course, I wouldn't expect otherwise. I raised you to be an excellent busi-nesswoman.'' He cleared his throat. ''Mary Chris-

tine, I just called to tell you something. I love you."
He uttered this statement without changing his tone in
the least, as if he'd merely informed her of his latest
stock purchase. But Christie was stunned. He'd never,
ever told her those words before.

"Dad... I love you, too," she was able to say.

"Well, yes, that's good then, Mary Christine. I'll
call you again sometime soon."

"Please do. I'll look forward to that... goodbye,
Dad." She replaced the receiver slowly. It seemed she
was at peace with her father after all these years. That
was a wonderful gift. She stood by the phone for a
long moment, quietly enjoying this new sense of calm.

Eventually she glanced at her watch, and realized
with a start how late it was getting. She finished off the
last stuffed animal and deposited her entire herd of
dragons into a large plastic bag. Hauling the bag with
her, she left the house and hurried down to Main
Street.

Brightly colored pennants fluttered in the breeze
from booths all up and down the road. Already
crowds were milling around, sampling ale that was
actually apple cider, shish kebabs that represented
medieval spits of meat, and authentic fourteenth-
century pudding made out of milk and bread contributed by Carl's Grocery Store.

Tomorrow the children's pageant would take place,
but today all Christie had to do was take charge of the
archery booth. She arrayed her dragons in an inviting
manner underneath the target and propped up her
sign: WIN A DRAGON WITH EVERY BULL'S-
EYE! ONLY 50 CENTS A TRY. PROCEEDS TO
BENEFIT NEW RED RIVER MUSEUM. Then she

plunked herself down on a stool to wait for takers. Business was noticeably slow—probably because she was thinking about Matt again and her mouth had begun to droop. She wouldn't attract any customers this way. Christie tried to plaster an inviting smile on her face. It wasn't easy. Her natural inclination was to gaze morosely at the ground, wishing with all her heart that she'd never heard the name Matt Gallagher.

"Say, fair damsel, how about passing a quiver of arrows my way?" boomed a deep, masculine voice above her.

Christie's head jerked up, and she stared at the cowboy who'd appeared in front of her. His hat was pushed back off his forehead, revealing a glimpse of russet hair. His jeans were slung low with the weight of an enormous silver belt buckle, his thumbs hooked casually in his belt loops. His dark amber eyes held a mischievous glint.

Christie's heart began stampeding, but somehow she managed a nonchalant demeanor.

"Why, hello there, Matt. I didn't know you'd ridden into town."

He deposited two quarters on the counter. "I'm going for a bull's-eye, Christie. Just watch."

Silently she provided him with a bow and an arrow. Her hands were shaking. Matt, however, was completely steady as he drew back on the bowstring and squinted at the target. POP! The suction-cup tip of the arrow landed right in the middle of the bull's-eye.

"Good shot," Christie said. She pushed a dragon toward him. It was a bit wobbly on its paws, but managed to remain in an upright position. Matt snapped a crisp one-dollar bill out of his pocket.

"Two more tries, Christie. I feel lucky today."

A few moments later she thumped two more dragons down on the counter. One of them toppled over. "Look here, Matt—"

"Let's go for three this time. I'm on a roll." Six quarters clinked onto the counter.

He missed a shot, but now there were five corduroy dragons lined up in a row in front of him. He picked one up and tugged on its tail.

"I think I could grow fond of these critters," he remarked. "They need a good home."

She snatched the dragon away and placed it next to its fellows. "They already had a good home before you came along," she declared.

"Still hiding your feelings, Mary Christine?" he asked in a gentle voice.

"Confound you, Matt!" She folded her arms tightly against her body. She was trembling all over now, as if she'd caught a major chill. "What are you doing here, anyway?" she demanded grumpily.

"I have some news to share with you." He grinned, looking roguish and much too attractive. "I sold a piece of my writing."

"Oh . . . Matt, that's wonderful!" she exclaimed, leaning over the counter toward him. "I knew you could do it. I just knew you could! You have what it takes. You're a fantastic writer. You're—"

"Hold on, don't get so excited. It's only a two-page article for an obscure financial journal. It's about the need for tighter reporting regulations on stock transactions—not exactly television miniseries material. Maybe ten people will read it."

"I'll read it," Christie said fervently. "Oh, Matt..."
She flung her arms around him, but the counter was a
serious impediment. Matt solved the problem. Swinging first one leg and then the other over the five dragons, he was now inside the booth. Christie pressed
herself against him, her face buried in the soft material of his plaid shirt. He smelled like pine trees.

"I told you I didn't want to interfere in any of your
decisions," she murmured. "I still feel that way, you
know. Except you'd better just keep holding me.
That's all I can say."

He chuckled, tilting her chin up with his finger.
"Christie, you started interfering with my life the
minute I walked through your front door. And it's a
damn good thing. Sometimes a person needs a little
push...or a hefty kick in the rear end, whichever way
you want to look at it. You were right about me. I
needed to make some changes in my life. I was burning out as a stockbroker, but I was too stubborn to
admit it. I didn't want all those years of my life to be
a waste. That was the one thing I couldn't face. I guess
I had to discover the truth for myself—that I could
change my direction without turning my back on
everything I'd done before. The stock market will always fascinate me, always be a part of me. I've found
a new way to be involved in it, that's all. A better way.
I even made enough from that magazine article to buy
myself another fishing rod."

He interrupted himself to give Christie a thorough
kiss. She closed her eyes blissfully, savoring the clean,
spicy taste of him. She wasn't shaking anymore. A
sensation like golden honey was melting all through

her veins. She didn't break away until an interested voice asked, "Hey, is this the kissing booth?"

Matt smiled down at Christie, his hands linked around her waist. He spoke to the eager young boy peering in at them. "This lady's all mine, I'm afraid." The boy wandered off with a disappointed look on his face.

"You sound awfully proprietary," Christie grumbled.

"That's because I can't live without you. I love you, Christie."

His warmth spread all through her. She felt as if she must be glowing with her own inner light. "That's the second time someone's said that to me today, you know."

Matt's russet eyebrows drew together. "You mean I have some serious competition?"

She grinned. "It was my father, actually. And I love you, too, Matt Gallagher. I never want to be away from you again! Red River isn't home without you— that's what *I've* discovered. I'll go live in the Sahara, as long as you're with me."

His finger gently traced her eyebrow. "Marry me, Christie. Right away. Spend a honeymoon with me up at my new gold mine—"

"So *you're* the one who bought Big Shelby's," she said accusingly, "right out from under my nose!"

"I guess we'll just have to make it community property. And I bought something else, too." He rummaged around in his back pocket. With a flourish he brought out a small packet. "Catnip," he announced.

Christie regarded the packet gravely. "You told me you hated cats," she reminded him.

"I do. However, I've decided to tolerate yours. But can't we at least find a bedroom door in your house that the damn animals don't know how to open?"

"I think that can be arranged..." Her hands moved up over his shoulders and she reveled in the feel of him. Happiness was making her positively unsteady and she leaned against his chest.

"Christie, I'm starting from the bottom up with this writing career—you realize that, don't you? It's not going to be easy, any way you look at it."

"But it's going to be lots of fun, as long as we're together," she said with conviction. "Oh, I can just see it, Matt! You'll have your own study in the house for writing, absolutely *no* cats allowed. And, you know, we ought to get you started on the lecture circuit as soon as possible. There's so much you have to tell people about the stock market. I think I'll make a darn good publicity agent for you, I really do. What do you say?"

Matt chuckled. "I say that you're always going to be full of plans and goals, just like your dad. I'll have to work awfully hard to keep up with you."

She smiled into his plaid cowboy shirt. "Don't worry. I'm going to learn to relax, too. Maybe I'll even take up fishing." She listened to the rumble of laughter deep in his chest. Then Matt kissed her nose and grinned at her.

"Christie, I believe you're capable of anything. But I don't know how you'll feel about all the trips to New York I'll have to make. I need to maintain my contacts there, and keep up with the stock market—"

"Hey, I'll be taking every trip right along with you. My father and I have a lot of catching up to do...and I think I'm actually looking forward to that. Besides, something tells me that Christopher Daniels the Third is going to be pretty interested in seeing his grandkids as often as possible."

Matt kissed her ear. "Just do me one favor. Make sure our children are tested for motion sickness before we drag them onto any ferries."

Christie laced her fingers together behind his neck. "First thing I have to do is marry you before some pretty cowgirl snatches you away from me. A few of them are looking you over this very minute."

Matt didn't seem at all interested in what was happening outside the archery booth. He gathered Christie even closer in his arms. "Mary Christine Daniels Gallagher...hmm, I like the sound of that. I like it a lot." He bent his head and kissed her once again. There wasn't any need for words now. They were no longer two against love.

HARLEQUIN
Romance®

This May, travel to Egypt with Harlequin Romance's **FIRST CLASS** title #3126, **A FIRST TIME FOR EVERYTHING** by Jessica Steele.

A little excitement was what she wanted. So Josslyn's sudden assignment to Egypt came as a delightful surprise. Pity she couldn't say the same about her new boss.

Thane Addison was an overbearing, domineering slave driver. And yet sometimes Joss got a glimpse of an entirely different sort of personality beneath his arrogant exterior. It was enough that Joss knew despite having to work for this brute of a man, she wanted to stay.

Not that Thane seemed to care at all what his temporary secretary thought about him....

H A R L E Q U I N

Coming Next Month

Available in May wherever paperback books are sold, or through Harlequin Reader Service:

In the U.S.
P.O. Box 1397
Buffalo, N.Y.
14240-1397

In Canada
P.O. Box 603
Fort Erie, Ontario
L2A 5X3

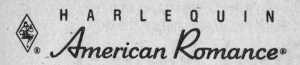

HARLEQUIN
American Romance®

THE ROMANCE THAT STARTED IT ALL!

For Diane Bauer and Nick Granatelli, the walk down the aisle
was a rocky road....

Don't miss the romantic prequel to WITH THIS RING—

I THEE WED
BY ANNE McALLISTER

Harlequin American Romance #387

Let Anne McAllister take you to Cambridge, Massachusetts, to
the night when an innocent blind date brought a reluctant Diane
Bauer and Nick Granatelli together. For Diane, a smoldering
attraction like theirs had only one fate, one future—marriage.
The hard part, she learned, was convincing her intended....

Watch for Anne McAllister's I THEE WED, available *now* from
Harlequin American Romance.

You'll flip . . . your pages won't!
Read paperbacks *hands-free* with

Book Mate • I

The perfect "mate" for all your romance paperbacks

Traveling • Vacationing • At Work • In Bed • Studying • Cooking • Eating

Perfect size for all standard paperbacks, this wonderful invention makes reading a pure pleasure! Ingenious design holds paperback books OPEN and FLAT so even wind can't ruffle pages — leaves your hands free to do other things. Reinforced, wipe-clean vinyl-covered holder flexes to let you turn pages without undoing the strap . . . supports paperbacks so well, they have the strength of hardcovers!

Pages turn WITHOUT opening the strap

SEE-THROUGH STRAP

Reinforced back stays flat

Built in bookmark

BOOK MARK

BACK COVER HOLDING STRIP

10 x 7¼ opened
Snaps closed for easy carrying, too

OLSON / MELVILLE

OLSON / MELVILLE

A Study in Affinity

Ann Charters

oyez

Acknowledgments

My indebtedness to Charles Olson began with my first letter to him, January 7, 1968, full of questions about the nature of his admiration for *Moby-Dick*. The letter must have struck him as coming from out of nowhere, since I was asking him to think back more than thirty years to the genesis of his feelings for Melville. But it was a long, cold winter in Gloucester, and he generously took time to answer my letters—"Those initial questions made time as fresh as it was then." Our correspondence, and then my visit with him in Gloucester on June 13 and 14, 1968, were the most help in clarifying my thoughts. I am also especially grateful for his permission to print the unpublished lectures from Black Mountain College that are included in the last section of this book.

Robert Hawley of Oyez arranged for the evening in San Francisco when I spoke with Robert Duncan about Olson's work, and Robert Wilson, of the Phoenix Bookshop, New York City, made John Wieners' Black Mountain College notes available to me. Also of considerable use was the bibliography of Olson's works compiled by George F. Butterick and Albert Glover (Phoenix, 1967). Samuel Charters listened patiently to my embryonic notions about the Olson/Melville affinity and gave sympathetic advice throughout the various stages of my study. Last, I would like to acknowledge the assistance of Mary Forte, who kept Mallay Charters—age one year—amused while I was working.

BROOKLYN HEIGHTS, NEW YORK
JUNE 27, 1968

For Robert Hawley
who suggested this study
and Dorothy & Jessica

Extracts

"*Call me Ishmael* records, often brilliantly, one way of taking the most extraordinary of American books. In spite of difficulties and excesses, it needs to be read and pondered."

Walter Bezanson, *New England Quarterly*

Ishmael is "something of an anomaly; for though the author makes some use of his fresh knowledge, the work mainly follows the intuitive line of D. H. Lawrence and Edward Dahlberg, and the reader is forced to take or leave Mr. Olson's thesis without benefit of persuasion or scholarly argument."

Lewis Mumford, *The New York Times*

Olson's work is "not only important, but apocalyptic."

New York Herald Tribune

"Olson's style ranges from Sears-Roebuck cataloguing to prose as fantastic and willful as e e cummings' verse. . . . But the author's arrangement and style repeatedly turn delight into either irritation or inappropriate amusement. He seems bent upon becoming nominated prose laureate of eccentricity. Old friends of Melville, never the less, may run upon fallen fruit in this tangled luxuriant jungle. Others should beware getting lost in the undergrowth."

Robert Berkelman, *Christian Science Monitor*

"In so full a book it is impossible to follow precisely each thread of the discussion. . . ." (but *Ishmael* is) "one of the most stimulating essays ever written on *Moby-Dick* and for that matter on any literature and the forces behind it. I've seen the results of a lot of Guggenheim awards, but I've never seen one better justified by its result than Mr. Olson's."

J. H. Jackson, *San Francisco Chronicle*

Charles Olson has written "a book to rejoice those admirers of Melville who like to identify him with Ahab. It will have quite a different impact on the scholars and critics who have been trying to disperse the fogs which the myth-makers have been sending up around Melville for the past quarter of a century."

Willard Thorp, *Saturday Review of Literature*

"Charles Olson has devoted thirteen years to the study of Melville—his is a work of understanding and of a well-nigh religious devotion. Finally, it is that rare and perfect thing—a work of scholarship that is full both stylistically and conceptually of the greatest excitement and movement."

Reynal and Hitchcock dustwrapper
Call me Ishmael, 1947

"Actually *Ishmael* is a great deal different than it ever seems to be taken to be."

Charles Olson, 1968

OLSON / MELVILLE

Introduction

Charles Olson is a poet who lives in Gloucester, Massachusetts, by the Atlantic Ocean. His kitchen windows look out over rooftops onto a wide bay where fishing vessels and small craft move out to sea, and he often walks the strip of beach near his home. The water is usually grey and cold, reflecting the sky, rolling onto the beach in almost silent waves. Olson's affinity for Herman Melville is similar to his need for Gloucester and the sea. They are essential to him both as a man and as a poet, and they have been in his writing ever since he began.

He is Mister Olson to his neighbors in the Fort, the district in Gloucester where he lives when he isn't lecturing or teaching, but to the world beyond he is best known, of course, as one of the group of modern poets like Ezra Pound, William Carlos Williams, and Hart Crane, who "are laying bases of new discourse," part of "the whole of the American push to find out an alternative discourse to the inherited one, to the one implicit in the language from Chaucer to Browning, to try, by some other means than 'pattern' and 'the rational,' to cause discourse to cover—as it only ever best can—the ideal."[1] A great teacher, Olson has been an influence, through the force of his personality and his writing, on younger poets; he terms it a "father" to—among many others—Allen Ginsberg, John Wieners, Ed Dorn.

A poet and philosopher, Olson has the larger purpose, as he once told his students at Black Mountain College, "to acquaint

---

[1] "On Poets and Poetry," *Human Universe,* page 64.

you with what can now be said to be known."[2] He disclaims being a philosopher ("I am a mythologist"[3]), but his interest as a poet and critic is always in a methodology that "points a way by which, one day, the problem of larger content and of larger forms may be solved."[4] Writing about Melville, Olson takes this perspective. His work includes a book about Melville published in 1947, *Call me Ishmael*, a long poem *Letter for Melville 1951*, and several short essays on Melville over the last twenty years, in addition to the countless times he has referred to Melville in other poetry and prose. But with the possible exception of his first published article, the essay "Lear and Moby-Dick," written thirty years ago when he was a student, Olson has never written about Melville solely as a scholar or academic critic. His intellectual concerns always extend beyond aesthetics to what amounts to a basic restructuring of the entire human universe. Except for his first article, implicit in all his writing about Melville is his major premise:

It is not yet gauged how much the nature of knowledge has changed since 1875. Around that date man reapplied known techniques of the universe to man himself, and the change has made man as non-Socratic (or non-Aristotelian) as geometers of the early nineteenth century made the universe non-Euclidean. Man as object and subject inquires in a locus of space and time, is the premise. . . .[5]

The sweep of Olson's "premise" is enormously complex, but his writing on Melville is possibly the most accessible introduction to his ideas. He has felt the close affinity, almost the blood tie of family kinship, with Melville because he feels Melville had the same view of the American experience as himself. Olson reads *Moby-Dick* as a poetic statement of the experience of space and the awareness of a human universe that in 1850 was prophecy. To Olson, Melville's achievement went unrecognized until interpreted in *Call me Ishmael* nearly a hundred years later.

---

[2] "An Institute of the New Sciences of Man," Black Mountain College, March 1953.

[3] Black Mountain College lecture, 1956; see Postscript.

[4] "Projective Verse," *Human Universe,* page 61.

[5] "Reading List in the New Sciences of Man," 1953 (John Wieners' notes).

Edmund Wilson's book *The Shock of Recognition* documented a self-consciousness among American writers that often manifested itself in literature reflecting "moments when genius becomes aware of its kin."[6] The tie between Charles Olson and Herman Melville is such a kinship. It may be speculated whether this affinity is more or less real than the one Melville felt between Hawthorne and himself, but what is evident is that Olson has taken Melville as the subject for a large portion of his most successful work, creating out of the relationship literature of intricate design and profound, prophetic vision.

————

How did Olson first encounter Melville? He explains in a letter.

I don't honestly know what hooked me on Melville. My father had given me *Moby-Dick* with some bad pun of his own rhyming cast your eyes and Mobylize when I was 17. My own sense of actually first reading it, with any sense — and that also is practically the last time! —was a winter here (in Gloucester) having just bought via John Grant the Bookseller Edinburgh George the IVth Bridge   the Constable edition complete.   For I think $25.   In 1939. (or 1938 probably.   See later.)

It doesn't matter. The vivid entry was *either Benito Cereno* or *Bartleby   Middleton Conn spring 1933* getting out of the infirmary after weeks of illness, and (as it might be) starved, and throwing myself down on my cot in my own room of a spring afternoon with the lovely Constable small edition of the Piazza Tales.

That did it. (It wasn't actually the Master's thesis nor any PhD — I *have* none — it was a summer — what 1938? doing a complete Melville & Shakespeare paper for F. O. Matthiessen. Dahlberg thought the section later published in Twice a Year was such, and I pulled it out the fall, 1938.

So it goes 1933-1938 really. I wrote a first version of a book by 1940. Which I showed to Dahlberg. Who then and there taught me how to write! (The ms. has since seen no one else's eyes.[7]

At Wesleyan University, Olson wrote a Master's thesis titled

---

[6] Wilson, *The Shock of Recognition,* viii.
[7] Olson letter, January 10, 1968.

"The Growth of Herman Melville, Prose Writer and Poetic Thinker," which led to a research fellowship at Harvard the following winter, 1933-34. During this time, with considerable ingenuity, he tracked down several of the most important books in Melville's library. His search began with a visit to one of Melville's granddaughters, Eleanor Melville Metcalf. Olson remembers that "She's the one whose door I knocked on in Cambridge to start the search for Melville's books."[8] He learned that some were still owned by the Melville family, others had been sold after Melville's death in 1891. Olson succeeded in locating the booksellers and tracing certain key volumes once in the library — Melville's collection of Hawthorne's books and his seven-volume edition of Shakespeare, printed "in glorious great type" in Boston, 1837, by the publishers Hilliard and Gray. In terms of its importance to Melville scholarship, Olson's discovery (he was then 23 years old) was the most significant find since 1919, when Raymond Weaver, who was to write the first complete Melville biography, discovered the mss. of the unpublished novella *Billy Budd* among Melville's papers. The volumes of Hawthorne and Shakespeare contained valuable insights into Melville's use of these authors in his writing, since he annotated and underlined what impressed him as particularly significant. As Olson later stated in *Ishmael*, "Melville's reading is a gauge of him, at all points of his life. He was a skald, and knew how to appropriate the work of others. He read to write."[9]

Olson was one of the earliest researchers who took a close, first-hand look at the notes Melville had jotted down in the margins and end-papers of his books. Eventually the editions of Hawthorne and Shakespeare became the property of the Harvard College Library, but they were originally given to Olson for study by Melville's granddaughters. As Olson describes the experience:

I had already, by the winter 1933-34, had the chance to examine all

---

[8] Olson conversation, Gloucester, June 14, 1968.
[9] *Call Me Ishmael,* page 36.

of Melville's library which had survived in the family. I was able to
have the time to do this due to a grant arranged for me by Wilbert
Snow, God bless him – a Fellowship, in *Economics* no less, and in one
of the finest slickest iced countrysides I ever knew Edward Matthews
& I drove to East Orange New Jersey and came away, at the end of
a Sunday afternoon, with *95* volumes of that library including the
Shakespeare! (One of his granddaughters)

I may already have set out to retrace the sale, in New York, of
Melville's library after his death. In any case the spring of '34 – I was
then 23 – I succeeded. It was John Anderson (who had, in 1891, been
a bookseller, but the founder, afterwards, of the Anderson Galleries,
now Parke-Bernet . . .) He was the one who put me on to Oscar Wegalin, who had then – in 1891 – been his delivery boy. . . .[10]

Olson's research was a milestone in Melville studies. At the
end of the winter afternoon in East Orange, New Jersey, he
drove away from his visit with Melville's granddaughter with
95 volumes from the library in his car. Thirty years later, only
124 other volumes have been located.

Reserving the Shakespeare for his own use, Olson gave his
other significant find, Melville's annotated copies of Hawthorne's books, to his Wesleyan professor, F. O. Matthiessen.
In 1941, when Matthiessen published his literary study *American Renaissance*, he acknowledged "Olson's generosity in letting me make use of what he has tracked down in his investiga-
tion of Melville's reading, particularly Melville's markings in
his volumes of Hawthorne, which alone made possible my
study of that interrelation."[11] More recently, the scholar Merton M. Sealts, Jr., referred in his book *Melville's Reading* to
Olson's interviews with the booksellers Anderson and Wegalin
for information about Melville's library.

Olson looked into more than Melville's books, however. In
Cambridge, with Eleanor Melville Metcalf's assistance, he began research into the family papers.

I got an awful break one day sitting in Eleanor's house. In some
dumb way, with my high school French, I began to read Philaret
Chasles' review of *Typee* or *Omoo*. Here I suddenly realize that what

---

[10] Olson letter, January 10, 1968.
[11] Matthiessen, *American Renaissance,* xviii.

the French is actually saying is that Melville's brother-in-law was in his house and confirmed all Melville's experiences in the Pacific, 1847. I realize this is Lemuel, or Sam, Shaw. Eleanor's in the kitchen, and I asked her where the Shaw Papers were. "I sent them to the Massachusetts Historical Society—this was long ago, when I was first married." So she calls up to see if I can look at them, and I grab a cab, and within 45 minutes of reading that French review, I was looking at the boxes Eleanor had sent them.[12]

From 1936 to 1938, after teaching English at Clark University, Olson completed the course work for his doctorate at Harvard, but he left without the degree in 1939, when he received a Guggenheim grant for independent Melville studies. The Guggenheim was the result of the "complete Melville and Shakespeare paper" he wrote the previous year, published in the first issue of the magazine *Twice a Year* because Edward Dahlberg, who was helping to start the magazine, saw the essay and liked it.

Living on the Guggenheim, Olson left Cambridge to join his mother in Gloucester (his father had died in 1935). There he worked on the first draft of his Melville book. It was at this time, in the fall, 1939, that he read Freud's *Moses and Monotheism*, a book which greatly shaped his thought in *Call me Ishmael*. Olson insists that Freud's influence is "protogonic, suggesting the earliest conceivable possibility of creation." Although it is the "psychic root" of his conception of Melville, it would be wrong to "make too much of it."[13] But when Freud stated that "the great man influences his contemporaries in two ways: through his personality and through the idea for which he stands,"[14] the sentence is a comment on the Olson-Melville affinity. Melville is not Olson's historical contemporary in point of chronological time, but history to Olson is ritual and repetition,[15] and certainly he has felt the force of Melville (and Freud) as contemporary. Melville, Freud, and Eisen-

12 Olson conversation, Gloucester, June 14, 1968.
13 *Ibid.*
14 Freud, *Moses and Monotheism,* page 139.
15 *Ishmael,* page 13.

stein (whose films he had encountered in Cambridge) were the
three intellects who enabled Olson to see himself as *object:*
"One of the great things about growing up is that you discover
there are other people. These men are for me the men who
sprang up like violets."[16]

The first draft of the Melville book was completed in 1940,
and Olson went over the 400 page ms. with Edward Dahlberg.
Dahlberg's opinion was that the literary style was inappropriate—"too Hebraic, Biblical Old Testament."[17] The book was
put away for five years, from 1941-44, when Olson worked in
New York and Washington for the Foreign Language Information Service and the Office of War Information. He "resigned
in protest" from government service on May 18, 1944, and
went to Key West, Florida, to write poetry. Returning to
Washington a year later, he read in the newspapers the morning of his return that Roosevelt was dead. "I started *Ishmael*
that afternoon, the afternoon I kissed off my political future."[18]
Olson didn't re-work the earlier version of the book. Instead
he started fresh, and *Ishmael* came as

one piece, and was written at a clip starting April 13th, 1945, and
finished before the 1st A-bomb, 1st week in August that same year.
The only thing I didn't have right was the opening *Essex* narrative,
and I had left Washington and was in Newport the evening of the false
Japanese armistice (Thursday of that week), and in Nantucket that
weekend following. I wrote the opening story on the boat back from
Nantucket, the morning of Monday, must be say August 10th, that
year. In other words no connection to the ms. of 1940 at all. And in
the interim—until April 13th, '45, I had been wholly absorbed in Foreign Nationality business & politics. (Actually, until November, 1944,
or rightly date Jan 1st, 1945, when I set, in Key West, to write like
forever! (Wrote "The K," the go-away poem shortly after the Inauguration of that year.) [19]

In Washington the summer of 1945, Olson "really did" his

---

16 Olson conversation, Gloucester, June 13, 1968. The "violets" image is
   explained in the 1956 BMC lecture in the final section of this book.
17 *Ibid.*
18 *Ibid.*
19 Olson letter, February 14, 1968.

subject. "I kept myself in the proper place."[20] Following hunches, he continued his research much as he had as a student in Cambridge several years before.

In Washington in 1945 I had the thought that if the *Essex* thing was the plot of the book, the mutiny on the *Globe* was the psychic button for Melville that pushed the book. I knew the *Globe* had been sailed back by the two cabin boys to the port of Valpariso. I was alone in the house, so I grabbed a cab to the National Archives and asked for the Consular Papers of Valpariso for 1819 (?). Yes — out they came — I read the total first testimonies, the eye-witness of the crew as they were taken down. This was the basis of FACT #2 in *Ishmael*.[21]

"Written at a clip," the publication of *Ishmael* took more time. A year after the book was completed, Olson began visiting Ezra Pound at St. Elizabeth's Hospital. One afternoon Pound asked him, "What do you do?"[22] Olson answered, "I write." Pound said, "Show me something," and Olson gave him the *Ishmael* ms. At their next meeting, Pound returned it. "There's only one bad sentence in your book," he told Olson. " 'Now, in spite of the corruption of myth by fascism, the swing is out and back'."[23] Immensely flattered, Olson left the sentence as it was and agreed to let Pound send the ms. to England so that T. S. Eliot might consider it for publication. In the covering letter to Eliot, Pound wrote that *Ishmael* performed a valuable service as a labor saving device; now there was no need to read *Moby-Dick* (a book Pound knew Eliot did not care for). Eliot turned it down, considering it "too little, and too American a book."[24] That year (1946), *Ishmael* was also rejected by Harcourt, Brace on the advice of their academic readers Lewis Mumford and F. O. Matthiessen. However, in 1947, sponsored by Harry Levine and Jay Leyda, *Ishmael* finally found a publisher. Charles Olson was included, along with Alfred Kazin, Eric Bentley, Cleanth Brooks, and

---

[20] Olson conversation, June 14, 1968.
[21] *Ibid.*
[22] *Ibid.*
[23] *Ishmael,* pages 14-15.
[24] Olson conversation, June 14, 1968.

Robert Penn Warren, in the list of Reynal and Hitchcock. Olson recalls that he

"set" it, for Harry Ford [the designer] of Reynal & Hitchcock, with some rigidity. (It may interest you to know that something which the book is was immediately reflected in a cable from Serge Eisenstein / on his receipt of the book through his former assistant, Jay Leyda /, that John Huston held me in Hollywood in 1947 when he hoped to get Jack Warner to let him make *Moby-Dick* — and that Jean Renoir, there at that time, looked over the *Essex* part for a film by himself. — Crazy, no? that the very men I wld have wanted to respond, in some curious "means" of the book itself, came down on me like shooting stars!

(I had hoped of course that the World would stand still!) [25]

The world didn't stand still for Olson, but he has gone his independent way much as if it had. To the staid academic community, his work is "a little startling,"[26] but for the last twenty years he has interpreted the ideas for which Melville stands — his knowledge of the space of ocean, man's past, the unfound present — in essays and poetry. Since these are also Olson's concerns as a poet, his interpretation of Melville is a compelling, highly personal study of affinity. Like Melville's fascination with the "blackness in Hawthorne," Olson has been held fast by the prophetic vision of Herman Melville.

---

[25] Olson letter, February 14, 1968.
[26] Stovall, *Eight American Authors,* page 230.

Call me Ishmael: I

In his writing, Olson is as much a blend of philosopher and poet as an earlier New England iconoclast, Ralph Waldo Emerson. Certainly without understanding Olson's philosophic framework, a reader's encounter with *Call me Ishmael* is likely to be an incomplete, even baffling, experience. Or he may be left with a misapprehension of the book, perhaps calling it, as a *London Times* reviewer did, a "mishmash." Whatever else it might be, *Ishmael* is definitely not a mishmash. Olson has not jumbled his thoughts about Melville; they are as systematically sorted as the whaling gear aboard the *Pequod*.

Perhaps the best approach to understanding how *Ishmael* is organized is through the shorter prose piece "Equal, That Is, to the Real Itself." Olson considers this article, originally a book review written ten years after *Ishmael* was published, the "last chapter" of *Ishmael*,[1] and it would be appropriately included in some further reprinting of the book. "Equal, That Is" is a statement of Olson's philosophical belief in the principle of "quantity as intensive," quantity as the basic characteristic of the universe, giving it force and emphasis, the basic condition of things. This principle he sees operating in *Moby-Dick*, since with his interpretation, Melville's book is "the first art of space to arise from the redefinition of the real." To Olson, the redefinition of the real was begun in nineteenth century mathematics, a discovery of no less importance than man's "reentry of or to the universe." The break-through was first made

---

1 Olson letter, January 10, 1968.

in 1829-1832 by two geometers, Bolyai and Lobatschewsky, who after dissatisfaction with Euclid's "picture of the world," created a new system of geometry known as hyperbolic geometry. Several years later, in 1851, the German mathematician Bernhard Riemann extended their ideas in another system, elliptical geometry, defining "two kinds of manifold," the discrete and the continuous. Energy and motion, QUANTITY — the measurable and numerable — became the striking character of the external world. In Olson's words, "all things do extend out," all things exist to promote feeling and be felt, and the physicality of the universe (including the human beings in it) is without interruption, continuous.

Riemann's non-Euclidean geometry sounded like an exercise in pure mathematics in his own time, but fifty years later it was found not to be divorced from reality when Einstein showed that it represented a truer picture of the universe as a whole than Euclid's geometry. It has been Olson's intent as a poet, philosopher, and teacher, to propose a new discourse, or way of writing, that would make use of the discoveries of the new mathematics and physics. It is almost as if Olson has tried to formulate aesthetic theories that would parallel mathematical concepts. Non-Euclidean and Euclidean geometries are all branches of a larger projective geometry, for example, which is the study of the properties of a geometric figure when it is transformed by projection and section. In a famous essay "Projective Verse," Olson has defined a poem as "energy transferred from where the poet got it (he will have some several causations), by way of the poem itself to, all the way over to, the reader." This essay contains a striking incidence of terms from mathematics and physics: composition by field, kinetics, law of the line, propositions, the principle, the law, the corollary. In turn, projective geometry is an aspect of topology, the most general kind of geometry, with the widest range of application in mathematics. To Olson, topology is also the general method of the new linguistic discourse, concerned with quantity, the measurable and numerable. In "Equal, That Is," he asks, "Who still knows what's called for, from physicality, how far it does cover and reveal?" The basic question in Olson's approach to writing parallels the physicist's fundamental attempt to understand the structure of the universe. Olson encompasses both disciplines of science and the arts when he writes, "The projective involves a new stance toward reality outside a poem as well as a new stance towards the reality of a poem itself."[2]

With the discoveries of the nineteenth century mathematicians, Olson argues, logic and classification become useless, relativity holds sway, and the universe is a "flow of creation itself, in and out."[3] Quantity is intensive, serving to give force or emphasis, in the universe. Space is continuous, as in Einstein's system, where space cannot be considered apart from matter. A purely deterministic philosophy of the universe, as in Newtonian physics, where physical space was considered discrete, independent of the phenomena that occur in it, is meaningless. For Olson, interpretations of experience according to Einstein's theories of Relativity and Heisenberg's Uncertainty Principle offer the highest challenge to the creative artist: "to believe that things, and present ones, are the absolute conditions; but that they are so because the structures of the real are flexible, quanta do dissolve into vibrations, all does flow, and yet is there, to be made permanent, if the means are equal to the real itself." This interpretation has for Olson the strength of a religious conviction. At the core of the actual structure of the real itself, he describes a calm or passivity that parallels the mystical experience of many religions. The ultimate experience is realizing that *"The inertial structure of the world is a real thing which not only exerts effects upon matter but in turn suffers such effects."* The italics are his, and he goes on to say, "I don't know a more relevant single fact to the experience of *Moby-Dick* and its writer than this."[4]

---

2 "Projective Verse," page 59.

3 "Equal, That Is, to the Real Itself," *Human Universe*, page 119.

4 *Ibid.*, page 122.

It takes considerable courage to take off, as Olson does, from the premises of modern science, discarding God as excess baggage and accepting "the necessary secularization of His part in the world of things."[5] Certainly religious dogma has stifled thought in the past (Olson maintains more particularly that it unmanned the creator in Herman Melville after *Moby-Dick*). But readers of Olson's essays and poetry may question whether he has freed himself with the relativism of the nineteenth century "redefinition of the real," or if he has instead substituted another dogma for that of Euclid, Plato or St. Matthew. Nearly every line of Olson's prose partakes of the same consistency of thought, every paragraph turns upon itself to reveal the same emphasis. The message is repeated in essay after essay, at the center of major pieces like "Equal, That Is," "Projective Verse," and "Human Universe," and even the ingenious hypothesis of Olson's interpretation of the glyphs in his Mayan letters to Robert Creeley.

Why has Olson structured his interpretation of human experience so dogmatically? Why does he insist upon his philosophy—topology—as the key to Melville's greatness in *Moby-Dick?* Certainly Olson's concern with the topological in his own poetry has become more pronounced over the years. His longest work, the Maximus poems, have flowered as great lists of things, their importance left unexplained, sufficient unto themselves for Olson in their abstraction. In his Gloucester home, Olson has pinned on his wall large aerial survey maps of Dogtown, the location of some of the Maximus poems, and over the maps he has pasted bits of paper, recreating the physical landscape, the topography, of the region. Is this concern with the *measure* of things a substitute for an imaginative apprehension of their reality? Early critics of *Moby-Dick* were much taken with Melville's factual knowledge of what went into a whaling voyage. Olson's fascination with the book's "physical qualities" is less naïve; for him Melville's concern with visible truth is the mark of a profound affinity of two similar minds.

---

[5] *Ibid.*, page 121.

With his involvement in topology, Olson of course does not mean to be read merely as a mathematician or physicist—no more than Melville meant his facts about the whaling industry to limit *Moby-Dick* to the dimensions of a scientific or economic treatise. Olson once told his students at Black Mountain College that his philosophy was primarily meant to be grasped as metaphor and as method. "Just as I wrench history from any meaning of the past, I wrench knowledge from any meaning of know-it-all, even though my premise is that you know-it-all or you miss. . . . It may turn out in the end that this dogmatic system of mine is no more [than] 'images for your verse.' Yet I am impelled to think that what I am offering you is, as I also have said, STANCE, stance toward reality by which it will yield to you that from which I take it any of us are, in varying degrees, estranged."[6]

As a "post-modern" philosopher, Olson has little patience with the nineteenth century transcendental idealism of Emerson and Thoreau, but his methodology is often similar to theirs. Like them, he writes as a dogmatist, lecturing in the manner of a Yankee original, theorizing independent of the academy. He is a bookish man, with a wildly diverse taste for books (his writing often seems an immediate, direct response to something he has just read), but he remains at heart an enthusiast, a poet-preacher rather than a professor. In scientific matters, Olson is a self-educated man, as much an amateur mathematician and physicist as Thoreau was a gentleman botanist and zoologist. Olson's friend Robert Duncan once recalled affectionately, "Charles is just like I am. He sits around and reads all day."[7] Like Melville, Olson reads to write.

Like Emerson and Thoreau, Olson is fiercely involved in the uniqueness of the American experience. He has stated in *Proprioception* that America is the inheritor of "a secularization which not only loses nothing of the divine but by seeing process in reality redeems all idealism from theocracy or mob-

6 Black Mountain College lecture (John Wieners' notes).
7 Robert Duncan conversation, San Francisco, January 25, 1968.

ocracy, whether it is rational or superstitious, whether it is democratic or socialism." But while he can be rhapsodic over the promise of the democratic experiment, he is also disillusioned over the exploitation of natural resources and the prevalence of human greed. With the passionate conviction of a Massachusetts sage, for example, he wrote in "A house built by Capt. John Somes 1763," that the "spirit anyway of this nation went away at some point of time between 1765 and 1770 and a man born about then, therefore a son rather of those men who made the Revolution was already, in the first years of the Nineteenth Century, crying us down accurately — James Fennimore Cooper, that early. All which writing including the hump-up of the middle of the 19th Century did insist upon and Melville had already passed American art out into the geometry which alone — until time re-entered about 1948 — was what was making things possible again."

Olson would also, like Emerson, ascribe to the notion that a foolish consistency is the hobgoblin of little minds. Certainly historical facts or dates mean little to him when he is on the trail of an intuitive relationship between Melville and the nineteenth century mathematicians who created the new geometry. Melville wrote *Moby-Dick* three years before Riemann lectured on the metrical structure of the universe, and there is no evidence he either read or even heard of the German's work. In matters of bibliographical scholarship about Melville, Olson is meticulous. But in theoretical matters, he is usually intuitive; like Emerson, a poet proposing Beauty as well as philosophical Truth. It suits him as poet to recognize the function of physical science in the modern world. He wrote in "This is Yeats Speaking" that at the millenium a physicist will come on as stage manager of the tragedy, while Freud is left in the wings.

Olson's belief that *Moby-Dick* illustrates the principle of quantity as intensive is also severely challenged when tested against close textual analysis of the novel itself, perhaps a more serious objection to *Call me Ishmael.* Olson bases his concept of what Melville achieved on just one book, *Moby-Dick*. Melville "only rode his own space once." (13) * Furthermore, his achievement is seen in only one chapter of that work, "The Tail." "Melville on the tail of the whale . . . is the purest non-Euclidean act in writing yet."[8] The rest of his writing does not illustrate so strikingly "the notion of actuality as in its essence a process."[9] But as a philosophic theory, Olson's belief can be criticized even without recourse to Melville, who may even have been innocent of the association with projective space. The universe may well be a collection of things, with man merely another *thing* in it. Melville might have been impressed with this when he wrote Hawthorne that "By visible truth we mean the apprehension of the absolute condition of present things," a sentence Olson quotes as indisputable evidence for Melville's belief in topology. The difficulty with Olson's philosophy is not with the basic comprehensiveness of topography as a realization of what *is;* the difficulty lies with the limitation of topology as a philosophy in itself. Although the universe is discernible to human beings through their sense receptors, human perception is more complex than a series of sensory reactions to a collection of things. The world is organized for us as a sphere of meanings and relationships, but Olson's topography shies away from "meanings" and "relationships," leaving them for his reader's instinctive, intuitive, nonverbal responses. The implication is that the unexamined life is the only one worth living. It is true, as Pound maintained, that generalization is like a greased slide; but when the poet selects a particular thing to adnumerate in his writing as meaningful, its meaning succeeds only in proportion to its generality, its relevance for each different reader. The references to historical events in Olson's Maximus poems are presented so that their relevance is intuitive, mysterious as ritual, the primitive ritual of belief in the magic of the word itself.

*Numbers in parentheses refer to pages in *Call Me Ishmael.*

---

8 Olson letter to Robin Blazer, May 3, 1957.

9 *A Bibliography on America for Ed Dorn,* page 9.

If I have raised serious objections to Olson's philosophy, in the larger sense his efforts are wholly admirable. Keenly aware that "the change the 19th century did bring about is being squandered by the 20th, in ignorance and abuse of its truth,"[10] Olson stands firm by his belief in physicality, man a thing among things. And, as he wrote in *Ishmael,* Melville had shown with Ahab the "END of individual responsible only to himself." (119) Since the humanism he deplores has brought mankind to the edge of extinction, Olson urges

> turn now and rise
> Wrest the matter into your own
> hands – and Nature's laws.

Olson theorizes about the universe without quite the total comprehensiveness necessary to account for the complexity of life with God in the street, the result of the secularization of His part in the world of things. But he is on the right side of the fence after Aristotle, whom he criticizes for systems of logic and classification that have fastened themselves on man's habits of thought and interfered with man's actions. Idealism is only a means to an END –

> which is never more than this instant,
> than you on this instant, than you,
> figuring it out, and acting, so.
> If there is any absolute, it is never more
> than this one, you, this instant, in action.[11]

————

Olson's philosophy of projective space, that quantity is the basic principle of the universe and that process is its most interesting fact, brings him directly to his method in *Call me Ishmael.* As Robert Creeley has pointed out in his introduction to Olson's *Selected Writings,* the theory of projective space eschews criticism as a descriptive process. Attacking Plato and Aristotle's systems of logical notation and categori-

---

[10] "Equal, That Is," page 118.
[11] "Human Universe," *Human Universe,* page 5.

zation, Olson insists instead on criticism as an "active and definitive engagement with what a text proposes." This engagement strikes cautious readers as a mishmash if they expect a book like *Ishmael* (subtitled "A Study of Melville") to be organized according to some perceivable system of developing logical relationships. The organization of *Ishmael* is perceivable, but only to the inquiring, intuitive eye.

What Ezra Pound wrote about William Carlos Williams' *In the American Grain* (like *Ishmael*, a poet's strongly personal approach to literary criticism), is true also about Olson. Both he and Williams are concerned with their "own insides," totally uncommitted to "established solutions" to the problems of evaluating American literature.[12] Olson's "insides" are his theories of projective space. He states in "Human Universe" that "Art does not seek to describe but to enact." As a philosopher/poet, his concern is methodology, the use of human experience. Art is the only twin life has; impressions come into man by way of his skin, and go out again by his own "powers of conversion." Art is action, alive only when it "proceeds unbroken from the threshold of a man through him and back out again, without loss of quality, to the external world from which it came." If man chooses to treat external reality any differently than as part of his own process, his own inner life, then he is mistreating external reality for his own arbitrary willful purposes. To Olson, academic criticism destroys "the energy implicit in any high work of the past" because such criticism uses the methods of description, generalization, and logic — all inimical to the creative process since they blur or destroy the outlines of external reality. Such writing is unsatisfactory because to arrive at a generalization, the critic must have selected from the full content "some face of it, or plane, some part. . . . It comes out a demonstration, a separating out, an act of classification, and so, a stopping." Olson went a different way in *Ishmael*. His book is constructed like the acts of experience

---

12 Pound, "Dr. Williams' Position," *Literary Essays of Ezra Pound,*
   pages 392, 398.

themselves, "on several more planes than the arbitrary and discursive which we inherit can declare."

To comprehend fully how Olson conceived *Ishmael*, the reader must keep in mind that what really matters for him is not generalization or logic or a coherent intellectual framework, but the Thing Itself. In "Human Universe" he writes that the most important fact is the "self-existence" of the thing, "without reference to any other thing, in short, the very character of it which calls our attention to it, which wants us to know more about it, its particularity. This is what we are confronted by . . . the thing itself, and its relevance to ourselves who are the experience of it (whatever it may mean to someone else, or whatever other relations it may have." Olson doesn't care what his facts may *mean* to "someone else." His method is to present them for the reader's experience.

———

Call me Ishmael is Olson's study of Melville as prophet — the first American writer to realize the principle of projective space. But *Ishmael* is also Olson's own emergence as prophet. If his first birth was his entrance into life, his second was his appearance as philosopher and poet in his first book: "Art is the only twin life has."

According to Robert Duncan, Olson's reading of Melville, especially Melville's notes in his volumes of Shakespeare's plays, acted as a catalyst. Olson quotes Melville in *Ishmael* to explain the genesis of *Moby-Dick*, but Melville's words apparently also describe what happened to Olson:

I somehow cling to the strange fancy, that, in all men hiddenly reside certain wondrous, occult properties — as in some plants and minerals — which by some happy but very rare accident (as bronze was discovered by the melting of the iron and brass at the burning of Corinth) may chance to be called forth here on earth. (38)

Olson's realization that Melville could proceed to an original creative act — *Moby-Dick* — after reading Shakespeare, apparently motivated his own creative expression. His encounter

with the seven volumes of Melville's copy of Shakespeare was
the "very rare accident," since this experience led Olson to discover "all that has been said but multiplies the avenues to
what remains to be said."[13] From Melville, Olson first realized
what he later came to understand was known by Lawrence
and Pound, that the past was usable. *Call me Ishmael* is
Olson's first book, not completed until he was nearly 35 years
old. As Creeley observed, the book is totally integrated in its
writing,[14] the work of a fully mature mind. The philosopher in
Olson was ready long before the poet took courage, but with
Melville as spiritual mentor, Olson found his voice.

This voice was Ishmael's, the philosopher, the witness. The
title of his study of Melville is the key: "Call me Ishmael."
The title is also of course the first sentence of *Moby-Dick*, so
its implications for Olson can easily be over-looked if read
merely as homage to Melville. But in Olson's book he speaks
throughout as Ishmael. Ishmael is the mask assumed in the
drama of his book about Melville and *Moby-Dick*. As a study
of Melville, the book is not a critical dissection. It is rather a
dramatic enactment, a definite engagement: "Art does not seek
to describe but to enact."[15]

Olson's Ishmael is as complex as Melville's. Both writers
speak through their Ishmaels, using him to state their own
philosophy. Melville is more easily separated from his Ishmael
in that he also functions as a character in the novel who comments (he alone survives the wreck of the *Pequod*) on Ahab's
blasphemy. As Olson points out, "By this use of Ishmael, Melville achieved a struggle and a catharsis which he intended, to
feel 'spotless as the lamb'." (58) Olson lacks this imaginative
use of Ishmael as a fictional character in his book, but he adds
a different dimension by virtue of his historical perspective,
the advantage of living a century after Melville and having
Moby-Dick as part of his own cultural experience of being an

---

13 "Lear and Moby-Dick," *Twice a Year* (Fall-Winter 1938) page 172.
14 Creeley (editor), *Charles Olson Selected Writings,* page 280.
15 "Human Universe," page 10.

American. Melville had "the power to find the lost past of America, the unfound present, and make a myth, *Moby-Dick*, for a people of Ishmaels." (15) A visionary alienated from twentieth century America, Olson sees the country as inhabited by a "people of Ishmaels" fulfilling the Biblical prophesy told in Genesis. There the angel announced to Hagar, Abraham's concubine, "Behold, thou art with child, and shalt bear a son, and shalt call his name Ishmael; because the Lord hath heard thy affliction. And he will be a wild man; his hand will be against every man, and every man's hand against him; and he shall dwell in the presence of all his brethren."

Moreover, Olson—like his friend Edward Dahlberg, who had written, "Our artists are American Ishmaels doomed to be cut away from the human vineyard"[16]—had the concept of an "Ishmael of solitude" (46), a philosopher alienated from his fellow men to a much greater extent than Melville's Ishmael. In the opening chapter of *Moby-Dick*, Ishmael suffers "a damp, drizzly November" in his soul, but he signs up with the whaling voyage in an effort to rejoin his fellow men. An ocean voyage is his way "of driving off the spleen, and regulating the circulation." Olson's Ishmael, on the other hand, is not in a temporary state of mind. Olson's Ishmael *is* Olson. With his philosophy he places himself in an unpopular camp; for insisting upon God's place in the street, he is as much an infidel as Mohammed, who claimed descent from Ishmael the son of Abraham and thus brought the name into disrepute.

Through the mask of Ishmael and while in the guise of a Melville biographer and scholar, Olson speaks as a philosopher of projective space and an interpreter of the American experience. The drama of Olson's book, its becoming in its own way as extended a prose-poem as *Moby-Dick*, lies in its structure. *Ishmael* may be felt as a re-creation of *Moby-Dick* according to the theory of projective space, with Olson as Ishmael and Melville as Ahab. The re-creation is intuitive, not rigorously schematic. It is the record of Olson's response to Melville

---

[16] Dahlberg, *Can These Bones Live,* page 45.

offered in the terms of quantity as intensive. A book like *Call me Ishmael,* conceived "on several more planes than the arbitrary and discursive which we inherit can declare,"[17] is done an injustice by any one systematic explanation. Yet although the book projects a complex impression in its totality, it seems to have germinated from a simple original response. The response accumulated in Olson over the dozen years between his first awakening to Melville in 1933 and his writing the final version of *Ishmael* in 1945. In one extended, totally assimilated breath, the response "proceeds unbroken from the threshold of a man through him and back out again, without loss of quantity, to the external world from which it came."[18] Olson's Ishmael is witness to the triumph and tragedy of Herman Melvlle, like Ahab finally defeated—according to Olson—in his effort to master space.

———

Olson introduces his study of Melville with a poem.

> O fahter, fahter
> gone amoong
> O eeys that loke
>
> Loke, fahter:
> your sone!

Olson has said that the poem is literally addressed to the memory of his own father, Charles Joseph Olson.[19] Highly suggestive, it contains an image central to the later poetry—eyes, looking—an individual's instinctive sensory perception of reality. Years later, for example, in "Maximus Letter 6," Olson expanded:

> There are no hierarchies, no infinite, no
>   such many as mass, there are only
> eyes in all heads,
> to be looked out of.

---

17 "Human Universe," page 5.
18 "Human Universe," page 11.
19 Placed beside the introductory poem in Olson's personal copy of *Call me Ishmael* is a photograph of his father.

Whatever its literal meaning, the *Ishmael* poem also suggests Olson's relationship with Melville, much as Melville himself was quick to recognize the chain of influences that link
different writers separated by many generations. A year before
starting *Moby-Dick*, he wrote his friend Evert Duyckinck,
"The truth is that we are all sons, grandsons, or nephews or
great nephews of those who go before us. No man is his own
sire." Toward the end of *Ishmael*, Olson quotes from *Moby-
Dick:* "It is your own grim sire, who did beget ye, exiled
sons." (85)

The contents page is Olson's brief or summary of his book.
Its organization also suggests its parallel with the structure of
Moby-Dick. The suggestion must be inferred, however, since
Olson's avoidance of logic and systems, his insistence on "planes
of experience," results in a contents page that looks baffling at
first sight. It begins with
    "FIRST FACT" is prologue,"
clear enough. But then follows
    "part I is FACT."
Is this second fact? Not possible, since further down on the
page is
    "FACT #2 is dromenon."
Dromenon? The word isn't in Webster's Unabridged. What
does it mean?
    "part II is SOURCE: SHAKESPEARE."
Shakespeare is important enough in Olson's scheme to appear
on the contents page.
    "Part III is THE BOOK OF THE LAW OF THE BLOOD."
No name alongside this part. It will appear later: Moses.
    "part IV is LOSS: CHRIST."
Shakespeare and Christ, Olson feels, were the two biggest in-
fluences in Melville's life. One giveth, the other taketh away.

Then follows A LAST FACT. Is this *Ishmael's* conclusion?
No. One more item on the contents page remains—
    "part V is THE CONCLUSION: PACIFIC MAN."
We learn later he is Noah.

What similarities does this organization have with *Moby-Dick?* The only obvious resemblance are the FACTS interspersed throughout *Ishmael,* corresponding to the facts on the whaling industry and cetology Melville included throughout his book. In Olson's study, the scale is much diminished, but of course *Ishmael* is much shorter than *Moby-Dick,* less than one-tenth its length. Other parallels are not obvious from the contents page; they must be inferred after reading *Ishmael.* But even before proceeding too deeply into Olson's text, it is clear that the contents page is not what it reads. The title pages before each part do not agree with the table of contents.

Part I, called "FACT" on the contents page, later reads "Call me Ishmael."

Part II, called "SOURCE: SHAKESPEARE," later reads simply "Shakespeare."

Part III, called "THE BOOK OF THE LAW OF THE BLOOD," reads "Moses."

Part IV, called "LOSS: CHRIST," reads "Christ."

Part V, "THE CONCLUSION: PACIFIC MAN," reads "Noah."

Ishmael, Shakespeare, Moses, Christ, Noah. There is no historical continuity in the five names, but there is an emotional continuity paralleling the acts of experience in *Moby-Dick.* Olson has recreated the rise and fall of Ahab's voyage after the white whale. *Moby-Dick* has supplied the basic rhythm for him to orchestrate his interpretation of Melville's experience as the first American prophet of projective space.

Heading the contents page is "FIRST FACT is prologue." On the section page following it in the book is "FIRST FACT as prologue." Not a misprint,[20] for Olson explains in the essay "Projective Verse" that "is" comes from the Aryan root "as," meaning "to breathe." The FIRST FACT breathes prologue. As a poet, Olson teaches that verse will only succeed when "a poet manages to register both the acquisition of his ear *and* the pres-

---

[20] Olson verifies that the Cape Edition (London, 1967) of *Ishmael,* which has "FIRST FACT is prologue" on both pages, is in error.

sures of his breath."[21] His theory of projective verse proposes a complex view of FIELD COMPOSITION in which breath plays a major role. Here, in *Ishmael*, the implications are simpler. "Breath" means, literally, life. The critic's act is not to generalize, or kill, experience; rather, he must animate it, make it live. "FIRST FACT is/as prologue" is Olson's way of starting his book so that his reader steps off into space.

Stepping off into space can be an exhilerating experience, like flying, or a disaster, like falling down. Olson's FIRST FACT manages to give the illusion of flying while keeping the reader's feet solidly on the ground, no small accomplishment. The first section of *Ishmael* is an extended narrative of the shipwreck of the whaler *Essex*. On November 20, 1820, a little more than a year after Melville was born, this ship was struck "head on twice by a bull whale, a spermeceti about 85 feet long, and with her bows stove in, filled and sank." What happened to the twenty men in her crew, how four survived the sea by recourse to cannibalism, is the story Olson narrates as first fact.

The tone of the writing is what keeps the reader's feet on the ground. The three sections of *Ishmael* called "Facts" are written differently than the other "Parts" of the book. In these three sections, Olson assumes a tone similar to that found in historical documents written by the earliest English explorers and settlers in America, men like John Smith, William Bradford, John Winthrop. Fascinated by the roots of the American experience, Olson has read widely in Colonial history; even "plugging John Smith as the first American writer," "that great successor to William Shakespeare."[22] John Smith's way of handling historical narrative could have been Olson's model. Describing a scene he witnessed among the Indians, for example, Smith wrote:

At his entrance before the King, all the people gave a great shout. The Queene of Appamatuck was appointed to bring him water to wash his hands, and another brought him a bunch of feathers, in stead of a

21"Projective Verse," page 53.
22*Charles Olson Reading at Berkeley,* page 40.

Towell to dry them: having feasted him after their best barbarous manner they could, a long consultation was held, but the conclusion was, two great stones were brought before Powhatan: then as many as could layd hands on him, dragged him to them, and thereon laid his head, and being ready with their clubs, to beate out his brains. . . .

Olson writes of violent action with the same understated directness. With a repetition of words like "eat," "flesh," and "body," his prose structure is as fundamental as the act of survival it describes.

It was not until February 8th, when Isaac Cole died in convulsions, that Owen Chase was forced, some two weeks later than in the other boats, to propose to his two men, Benjamin Lawrence and Thomas Nickerson, that they should eat of their own flesh. It happened to them this once, in this way: they separated the limbs from the body, and cut all the flesh from the bones, after which they opened the body, took out the heart, closed the body again, sewed it up as well as they could, and committed it to the sea. (6)

A different historical method was Melville's in the earliest pages of *Moby-Dick*. He didn't write in the prose style of John Smith, but the Extracts on Leviathan compiled by the Sub-Sub Librarian were a "veritable gospel cetalogy," ranging in history from the Creation to nineteenth century Nantucket. Melville's intent was mostly humorous, however, and here Olson also differs from him. Handled with a poet's compression and intensity, the *Essex* narrative is meant to hold the reader with its power as story; the material speaks for itself, is animated without comment from Olson (just as Melville merely listed his extracts, without explaining their implications).

The *Essex* disaster suggests the American experience of ocean as space, but it is also appropriate to what follows because it contains one of the themes of *Ishmael*: cannibalism, "the book of the law of the blood," central to what Olson saw in Melville and in the American experience. "The First Fact breathes Prologue" is Olson's poetic suggestion that the *Essex* disaster portends the tragedy that *Ishmael* will unfold.

In the table of contents, Part I is FACT; however, the section page reads "Call me Ishmael." What Olson takes as fact about Part I is stated in the first paragraph: "I take SPACE to be the central fact to man born in America, from Folsom cave to now." The tone is an abrupt change from the *Essex* narrative. But Olson's section heading should be read like the title in certain poems, as the first statement in the paragraph. Then the dogmatic pronouncement is totally in character.

Call me Ishmael. I take SPACE to be the central fact to man born in America, from Folsom cave to now. I spell it large because it comes large here. Large, and without mercy. (11)

Although Olson's concerns are those of a philosopher, his prose is that of a poet. "I spell it [SPACE] large because it comes large here." Typography, the image of the word, the thing-ness of physical perception are in Olson's concept the basic materials of poetry. His underlying philosophic concern with continuous space leads him to history, geography, economics — *facts* rather than imagination. Unlikely materials for a poet, but as Ishmael, Olson animates them for his interpretation of Melville.

If the prologue to *Ishmael* corresponds to the extracts in *Moby-Dick*, then "part I is FACT" is the counterpart of the first 28 chapters of the novel, up to the chapter titled "Enter Ahab; to him, Stubb." Chapter 29 and following correspond to "part II is SOURCE: SHAKESPEARE." Olson's underlying structure in *Ishmael* runs an intuitive, emotional parallel with *Moby-Dick*. Correspondences are not rigorously maintained on a one-for-one basis, but certain relationships are clear. The words "Call me Ishmael" begin both books, and Olson's first two chapters, like the first events of *Moby-Dick*, are presented through the eyes of a philosophic Ishmael.

As Ishmael, Olson speculates about the "first American story," exploration: America is a country with "seas on both sides, no barriers to contain as restless a thing as Western man." (11) Although Melville's Ishmael "is tormented with an everlasting itch for things remote," he is a much more eclectic philosopher than Olson. Melville is fascinated by the philosophic state of mind and leaves Ishmael's perceptions soon after the *Pequod's* voyage gets under way. The essential difference is that Olson has committed himself to a particular philosophy, whereas Melville holds no single belief. For Melville, dogma of any kind is impossible. Like the character Bulkington in *Moby-Dick*, he has had glimpses of "that mortally intolerable truth; that all deep, earnest thinking is but the intrepid effort of the soul to keep the open independence of her sea; while the wildest winds of heaven and earth conspire to cast her on the treacherous, slavish shore."

Olson's chapter "What Lies Under" corresponds to Melville's description of the whaling industry, dramatized as Ishmael travels to Nantucket, meets Queequeg and signs aboard the *Pequod*. Olson even refers to Melville's Chapter 24, "The Advocate," for facts and figures to corroborate his own. The third and final chapter in "part I is FACT," titled "Usufruct," parallels Melville's chapters 26, 27, and 28, describing the *Pequod's* crew and Ahab. But although Pound once told Eliot that if he read *Ishmael* there would be no need ever to read *Moby-Dick*, the correspondences between the organization of the two books can be only loosely discerned. Olson, like Melville, might have decided that "There are some enterprises in which a careful disorderliness is the true method."[23] "Part II is SOURCE: SHAKESPEARE" parallels Chapters 29-53 in *Moby-Dick*. Fact #2 in *Ishmael* corresponds to Chapter 54, the Town Ho's Story. "Part III is THE BOOK OF THE LAW OF THE BLOOD" approximates Chapters 55-92; "Part IV is LOSS: CHRIST," Chapters 93-135. Finally, Olson's "Part V is THE CONCLUSION" suggests Melville's Epilogue.

Establishing a close parallel between *Ishmael* and *Moby-Dick* was less important to Olson than animating his thoughts about Melville. He implied as much in his *Bibliography on America for Ed Dorn*, when he advised Dorn that "one must henceforth apply to quantity as principle and to process as the

---

23 Melville, *Moby-Dick* (Hendricks House, 1962), page 359.

most interesting fact *all attention.*" "Quantity as principle" is his basic concern with continuous space, defining "process" as "the most interesting fact of fact (the overwhelming one, how it works, not what, in that what is always different if the thing or person or event under review is a live one, and is different because adverbially it is changing." The "process" of *Call me Ishmael*, "how it works," was Olson's main concern. Instead of a strict logical organization of his thoughts or a rigid parallel with *Moby-Dick*, he tried to express his feeling about Melville directly. If he had wanted to be logical, for example, he would never have buried his main idea — the three forces that contributed to *Moby-Dick* — in the middle of his first chapter, cryptically tossed off in two short paragraphs.

He had the tradition in him, deep, in his brain, his words, the salt beat of his blood. He had the sea of himself in a vigorous, stricken way, as Poe the street. It enabled him to draw up from Shakespeare. It made Noah, and Moses, contemporary to him. History was ritual and repetition when Melville's imagination was at its own proper beat.

It was an older sense than the European man's, more to do with magic than culture. Magic which, in contrast to worship, is all black. For magic has one purpose: compel men or non-human forces to do one's will. Like Ahab, American, one aim: lordship over nature. (13)

The three forces acting on Melville "to bring about the dimensions of *Moby-Dick*" were tragedy (Shakespeare), myth (Noah and Moses), and space (lordship over nature). *Ishmael's* part I is the force of space on Melville. Part II is source, Shakespeare. Part III is Moses, Part V is Noah — myth. Olson hints at his interpretation on page 13, but doesn't make it fully clear until page 71: "Three forces operated to bring about the dimensions of *Moby-Dick*: Melville, a man of MYTH, antemosaic; an experience of SPACE, its power and price, America; and ancient magnitudes of TRAGEDY: Shakespeare." This is what *Call me Ishmael* is explicitly about. As Olson told Dorn, "the overwhelming concern is how it works, not what." Olson organizes his book like a poet. The process of simply getting through the text is a major part of the reader's experience, and probably for most readers the act of reading the book gener-

ates in itself a more vivid impression than what the book is
specifically about.

   The impact on the reader of encountering how Olson organized *Ishmael* is sustained by his literary tone. It is the tone of
his early poems, modified with the rhetorical echoes of Edward
Dahlberg and D. H. Lawrence. The assertion of "The K," a
poem written a few months before his study of Melville, early
1945, shows that poetry and prose were one breath for Olson.

> Take, then, my answer:
> There is a tide in a man
> moves him to his moon and,
> though it drop him back
> he works through ebb to mount
> the run again and swell
> to be tumescent

But *Ishmael* has an edge, a ring to the voice, lacking here.
Olson is an "impressionist" critic like Williams, Lawrence, and
Dahlberg, and while his was not what Yvor Winters has called
the "heroic prose" of Williams, Olson did adapt elements of the
style of Lawrence and Dahlberg to his own use. From Lawrence he absorbed audacity, the tone of a man utterly sure
of his own voice. Lawrence's way with Melville in *Studies in
Classic American Literature* was a vivid blend of physical car-
icature and spiritual wonder:

It is the same old thing as in all Americans. They keep their old-
fashioned ideal frock-coat on, and an old-fashioned silk hat, while they
do the most impossible things. There you are: you see Melville hugged
in bed by a huge tattooed South Sea Islander, and solemnly offering
burnt offering to this savage's little idol, and his ideal frock-coat just
hides his shirt-tails and prevents us from seeing his bare posterior as he
salaams, while his ethical silk hat sits correctly over his brow the while.
. . . And meanwhile in Melville his bodily knowledge moves naked, a
living quick among the stark elements. For with sheer physical, vibra-
tional sensitiveness, like a marvellous wireless-station, he registers the
effects of the outer world. And he records also, almost beyond pain or
pleasure, the extreme transitions of the isolated, far-driven soul, the
soul which is now alone, without any real human contact.

Here is Olson's dogmatic pronouncement, sweeping "all Americans" under the same broom. But Olson is more literal, less figurature — never *ideal* frock-coats in the language of projective space. Lawrence also exercised a waspish humor, an irreverence for things (including ideas) that Olson is too serious to entertain. Actually the main influence throughout *Ishmael* is that of Edward Dahlberg, one of Olson's close friends.

The book that bears the closest resemblance to *Call me Ishmael* is not *In the American Grain* or *Studies in Classic American Literature*, but Dahlberg's *Can These Bones Live*. Published in 1941, the book acknowledges the influence of Olson's ideas about Melville. In 1940, Olson showed Dahlberg the first draft of *Ishmael*, and Dahlberg mentions his friend's unpublished ms. in a graceful inscription to Olson before Chapter VII, on Melville:

My dear Charles: Literature, we know, is the art of ripening ourselves by conversation; and originality is but high-born stealth. How much of our talks have yeasted and bloomed this little Herman Melville loaf; and how I have played the cutpurse Autolycus, making my thefts as invisible as possible, you and my blushes best know. But here is my hand with Mephistopheles' orison: When your own polestar Truths surge upon the whited page, may "God's spies" put the same vermilion Guilt upon your face!

Olson returns the compliment by dedicating part IV of *Ishmael*, "Christ," to "EDWARD DAHLBERG, my other genius of the Cross and the Windmills. If the Fool is in this book, you nurtured him. . . ." And on page 36, Olson quotes his friend's definition: "Highborn stealth, Edward Dahlberg calls originality, the act of a cutpurse Autolycus who makes his thefts as invisible as possible." Olson's debt to Dahlberg would seem very large. The Fool is the Shakespearean Wise Fool of *King Lear*, the character who is not afraid to speak the deepest truth.

Certainly Olson and Dahlberg shared the same judgments on the function of literary criticism, believing it "an act of creative faith."[24] In one clean sweep Dahlberg dismissed his-

---

[24] *Can These Bones Live,* page 51.

torical, scientific, proletarian, psychoanalytic and "genteel" academic critics, which included practically everyone writing about American literature except D. H. Lawrence and Raymond Weaver. In *Can These Bones Live*, he wrote: "We desire the same quickening from the critic that we have from the poet." Also,

> The critic is the Sancho Panza to his master, our Lord Don Quixote, the artist. Sancho is no bread, butter and beer realist. He too sees and knows with the magical folly of the heart that there is knowledge before reason and science, a secret wisdom that is prior to logic – the vibrant god-telling PULSE. "There are reasons of the heart of which Reason knows nothing," said Pascal.
>
> There are no abstract truths – no Mass Man, no proletariat. There is only Man. . . .

Sharing similar feelings about the function of literary criticism, that it should primarily reflect a philosophical interpretation of all human experience, Olson and Dahlberg went different ways. Dahlberg emphasized, like Lawrence, the sexual inhibitions brought about by a stifling industrial society, and he castigated the state as a social institution. The "Bones" in his title refer to the sensual, naked physicality of mankind.

> O ye oracles and Bacchic fakirs, return to these States of Dry Bones. Come back, Walt Whitman, and breathe upon them, shake them into a great prophetic commotion. Ye choric fools, Melville, Thoreau, Whitman, Anderson, take these slain, bleached bones of Philistia, and drive them mad, make them weep and say to the Heart, "Son of man, can these bones live?"

Dahlberg's prose is hortatory, a blend of earnest advice and passionate encouragement. Olson's is laconic, even understated. The main difference is in what they are saying, however, not in *how* they are saying it. For as Olson wrote in "Projective Verse," Dahlberg "first pounded into my head" the key to shaping material, transforming energy into form by the method of "composition by field." From Dahlberg, Olson said he learned that

> ONE PERCEPTION MUST IMMEDIATELY AND DIRECTLY LEAD TO A FURTHER PERCEPTION. It means exactly what it says . . . get on with it, keep moving, keep in, speed, the nerves, their speed, the perceptions, theirs,

the acts, the split second acts, the whole business, keep it moving as fast as you can, citizen.

This is the key to Olson's prose style. The technique goes back beyond Dahlberg to Emerson, whose prose also exhorted in a series of one sentence pronouncements instead of moving in units of the paragraph to logically develop an idea. Like Emerson, Dahlberg and Olson are philosopher-poets, American originals; describing *Ishmael,* Olson stated, "The way the book continues to live is like wildlife."[25] There is a bombardment of perceptions in *Can These Bones Live,* but it is fleshy with sentiment. Olson's book outlines the skeleton.

In other words, the essential difference between Olson and Dahlberg's literary studies is that *Ishmael* is not only interpretation, it also rests on solid fact. The skeleton of the book is composed of the documents and statistics Olson marshalls to animate his interpretation of Melville. Of course any biography or literary analysis is a mixture of fact and opinion, but Olson's way with them is highly personal. Half the time he doesn't mix them, but instead presents his facts straight, without evaluation or interpretation. The word "fact" has its roots in the Latin, "factum," or deed, act. It also stems from the past participle of "facere," to do or make. The roots imply action, activity, animation, at the heart of "fact"—the word literally means "that which is of actual occurrence."

A glance at Olson's contents page reveals the basic organization of *Ishmael* into "Facts" and "Parts" (interpretive sections). Significantly, they mix on the page only once: "Part I is FACT." In this part of the book, Olson presents his basic interpretation of the American experience in terms of projective space, which, by implication of the section heading, carries the same weight as fact. The rest of part I is, literally, fact: the chapter "What Lies Under" contains statistics on whaling as an American industry, and "a document of our history," Melville's notes on what became of the ship's company of the whaler *Acushnet.* The last chapter of Part I, "Usufruct" (de-

---

[25] Olson letter, February 14, 1968.

fined as "the right to use or enjoy something"), consists of
Melville's annotations of his copy of Owen Chase's *Narrative
of the ... Shipwreck of the Whale-ship Essex. . . .* But for the
most part, throughout *Ishmael*, Olson carefully balances—not
really mixes—his facts and judgments. The effect is deliberately asymmetrical; look at the lay-out of the contents page.

In the text, however, there is more variety than first meets
the eye, since Olson draws from several different kinds of
facts. First there is actual history in the *Essex* disaster, and
economics in the importance of the whaling industry to the
American economy in the nineteenth century. (Olson has
affection only for first-hand experience. In the *Bibliography
for Ed Dorn*, he begins with two assumptions: that politics
and economics are like love, and that sociology is a lot of shit.)
There are also biographical facts, like the startling paragraph
about Melville to illustrate Olson's point that whaling was
"a sweated industry," exploiting the workers. More than two-
thirds of the crews deserted every voyage.

Melville himself is a case in point. He deserted the *Acushnet*, his
first whaleship, at the Marquesas. He was one of eleven mutineers
aboard his second, a Sydney ship the *Lucy Ann*, at Tahiti. Nothing is
known of his conduct on the third, except that he turned up after it,
ashore, at Honolulu. (23)

Then there are literary "facts," the more conventional
basic documents of criticism and evaluation. Olson refers fre-
quently in the second half of *Ishmael* to myths. Throughout
the book he quotes profusely from Melville's texts, "Hawthorne and His Mosses," *Mardi, Clarel,* but especially *Moby-
Dick.* The most significant documents Olson introduces are
unpublished writings, however. These include Melville's account of "What became of the ship's company of the whale-
ship *Acushnet*, according to Hubbard who came home in her
(more than a four years' voyage) and who visited me in Pitts-
field in 1850." (22) Also, Melville's notes—six printed pages—
in his copy of the Owen Chase narrative of the *Essex* disaster,
as well as his extensive marginal gloss of Shakespeare's trage-

dies. This last includes what Olson takes as "rough notes for *Moby-Dick* . . . upon the last fly-leaf of the last volume, the one containing *Lear, Othello,* and *Hamlet.*" (52) Finally, the enigmatic jotting Melville left on the back pages of the second of the two notebooks he kept on his journey to the Holy Land; this Olson includes in *Ishmael* as "A Last Fact." (109) By virtue of this material alone, Olson produced a remarkable book, for no study of Melville before 1947 or since has included so much unpublished writing.

What is the final effect of Olson's methodology, organizing his different facts so carefully among the first parts of *Ishmael?* The desired effect was animation, letting the facts act upon the reader's consciousness. The juxtaposition of facts and parts create a multi-layered texture as complex in its intuited inter-actions as the experience of life itself. *Ishmael* is criticism as an active and definitive engagement, for the reader, as well as for Charles Olson.

With its structure a brilliant dramatization of Olson's philo-sophical theories, the contents of the book — Olson's demon-stration that Melville was the first American "poet of space"— next requires careful scrutiny. In everything Olson writes, his meanings are complex, never mere description or logical argument. Over a hundred years ago, Emerson said, "Let us answer a book of ink with a book of flesh and blood."[26] As a literary and biographical study of Melville, *Call me Ishmael* is no academic book of ink. It is Olson's personal vision of what Melville *is:* Melville's experience interpreted by an eye-witness.

---

[26] Perry, *The Heart of Emerson's Journals,* page 162.

Fort Point and Gloucester

Call me Ishmael: II

Facts dominate "Parts" in the first two-thirds of *Ishmael*. Toward the end of the book, when Olson moves deeper into his interpretation of Melville's experience, facts are made subservient much as Melville finished with the "scientific" chapters on whales and whaling before sweeping into the final climactic action of *Moby-Dick*. In the first Part of *Ishmael*, facts are included so abundantly in the text that reading the book is literally a dramatic enactment of Olson's theories of projective space. His tone is self-assured, so positive, that some readers retreat angrily from what they take is his arrogance. Robert Duncan has said, "Olson preaches, like Lawrence. If you don't want to be preached at, you won't go along with the dogma. We're all intellectually suspicious fact-finders now, so he's unpopular."[1] In the chapter "Call me Ishmael," for example, one assertive pronouncement follows another.

I take SPACE to be the central fact to man born in America. . . .
It is geography at bottom. . . .
PLUS a harshness we still perpetuate. . . .
The fulcrum of America is the Plains. . . .
Some men ride on such space, others have to fasten themselves like a tent stake to survive. As I see it Poe dug in and Melville mounted. They are the alternatives. . . .
To Melville it was not the will to be free but the will to overwhelm nature that lies at the bottom of us as individuals and a people. Ahab is no democrat. Moby-Dick, antagonist, is only king of natural force, resource. . . .

---

[1] Duncan conversation, January 25, 1968.

47

The beginning of man was salt sea, and the perpetual reverberation
of that great ancient fact, constantly renewed in the unfolding of life
in every human individual, is the important single fact about Melville.
Pelagic. . . .

In place of Zeus, Odysseus, Olympus we have had Caesar, Faust, the
City. The shift was from man as a group to individual man. Now, in
spite of the corruption of myth by fascism, the swing is out and back.
Melville is one who began it.

Whitman we have called our greatest voice because he gave us hope.
Melville is the truer man. He lived intensely his people's wrong, their
guilt. But he remembered the first dream. The *White Whale* is more
accurate than *Leaves of Grass*. Because it is America, all of her space,
the malice, the root.

Olson's approach is monolithic. A comprehensive sweep of
American topography leads him to the two alternatives in
American literature. Melville is presented as a participant in
the American experience before we are told the most "important single fact" about him. Then comes references to philosophy, myth, finally the tragedy—Melville's and America's—of
"space, the malice, the root." Olson's main concerns emerge as
cataclysms, violent upheavals. His images from geography and
history make these concerns tangible. Ahab assailed the White
Whale "as Columbus an ocean, LaSalle a continent, the Don-
ner Party their winter Pass." (12) Olson's similes, like Melville's, are Homeric—hyperbole, larger than life. His language
is vivid, poetic: "From passive places his imagination sprang
a harpoon." (15)

But the poetic metaphor and dogmatic tone of Olson's interpretation do not hide a serious difficulty for some readers with
Call me Ishmael. Each part of the book is written so that one
perception immediately and directly leads to a further perception. The sentences move the reader along rapidly, but nowhere
along the progression of Olson's ideas does he confront two
questions essential to his basic conception of Melville as what
he calls the first American "poete d'espace." (94) The questions are:

1. What precisely is a "poete d'espace"?
2. How did Melville become one?

Instead of a clear definition of (1) and a rational explanation of (2), Olson offers his own intuitive comprehension and
belief as sufficient argument. It is ironic that he should mar-
shall so many facts so brilliantly in the pages of *Ishmael* and
yet avoid introducing any facts to support his central idea.
Part I, "Call me Ishmael," avoids any definition of the word
"space," but it is used over and over again as if Olson hopes
that by the dogmatic weight of the word itself, the reader will
find it meaningful. "Space" reoccurs from the opening sentence to the conclusion of the chapter:

I take SPACE to be the central fact to man born in America. . . .
Some men ride on such space. . . .
(The machine) is the only master of space the average person
                                                        knows. . . .
The captain, Ahab by name, knew space. He rode it across seven
                                                        seas. . . .
. . . he had all space concentrated into the form of a whale. . . .
(Melville) only rode his own space once — *Moby-Dick*.
Melville had a way of reaching back through time until he got history
                    pushed back so far he turned time into space. . . .
The *White Whale* is more accurate than *Leaves of Grass*. Because it is
                    America, all of her space, the malice, the root.

The two gaps in Olson's interpretation are exposed with
these sentences about "space." The word is used in such varied
contexts that any precise meaning evaporates, leaving the
reader holding onto . . . empty space. Even if "space" or "poete
d'espace" were defined, Olson skips any account of how Melville became involved. He is fairly specific about the "average
person" and about Ahab's involvement, but about Melville he
is silent. He is perhaps guided by his own intuition in this
most important matter, but unless the reader accepts the basic
premise, he will not accept Olson's interpretation as his own.
    When asked about the precise meaning of his term poete
d'espace, Olson laughed. "I just made that phrase up. I put it
in French just to get away with it." How did Melville become
a poete d'espace? Olson: "He knew it experientially — the human race will forever be bumbling on."[2] Olson expanded a

---

[2] Olson conversation, June 14, 1968.

little, in "Equal, That Is, to the Real Itself" when he wrote that Melville possessed the powers of "spatial intuition by his birth, from his time of the world, locally America." But the matter basically remains unexplained and simply must be apprehended — as presented in *Ishmael* — as fact, that which is actual. "Space and time were not abstraction but the body of Melville's experience." (84)

If Olson's idea about Melville's involvement in space is meant to be taken on faith alone, as a religious belief, then *Call me Ishmael* has the power of myth. Melville's experience becomes archetypal, prophetic of the experience of "Pacific man"—including Charles Olson himself. The reader who decides to continue the experience of *Ishmael* beyond the first fifteen pages must take on faith (or be willing to suspend unbelief) Olson's view of Melville as the first American poet of space. He sees Melville as "an original, aboriginal. A beginner." (14) *Ishmael* is the account of how Melville "rode his own space" (13) in *Moby-Dick* and then denied its power by turning back to Christianity, looking "for solace to the Resurrection." (100) The longest extended interpretation is at the center of the book, "Part II is SOURCE: SHAKESPEARE," which could be read as an analysis of *Moby-Dick*, but Olson's study of Melville is intended primarily as biography, not textual criticism. In fact, there is a singular absence of textual criticism in *Ishmael*. Of course Olson does not believe in the systems and generalizations of academic New Criticism; he believes in animation: FACT/ACT. But he avoids literary analysis for another reason. *Ishmael* is a study of Melville, not *Moby-Dick*.

Perhaps the clearest way to understand Olson's approach is to compare the section "Part II is SOURCE: SHAKESPEARE" with his earlier treatment of the same material, written almost a decade before *Ishmael*. In his *Twice a Year* essay "Lear and Moby-Dick," Olson presented his discovery of Melville's Shakespeare notes, showing how the experience of reading Shakespeare contributed to the making of *Moby-Dick*. Most of *Ishmael's* "Part II" is a revision of this early academic study.

Olson added no new facts. What was new in *Ishmael* was the way he handled the facts: with a bold hypothesis at the beginning of the section, a change of emphasis at the end, and a different literary style throughout. "Part II is SOURCE: SHAKESPEARE" is divided into seven chapters, longer than the original article yet at the same time more concise. The basic interpretation is the same in both pieces. As expressed in "Lear and Moby-Dick," "Melville did not need Shakespeare to form his vision, though Shakespeare could enrich it; what he needed most Shakespeare could help him to — the free articulation of that vision."

Olson's new approach to this idea in *Ishmael* is most significant, stated in the first paragraph of the first chapter, "Shakespeare, or the discovery of *Moby-Dick*."

Moby-Dick was two books written between February, 1850 and August, 1851.

The first book did not contain Ahab.

It may not, except incidentally, have contained Moby-Dick.

This is a vastly different tack from the beginning of the *Twice a Year* article, "I propose a Melville whose masterpiece, *Moby-Dick*, was actually precipitated by Shakespeare." The *Ishmael* chapter begins as if Olson's theory were proven fact and he were writing with the ms. of the unpublished draft of the "first" *Moby-Dick* on the desk before him. In reality, of course, he was only making an intelligent guess (now substantiated but in 1947 bitterly contested in a review of *Ishmael* by the Melville scholar Willard Thorp), inferred from the available evidence — Melville's letters; letters of his close friend, the editor Evert Duyckinck; the article "Hawthorne and His Mosses"; and the notes he made in his edition of Shakespeare.

Olson's theory that *Moby-Dick* was two books was more than an audacious way to begin his discussion of Shakespeare in *Ishmael*. If it established him as an iconoclast (although his unique approach to literary biography would have been evident from the opening pages of *Ishmael*), it also reflected on another aspect of his intent in his study of Melville, the bio-

graphical emphasis. The *Twice a Year* essay was primarily a
literary analysis of *Moby-Dick*. In *Ishmael*, Olson was suggesting other implications. Melville's decision to re-cast the
first version of *Moby-Dick* and write what he wanted, instead
of "a quick book for the market," (38) was his "declaration
of the freedom of a man to fail." (38). This act marked his
emergence as a fully mature writer, the first American "poete
d'espace." Olson returns in later chapters of *Ishmael* to this
"declaration" when Melville turns to Christianity, led not by
a triumph of imagination but by a failure of mind. According
to Olson's interpretation, this is Melville's tragedy, the explanation for his "silence" in the remaining years of his life.

After stating that *Moby-Dick* was two books, Olson begins
his discussion of Shakespeare and Melville, closely paralleling
the material in the *Twice a Year* article. The new approach to
Shakespeare and Melville in *Ishmael*, however, is reflected in
the shift in Olson's prose style. Re-written, the interpretation
is more animated. There is a greater succinctness, more concrete language, a more dramatic tone. The change of emphasis is best shown in a direct comparison of how one statement
differed in the two versions. In "Lear and Moby-Dick," Olson's
paragraph read:

But Melville's words on the necessary silence of truth, even in a
Shakespeare, imply more than this ultimate limitation of all truth-
tellers. These passages contain a particular measure of Shakespeare
himself, and plucked out it will help to define Melville's approach to
Shakespeare. Melville as an artist chafed at the bonds of representation. His work up to *Moby-Dick* was a progress toward the concrete
and after *Moby-Dick* a breaking away. It might be reasoned that his
final renunciation of the form of the novel resulted from just such irritation in him at the need for dramatic location of truth. The more Melville pushed toward abstraction, the less was he artist and the more
"a searcher for Truth." This recognized, Melville's demand for a more
explicit Shakespeare, a more complete master of the great Art of Telling the Truth, is self-revelatory. Melville would have Shakespeare less
the playwright, although Shakespeare's deeper dramatic significance
was not lost upon him. Melville could have been more "content with
the still, rich utterance of a great intellect in repose." Then, more directly, he would have "the spiritual truth as it is in that great genius."

The discussion of the same point in the *Ishmael* chapter "American Shiloh" covers the ground much more quickly.

As an artist Melville chafed at representation. His work up to *Moby-Dick* was a progress toward the concrete and after *Moby-Dick* a breaking away. He had to fight himself to give truth dramatic location. Shakespeare's dramatic significance was not lost on him, but he would have been, as he says, "more content with the still, rich utterance of a great intellect in repose." Melville's demand uncovers a flaw in himself. (42-43)

Olson's basic argument in "Part II is SOURCE" is that reading Shakespeare caused a ferment in Melville that gave him, with *Moby-Dick*, the courage to express fully his "disillusion in the treacherous world." (44) He had written the two books before *Moby-Dick*, *Redburn* and *White-Jacket*, solely for money, "being forced to it, as other men are to sawing wood." (36) There is no doubt that Shakespeare's plays were a revelation to Melville, for in a late poem, "The Coming Storm," he wrote,

> No utter surprise can come to him
> who reaches Shakespeare's core;
> That which we seek and shun is there —
> Man's final lore.

But in the writing of *Moby-Dick*, not one but many strains from Melville's reading entered the composition: the Bible, Hawthorne, Emerson, Carlyle, Sir Thomas Browne, even Christopher Marlowe. And certainly his personal friendship with Hawthorne, whom he met in the Berkshires halfway through the writing of *Moby-Dick*, was in itself a great inspiration to re-cast the book. Olson mentions Hawthorne's influence only in passing; it is Shakespeare he stresses, even calling him SOURCE.

Six years before *Ishmael* was published, F. O. Matthiessen criticized his former student's interpretation at length. In *American Renaissance*, Matthiessen found *Moby-Dick* "too richly complex to be reduced to Olson's formula." Olson had ample time to revise his theory, but he brought it over as the central section of *Ishmael* essentially intact from *Twice a Year*.

Plainly he was unconcerned about censure from an old professor. Matthiessen may have put Olson down in *American
Renaissance,* but his analysis of *Moby-Dick* includes two points
that compliment Olson's idea of quantity as intensive. Matthiessen's discussion of the imagery in "The Tail" chapter emphasizes "an illusion of sheer size" obtained through Homeric
simile, a concept of size that corresponds to Olson's insistence
on "thing-ness." Second, Matthiessen explored the problem of
thought as an experience, writing that "an idea separated
from the act of experiencing it is not the idea that was experienced." This parallels Olson's theory of process, animation, in
his philosophy of projective space. Matthiessen's book is rich
in these and other insights, but his study is without the vivid
conviction of Olson's *Ishmael.* Olson made no concessions. He
was a visionary, intuitive; Matthiessen wrote as an academic
rationalist.

It suited Olson's purpose to stress the inspiration he sensed
Melville getting from Shakespeare, since what Olson himself
had found in Melville paralleled the relationship he saw working nearly a century before between the two writers. When
Olson refers to what Melville saw as an "American advantage"
over Shakespeare, (41) for example, it is to find a similar
"advantage" for himself over Melville.

I am willing to ride Melville's image of man, whale and ocean to
find in him prophecies, lessons he himself would not have spelled out.
A hundred years gives us an advantage. For Melville was as much
larger than himself as Ahab's hate. He was a plunger. He knew how
to take a chance. (13)

The advantage is, as Olson wrote in his *Bibliography for Ed
Dorn,* that "You is an American (no patriotism intended:
sign reads, 'LEAVE ALL FLAGS OUTSIDE — PARK YR KARKAS-
SONE')." There is no flag waving in *Ishmael,* but there is a
strong cry of political idealism. The chapter titled "Shakespeare, concluded" is Olson's most extended discussion of the
American advantage, the golden promise and the bitter reality
of the "strongest social force," democracy. This discussion is

not in the *Twice a Year* essay. Olson makes it the conclusion of the Shakespeare section, writing the equation:

America, 1850, was his [Melville's] GIVEN:
      "a poor old whale-hunter" the great man;
      fate, the chase of the Sperm whale, plot
      (economics is the administration of
            scarce resources) ;
      the crew the commons, the Captain over them;
           EQUALS:
tragedy. (65)

Ahab is "the American Timon," assailing through his extra-human hate "all the hidden forces that terrorize man," and dragging his crew and himself to violent death through his solipsism.

For the American has the Roman feeling about the world. It is his, to dispose of. He strides it, with possession of it. His property. Has he not conquered it with his machines? He bends its resources to his will. The pax of legions? the Americanization of the world. Who else is lord? (73)

Olson is writing as a social philosopher, not as a literary critic, using *Moby-Dick* to project a description of what he sees as the myth of America. He interprets Melville's experience of being witness to the failure—the tragedy—of the American experiment through greed, "solipsism," the lust to possess space. This is as explicit as Olson gets on the subject of what exactly Melville was as a "poete d'espace." Not until the article "Equal, That Is," did he approach Melville more technically as a writer following projective space insights. The idea was later extended in the Ed Dorn bibliography, when he mentioned Whitehead's principle of "actuality as in its essence a process" and went on to advise Dorn to read "The Tail" chapter in *Moby-Dick*, "that exactitude of process known."

But in *Ishmael*, Olson was following a different path. He traces relationships between characters in *Moby-Dick* and *King Lear, Macbeth, Timon of Athens,* and *Anthony and Cleopatra*. He examines parallels of theme, setting, and symbol between Melville's book and Shakespeare's tragedies. All of

this was in the *Twice a Year* essay. The end of "Lear and
Moby-Dick" was also about democracy, but there Olson wrote
with the perspective of a humanist.

At the end of the book, in the heart of the Whale's destruction, the
crew and Pip and Bulkington and Ahab all lie down together, "All
scatt'red in the bottom of the sea." They *are* all citizens, their state is
humanity, and what they find, in tragedy, is that the "humanities"
are their kinship and their glory. The citizenship of human suffering,
which is of no country, neither kingly caste nor representative government, gives *Moby-Dick* its meaning, as it does *Job* or *Lear*. For
human storms not states are the stuff of creation. Shakespeare knew
it deeply and from that man Melville learned.

Only the first sentence of this paragraph is in *Ishmael,* and it
concludes the Shakespeare section. Between "Lear and Moby-
Dick" in 1938 and *Ishmael* in 1947, Olson had abandoned
humanism for projective space.

——

Part II is SOURCE: SHAKESPEARE takes *Ishmael* more than
half way. The second half of the book repeats the movement
of the first with FACT #2 and two interpretive sections, Parts
III and IV. Then follows the asymmetry of A LAST FACT and
Part V, bringing *Ishmael* to a close. As the facts are over-
weighed by interpretation, Olson's study should by rights become more animated, taking off in a strong sweep like the final
three-day chase of Ahab after Moby-Dick. We shall see, however, that *Ishmael* ends very differently.

FACT #2 is dromenon, a "thing done," a rite. The total section is one sentence, the longest Olson ever wrote, like "writing *Macbeth* in one sentence."[3] He intended it to affect the
reader as a charge, a shock, stimulating propulsive energy to
move along the last sections of the book. Olson found the
meaning of "dromenon"—his "original experience of the word"
—in Jane Harrison's *Ancient Art and Ritual.*

The Greek word for a *rite* as already noted is *dromenon,* "a thing
done"—and the word is full of instruction. The Greeks had realized

---

[3] *Ibid.*

that to perform a rite you must *do* something, that is, you must not only feel something but express it in action, or, to put it psychologically, you must not only receive an impulse, you must react to it. The word for rite, *dromenon,* "thing done," arose, of course, not from any psychological analysis, but from the simple fact that rites among the primitive Greeks were *things done,* mimetic dances and the like. It is a fact of cardinal importance that their word for theatrical representation, *drama,* is own cousin to their word for rite, *dromenon: drama* also means "thing done." Greek linguistic instinct pointed plainly to the fact that art and ritual are near relations.[4]

Unlike FACT #2, "FACT #1 is Prologue" was not a psychological ritual. To begin *Ishmael,* Olson was concerned primarily with animating an historical fact about the American experience. This was the physical fact of space —"seas on both sides, no barriers to contain as restless a thing as Western man," (11) plus a certain "harshness," the matter of basic survival in the confrontation with nature. The *Essex* disaster was also an actual prototype of the fictional destruction of the *Pequod.* The crew of the *Essex,* adrift in three open boats on the wide Pacific, had final recourse to cannibalism, but their desperate action was the most basic instinct of self-preservation.

In FACT #2, Olson is doing something else, moving closer to Melville's personal experience, where the "thing done" is mutiny. Writing *Ishmael* in 1945, Olson "had the thought that if the *Essex* thing was the plot of the book, the mutiny on the *Globe* was the psychic button for Melville that pushed the book." Mutiny was one of Melville's dominant concerns, the rebellion of a strong spirit against repressive authority, real or imagined. Ahab's raging, "Talk not to me of blasphemy, man; I'd strike the sun if it insulted me." Even gentle Ishmael: "I myself am a savage, owing no allegiance but to the King of Cannibals; and ready at any moment to rebel against him." In the nineteenth century spirit of free enterprise, mutiny was common aboard American sailing vessels. Melville had mutiny in his family story. His cousin Guert Ganse-

---

4 Jane Harrison quoted in Olson letter, February 14, 1968.

voort was a key figure in the U. S. Navy training ship *Somers* mutiny in 1842, and Melville himself "was one of eleven mutineers aboard his second" ship, the *Mary Ann,* at Tahiti. (23)

For Olson, the concept of mutiny has deep psychological implications, both for his interpretation of Melville and America. In FACT #2, he presents mutiny as "a thing done" on the night of January 26, 1824, aboard the Nantucket whaleship the *Globe* in the Pacific Ocean. On this night, a boatsteerer, Samuel B. Comstock, age 21, split open the heads of the Captain and Chief Mate with a short axe, shot the Third Mate with a musket and "left the Second Mate dying from the wounds he gave him with a boarding knife," crying "I am the bloody man, I have the bloody hand and I will have revenge." (77-78)

In Olson's interpretation, cannibalism and mutiny are the essence of the American experience: "the will to overwhelm nature that lies at the bottom of us as individuals and a people." (12) "We act big, misuse our land, ourselves. We lose our own primary." (14) Part III is titled "The Book of the Law of the Blood." FACT #2 establishes the context of how Americans — including Melville — came "to be damned" with rage and hate, godless mutineers living under "the law of the blood."

As evidence for his interpretation of the American experience, Olson selects actual historical events, facts, for his narratives. When he turns from America to Melville, however, he is on intuitive—not so solid—ground. Part III is titled "Moses," whom Olson links directly to Melville thus:

The Melville who wrote *Moby-Dick* . . . was not weakened by any new testament world. He had reached back to where he belonged. He could face up to Moses: he knew the great deed and misdeed of primitive time. It was in himself. . . .

Another Moses Melville wrote in *Moby-Dick* the Book of the Law of the Blood. (85)

In Part III, Olson presents the third force in Melville that brought about *Moby-Dick:* myth. It is a short chapter, only five pages, divided into an introductory "effect" and six "efficient" causes. The over-all impression is often enigmatic, sometimes murky. In 1947 Olson's discussion of Melville's use

of myth was a ground-breaking effort, although the mythological references in *Moby-Dick* had struck many previous
readers as significant. Matthiessen had written in *American
Renaissance*, for example, that Melville "sank to the most
primitive and forgotten, returning to the origin and bringing
something back, seeking the beginning and the end." Unlike
Emerson, Melville didn't conceive of Art as an ever higher
and more refined ascent of the mind. He wanted nothing less
than the whole of life—he relived the values of "both Pan and
Jehovah" in his imagination. Melville cut through his contemporary civilization to rediscover the primitive and endur-
ing nature of man, the source of elemental energies. The source
was expressed in myth, a subject he drew from again and again
in his writing.

Olson names some myths most significant to Melville: Jupi-
ter and Europa; Uranus, Kronos, Saturn, and Enceladus;
Osiris and Seth; God and Satan; Prometheus; Daniel; Moses.
Underlying Melville's use of myth is his search for god.

Melville wanted a god. Space was the First, before time, earth, man.
Melville sought it . . . Christ, a Holy Ghost, Jehovah never satisfied
him. When he knew peace it was with a god of Prime. . . . Space was the
paradise Melville was exile of.

When he made his whale he made his god. . . .

When Moby-Dick is first seen he swims a snow-hill on the sea.
To Ishmael he is the white bull Jupiter swimming to Crete with rav-
ished Europa on his horns: a prime, lovely, malignant, white. (82)

The influence of Freud's *Moses and Monotheism* is appar-
ent here.[5] Melville, for Olson, "had lost the source. He demanded to know the father." (82) This was the root of his
experience, and the explanation of his involvement with mutiny. In *Moby-Dick*, he resolved his concern with ultimate
source, mysterious, ambiguous essence. The resolution occurred
when Melville acquired "the lost dimension of space." According to Olson,

There is a way to disclose paternity, declare yourself the rival of
earth, air, fire and water.

---

5 Olson has said that once he "dreamed of Melville with a scarab stuck in his
leg, like a bloodsucker. The bite of Isis."

Now he counted his birthdays as the Hebrews did: a son's years gathered not from the son's birth but from the father's death. Another Moses Melville wrote in *Moby-Dick* the Book of the Law of the Blood. (85)

Moby-Dick was Melville's triumph. Godless, he was a creative force sufficient unto himself. He had mastered space and time by realizing them as the body of his experience. His was the knowledge of stance, "that our aloneness is the aloneness of all of us."[6] The mutiny was complete, as Melville himself realized. "I have written a wicked book," he told Hawthorne upon the completion of *Moby-Dick*, "and I feel as spotless as the lamb."

———

As a poet whose subject is Melville, Olson's study is a uniquely animated blend of fact and interpretation. When his dogma is a stance, a tone of voice, a philosophic, psychological, or historic vision, *Call me Ishmael* succeeds brilliantly much as a good poem succeeds: it occupies more space than the words themselves.[7] But when his interpretation becomes merely biographical, his book diminishes. "Part IV is Loss: CHRIST" is such a diminishing. The book is nearly concluded when Olson constricts all the images he has projected of Melville's experience of space, its complexities and its ever-shifting process, into a rigid linear interpretation. Part III is a difficult, not always clearly articulated suggestion of Melville's endebtedness to myth, but the chapter expands the reader's awareness of Melville's involvement in history and time. In Part IV, however, Olson presents a biographical thesis, arguing it to the exclusion of everything else.

"Part IV is Loss: CHRIST" analyses Melville's experience after *Moby-Dick*. The last forty years of his life, from 1851-1891, are seen as "a bitterness of disillusion from which he never recovered." (99) Melville was certainly not a naïve opto-

---

[6] "Institute of the New Sciences of Man," BMC 1953.

[7] Samuel Charters, from an unpublished essay on Larry Eigner.

mist, and his close family were often concerned over what they termed his misanthropy. The brine of "the sea had soak'd his heart through."[8] A characteristic touch was Melville's underscoring, several months before his death, a passage in Schopenhauer's *Studies in Pessimism:*

> Myson, the misanthropist, was once surprised by one of those people as he was laughing to himself. "Why do you laugh?" he asked; "there is no one with you." "That is just why I am laughing," said Myson.[9]

What is difficult to accept in "Part IV is Loss" is not the facts of Melville's experience after *Moby-Dick*, but Olson's narrow interpretation of them. He feels that Melville's life was a tragedy because he abandoned the freedom of time and space and allowed Christianity to close in on him. Melville's

> natural sense of time was in its relation to space. It was not diverted as Christ's was, away from object, to the individual, and the passage of the personal soul.... Time was not a line drawn straight ahead toward future, a logic of good and evil. Time returned on itself. It had density, as space had, and events were objects accumulated within it, around which men could move as they moved in space. (101-2)

When Melville "surrendered" to Christianity, it was a failure of mind.

> The result was creatively a stifling of the myth power in him. The work from *Moby-Dick* on is proof. Melville was the antithesis of Dante. When he permitted himself to try to put his imagination to work in a world of Christian values, as he first did in *Pierre,* it is disaster. *Pierre* is a Christ syllogism: "I hate the world." *The Confidence Man, Clarel,* and *Billy Budd* are stories which follow from it. (102-3)

Olson's theory is an attempt to explain the second half of Melville's life, when he left the Berkshires and became a Custom House inspector in New York City, publishing only poetry in these years. But the theory that he was worried about mortality, caught "on the promise of a future life" offered by the Christian doctrine of Resurrection, doesn't explain much. Melville's poetry, like his fiction, is of a piece. In both he is,

---

8 Leyda, *Melville Log,* volume II, page 626.

9 *Ibid.,* page 832.

in the words of Robert Penn Warren, "a seeker of ultimates, the hater of illusion."[10] In his later work, as in *Moby-Dick*, there is "the effort to achieve awareness of the destructions and paradoxes of life and to resolve them."[11] His theme in his poetry is never the spiritual power of Christianity. It is rather, in his last years, marked by a stoicism and irony, or the muted, resigned pantheism such as that found in the late poem "Pontoosuce."

But the theory of Christianity was more than Olson's attempt to account for the biographical facts of Melville's later life. Olson was also finishing the portrait of a great American writer whose experience of space was that of a pioneer, a pathfinder, necessarily incomplete. Melville's genius was stimulated by the concrete, the specific. Olson's vision of him as "antemosaic" is penetrating, but Olson is a visionary, and the characteristic of a visionary is that he sharply limits what he sees.[12] In the last two sections of *Call me Ishmael*, Olson focuses only on the tragic aspects of Melville's life. "A Last Fact" is the briefest and most poetic of them all, Melville's entry in the back pages of one of the notebooks he kept as a *Journal Up the Straits*. In this short narrative, Olson reiterates the "eclipse" of Melville's last years, comparing him both to "Noah after the Flood" and Captain Pollard of Nantucket, one of the survivors of the *Essex* shipwreck described in "First Fact as Prologue." Olson has returned to poetry, for the reference to Pollard suggests an echo of an earlier mention of the name, in the chapter "Usufruct." Melville had met Pollard in Nantucket, when he wrote of the encounter: "To the islanders he was a nobody — to me, the most impressive man, tho' wholly unassuming, even humble, that I ever encountered." (32)

---

[10] Warren, "Melville's Poems," *The Southern Review* (October, 1967), page 801.

[11] *Ibid.*, page 821.

[12] The psychiatrist and Melville scholar Henry Murray once jokingly told Olson that *Ishmael* included everything important to Melville except one thing — his mother.

Pollard was the archetypal figure of "a man of the sea, but early driven from it by repeated disasters."[13] These are Melville's words, but this is Olson's conception of the final failure of Melville's life. To Olson, he shares Pollard's "eclipse," a loss or obscuring of powers after heroic experience. In the LAST FACT, Olson animates the interpretation of "Part IV: Loss."

The three narrative facts in *Ishmael* stress the destructive power of the sea — shipwreck, cannibalism, mutiny, blood, exhaustion, murder. Melville made much of what he once told Hawthorne was "the malignity of the sea,"[14] yet it is also his great image and source of creative energy, imaginative mystery, a basic symbol of life itself. In *Moby-Dick* the ocean is "the highest truth," "infinite as god." Not until the last chapter of *Ishmael* does Olson turn to the positive qualities of the sea in "what the Pacific was to Melville." (114)

Part V is THE CONCLUSION: PACIFIC MAN is *Ishmael's* final comment, the last look at Melville's experience. The central image is the Pacific, offering Melville concepts of space and myth, and confirming the future, which Olson presents in terms of economic history: Mediterranean trade routes, Columbus's exploration of the Atlantic Ocean, the opening of the Pacific. Olson summarizes his interpretation:

The Pacific is the end of the UNKNOWN which Homer's and Dante's Ulysses opened men's eyes to. END of individual responsible only to himself. Ahab is full stop. (119)

Melville's early romances *Typee, Omoo, Mardi, and White-Jacket* are also set in the Pacific, but they are not discussed in *Ishmael*.[15] Relating his subject to space, myth, and tragedy, Olson concludes:

The three great creations of Melville and *Moby-Dick* are Ahab, The Pacific, and the White Whale.
    The son of the father of Ocean was a prophet Proteus, of the chang-

---

13 *The Letters of Herman Melville,* page 157.

14 *Ibid.,* page 156.

15 Commenting on the emphasis on *Moby-Dick* in his study of Melville, Olson has said (July 27, 1968) :
    It was the *Piazza Tales* that turned me on. And, in a sense, in *Ishmael*

ing shape, who, to evade philistine Aristaeus worried about bees, became first a fire [Ahab], then a flood [the Pacific], and last a wild sea
beast [Moby-Dick]. (119)

Here *Call me Ishmael* closes. Olson, like Ishmael, is witness
to a tragedy, and like the conclusion of *Moby-Dick*, the final
part of *Ishmael* secures the larger philosophical perspective of
the preceding chapters. In the final words of his study of Melville, Olson is as much philosopher as poet. His book may be
read as either philosophy or poetry, for it is both. What it is
not is conventional literary criticism—Olson turned back to
this only after the "original, aboriginal" creative expression of
Call me Ishmael.

I went around and stopped in 1854. I must have basically wanted not to go
further than half his life. . . . I didn't say a word about the poetry in *Ishmael*. Today I would say that anything Herman Melville had put onto
paper is equally important. . . . I was too much a kid to know then. I still
have this enormous conviction that I knew what went on inside that cat.
I haven't had that feeling for anyone else, not even my own father. I had
the feeling for what he did do, and didn't do. And that's important—what
he *didn't do.*

on's House and Neighborhood

Essays and Letter for Melville

Although *Call me Ishmael* is Olson's major statement on Melville, there are also three short essays: "David Young, David Old," "The Materials and Weights of Herman Melville," and "Equal, That Is, to the Real Itself." These were written as book reviews for periodicals, and in one sense they are his explicit comment on the *other* kind of literary criticism: that produced by the academic establishment. "David Young, David Old" and "The Materials and Weights" are minor pieces; "Equal, That Is," discussed earlier, develops an aesthetic central to Olson's philosophy. A long poem, "Letter for Melville 1951," while also concerned with the Melville critics, holds its own as a poetic achievement as animated in its way as *Ishmael*.

"David Young, David Old" is Olson's review of F. Barron Freeman's book *Melville's Billy Budd* for the *Western Review* in 1949. "The Materials and Weights of Herman Melville" is a longer book review in two installments for *New Republic* in 1952. In the first piece, Olson continues to write with the biographical emphasis he used two years earlier in *Ishmael*, but the *New Republic* essay moves toward an explicit discussion of what Olson calls "the methodological question" more fully developed in "Equal, That Is" in *The Chicago Review*, 1958. Of the three articles, "David Young, David Old" redresses the imbalance of *Ishmael* where Olson emphasized Shakespeare's influence on Melville to the exclusion of Hawthorne. Two years after *Ishmael*, he suggests that Melville took "a double charge" from both Shakespeare and Hawthorne in writing *Moby-Dick*. Hawthorne's influence is expressed meta-

73

phorically in the title "David Young, David Old," Olson's reference to the Old Testament Book of Samuel, comparing Melville to King David:

For Hawthorne was as joined to Melville in his own mind as Jonathan to David, and though, in its beginnings, this love was good, when it was planted in Melville young, in the end the tree that flourished from it rove the giant out of Samuel.

Reviewing Freeman's edition of *Billy Budd*, Olson emphasizes the discovery that it might have been — like *Moby-Dick* — two books.

The story of the composition of *Billy Budd* turns out to be the exact contrary to the story of the composition of *Moby-Dick*. There, a first version done quick emerged, after a year of rewrite, as the book we know and can call Melville poet for. . . . But here, at the end of Melville's life, it now appears that the first version of another tale done in a little under four months . . . was for two full years worked over and over as though the hand that wrote was Hawthorne's, with his essayism, his hints, the veil of his syntax, until the celerity of the short story was run out, the force of the juxtapositions interrupted, and the secret of Melville as artist, the presentation of ambiguity by the event direct, was lost in the Salem manner.

"The presentation of ambiguity by the event direct"— Olson finds Melville's genius only in the first version of the tale, the 12,000-word short story "Baby Budd, Sailor." The conventional critical admiration for the novel *Billy Budd* he finds "more amorous than imaginative." His review is itself an amorous act; his love for Melville is as outspoken here as it is in *Ishmael* and the long poem "Letter for Melville." He asks, for example:

But *Billy Budd*, can anyone who has gone a little way into the cave of this man, has felt his air, had the thread in hand, heard the animal of the maze, can anyone be moved by anything here other than the myrrh of Melville's love for Billy (we always go farthest with our flesh).

Olson has no patience for "explainers," "those of dull mind who take what is obvious, Melville's intent, and prove it where he has not. I have nothing but scorn for such pietism." As a critic, he demands a more creative, personal involvement with the text. He cites with approval Auden's verses on Melville and Hart Crane's "natural and personal interest in Herman Melville's story of the Handsome Sailor."

"The Materials and Weights of Herman Melville" comes down even more heavily on traditional academic scholarship: "troubled rationalism" and "bead-telling books of the last years." Olson sees a few bright faces in "the Melville lobby": Raymond Weaver (the first sentence of *Ishmael* was modeled on the opening of Weaver's biography of Melville), Ronald Mason, Jay Leyda, Henry A. Murray, Merton Sealts. These men are Melville scholars who have written without the "pretentiousness, the ignorance, and the intolerable ill-proportion" found in the two books under review. Like A. E. Housman, Olson has a scathing tongue as a critic of critics. After castigating many and praising a few members of the growing Melville band, he turns in part two of the article to "offer whatever insights five additional years of work of my own might bring to correct or add to the measurement of Melville I offered in *Call me Ishmael*."

No real revision is presented (his discussion of Hawthorne in "David Young, David Old" is a more significant comment on *Ishmael*), but he rephrases his concept of Melville's methodology by itemizing "the materials and weights of Herman Melville."

Melville's importance, greater than ever, lies in (1) his approach to physicality, (2) his address to character as necessary human force, and (3) his application of intelligence to all phenomena as *the* ordering agent.

The article includes a short technical discussion of "the stance he [Melville] took toward object moving in space," but mostly it is a response to academic literary studies. Not until 1958 and "Equal, That Is," did Olson look more deeply into the situation of Melville's prose doing "things which its rhetoric would seem to contradict." This was after Olson had studied mathematical topology at Black Mountain College with Hans Rademacher, and encountered Whitehead's *Process and Reality,* Herman Weyl's *Philosophy of Mathematics and Natural Science,* and Merleau-Ponti's *Phenomenology of Perception.* The growth in Olson's ability to articulate concepts of projective space is strikingly evident in the last twenty years. As he has admitted "I was learning my lessons and writing hard."[1]

The difficulty with "The Materials and Weights of Herman Melville" is that Olson is lecturing as didactically as the classroom critics he disparages. Like the worst of them, he refuses to admit any interpretation of Melville that runs counter to his own. Projective space is the only way of life for Olson.

. . . until any of us takes this given physicality and moves from its essence into its kinetic, as seriously as we are all too apt to take the other end – the goal, we'll not be busy about the civilization breeding as surely now as that other one was between Homer and 500 B.C. And we'll not know what Melville had started a hundred years ago. . . . With Melville's non-Euclidean penetrations of physical reality ignored or avoided, all the important gains he made in expressing the dimensions possible to man and to story are also washed out.

The space, the breath, the vitality of *Call me Ishmael* have diminished here. Melville has been left behind, since instead of offering a more complete understanding of his work, Olson has become concerned with how the author of *Moby-Dick* may "more serve us." He emphasizes not technology but methodology, how "to use, to make use of, what is ours." He not only disparages any critic who interprets Melville in ways antithetical to quantity as intensive, but he also rigidly sets limits on what works of Melville's are successful. "Melville grasped the archaeological man and by doing it entered the mythological present. *Moby-Dick* is the evidence. The rest of his work is the defeat which is still our own."

Of all the many critics of Melville, Olson himself is probably the most dogmatic and the least concerned with text. In "The Materials and Weights," he refers briefly to "The Specksynder" chapter of *Moby-Dick,* and he writes at slightly longer length about the chapter "The Tail." These references

---

[1] Olson conversation, June 13, 1968.

are to chapter titles, with no quotations from the text. Olson is of course unsympathetic to the method of intensive textual explication, but for many readers, his avoidance of any quotations from *Moby-Dick* reduces the strength and comprehensibility of his interpretation.[2] Without illustrations from Melville's writing, Olson's essays do not develop a critical position; they rather exist as circular arguments. He is first and last asserting a moral system, not a critical position. Like Christions interpreting the Bible or Socialists referring to Marx, Olson leaves his reader with the thought that he could probably find chapter and line in *Moby-Dick* to prove anything he needs.

The truth is that Olson, like D. H. Lawrence, has had a revelation. The success of *Call me Ishmael*, like *Studies in Classic American Literature*, lies in its being a unique performance, Olson and Lawrence projecting a kind of poetic monodrama sustained by a creative vision (not rationale) of great force and decisiveness. In the shorter magazine pieces, Olson is less memorable since he is fixed within the context of the conventional critical review. These essays are finally vitiated by the framework he described as "the very rationalism Melville spent his life exposing, or just the facts of him without lending those facts an animation the equal of Melville's animation."[3] Olson is strongest in his *vision* of Melville, not in the re-view of what others have seen. We would not ask Elijah to review Captain Scoresby's accounts of whaling voyages.

2 For example, a major point in Olson's essay "Equal, That Is, to the Real Itself," that "the inertial structure of the world is a real thing which not only exerts effects upon matter but in turn suffers such effects," might have been illustrated by a reference to Melville's description of the carpenter in *Moby-Dick,* a man who

> seemed one with the general stolidity discernible in the whole visible world; which while pauselessly active in uncounted modes, still eternally holds its peace, and ignores you, though you dig foundations for cathedrals. (Hendricks House edition, pages 463-4)

Such textual illustrations, of course, are not Olson's method — nor necessarily should they be.

3 "The Materials and Weights of Herman Melville," *Human Universe,* page 113.

Olson has written about the Melville critics in a work that does possess the vitality and individual voice of *Ishmael*, however—his *Letter for Melville 1951*. It begins as occasional verse, but in its passionate outcry it becomes satire. Here Olson strikes through masks he knows very well. Hypocrisy? Who could be more blandly complacent than a group of Melville scholars at a "One Hundredth Birthday Party" for *Moby-Dick* at Williams College? Once again Olson has, as he does not in "David Young" and "The Materials and Weights," a real subject.

The full title of Olson's poem is

> LETTER FOR MELVILLE 1951
> written to be read AWAY FROM the Melville
> Society's "One Hundredth Birthday Party"
> for MOBY-DICK at Williams College, Labor Day
> Weekend, Sept. 2-4, 1951.

Approximately fifty copies were printed as a broadside (some were presumably distributed on the Williams campus) while Olson was teaching at Black Mountain College the summer of 1951. John Wieners, later his student at the college, remembered:

> This piece was written in a "moment of flame" at the end of August, 1951, as a bit of "verse pamphleteering." The students at Black Mountain College were so excited by the poem that they raised enough money among themselves to get it printed so that it might be sold at the birthday celebration which it attacks. This work, like *Apollonius of Tyana*, was under the direction of Larry Hatt, both being pushed out just at the end of August simultaneously.

Letter for Melville still reads as if it had been composed in "a moment of flame." It should be read aloud; then not only is it easier to understand the colloquial syntax (full of breaks in thought, asides under the breath, facial grimaces, and shrugs of the shoulder), but also the letter is then heard as intended—a dramatic public performance, an open letter to anyone who cares deeply about Melville. It isn't *to* Melville; it's *for* him, conceived in his support against the "bunch of commercial travelers from the several colleges" gathering at Williams for the weekend to do him in.

Beginning with a salutation, "My dear Eleanor Melville Metcalf," the first part is a reply to the invitation to attend the *Moby-Dick* birthday party. Olson wastes little time being polite before recoiling from the offer.

I do thank you, that we hear from you, but the Melville Society invitation came in the same mail with your news of this thing, and do you for a moment think . . . that I would come near, that I would have anything to do with their business other than to expose it for the promotion it is, than to do my best to make clear who these creatures are who take on themselves to celebrate a spotless book a wicked man once made?

The birthday party is a vulgar "false & dirty thing." "Can anything be clearer, as to how Melville is being used?" He mocks the institutional arrangements that have been made, a sight-seeing bus from Williamstown to Arrowhead, Melville's Berkshire farm; dormitories, catering services, and of course the main event of the celebration, speeches by the most ambitious Melville scholars. A very active weekend in the Berkshires; the situation had changed considerably from what it had been when Melville wrote in "Hawthorne and His Mosses," "There are hardly five critics in America; and several of them are asleep."

Olson satirizes the evasion of a typical academic defense of the party. For a few lines he speaks as one of the convention-ers, arguing with scarcely veiled self-mockery and contempt:

we cannot forget, even for this instant, that, in order,
too, that we can think that we ourselves are of some
present importance, we *have* to — I know, we really
would prefer to be free, *but* — we do have to have
an income, so, you see, you must excuse us if we
scratch each other's backs with a dead man's hand.

Olson's imagination is completely involved in his letter attacking the critics, the scholars whose main concern is not really Melville but rather making a living off Melville. As his feelings mount, his prose works itself over into poetry:

for after all, who but us, who but us has had the
niceness to organize ourselves in his name, who,
outside us, is remembering that this man a year ago

one hundred years ago (you see, we *are* very accurate
about our celebrations, know such things as dates)
was, just where we are gathering just ahead of labor
day (walked coldly in a cold & narrow hall by one
window of that hall to the north, into a room, a
very small room also with one window to the same
white north) to avoid the traffic who is, but us,
provided with dormitories and catering services?
      Timed in such a way to avoid him to see
      he gets a lot of lip (who hung in a huge jaw)
      and no service at all. . . .

A few months later, Olson used the same phrase, "a lot of lip
and no service at all," in the essay "Human Universe," referring to the homage given Rimbaud. Both he and Melville
"were prevented from work beyond what they do . . . by an
exasperation that a reality equivalent to their own penetra-
tion of reality had not come into being in their time." But
there was an essential difference between them, an American
quality to Melville with which Olson feels a stronger affinity.
Melville "was too American to have the logic Rimbaud had—
to quit, and to make money."[4]

Letter for Melville is a broadly comic performance, satiriz-
ing the personal folly as well as the professional vanity of the
conventioners. Olson mocks their delight in malicious gossip,
their homosexuality, their snobbish toadying to the "best"
colleges and the highest academic rank. His poem describes
the most prominent Melville critics (leaving out names to
protect the guilty), but readers even casually acquainted with
Melville scholarship can identify the individuals. It takes only
intelligent guesswork, for example, to place Eleanor Melville
Metcalf, Henry A. Murray, Olson, and Lewis Mumford ("by
another such") in the following lines:

      O such fools
      neither of virtue nor of truth
      to associate with
            to sit to table by
      as once before you, and Harry, and I

---

[4] *Ibid.,* page 116.

the same table the same Broadhall saw
water raised by another such to tell us
this beast hauled up out of great water was
society!

Yet with his angry concern for Melville, Olson is also aware
of the human side of the self-seeking scholars, and his poem
succeeds far more than his book reviews because he presents
a more complete view of the academic predicament. He asks
Eleanor Metcalf to

please say some very simple things, ask them
to be accurate:
ask one to tell you
what it was like to be a Congregational minister's son Midwest
how hard it was for a boy who liked to read to have to
          pitch, instead,
hay; and how, now that he has published books, now
          that he has done that
(even though his edition of this here celebrated man's verse
whom we thought we came here to talk about
has so many carelessnesses in it that, as of this date,
it is quite necessary to do it over)
let him tell you, that no matter how difficult it is
to work in an apartment in a bedroom in a very big city
because the kids are bothersome and have to be locked out,
          and the wife
is only too good, yet, he did republish enough of this other man
to now have a different professional title, a better salary
and though he wishes he were at Harvard or a Whale,
he is, isn't he, if he is quite accurate, much more liked
by his president?

The Melville scholars are scrambling, scratching "each
other's back with a dead man's hand," but their rewards are
small gains. Olson is free of their little skirmishes, and as his
poem makes clear, he is not crippled by their battle fatigue.
He sees Melville whole and alive. His poet's version of the
Moby-Dick birthday party has survived long after the sight-
seeing buses from Williams College have pulled away from
Arrowhead and the academic conventioners moved on to the
next English Institute at Columbia. Olson has the last word,

a description animated with his vision of projective space.

                 it is not the point
either of the hook or the plume which lies
cut on this brave man's grave
— on all of us —
but that where they cross is motion,
where they constantly moving cross anew, cut
this new instant open — as he is who
is this weekend in his old place
presumed on
                 I tell you,
he'll look on you with an eye you have the color of.
He'll not say a word because he need not, he said so many.

Postscript: Charles Olson at Black Mountain College 1953-56

Several years after Ishmael *was published,* Charles Olson *gave two lectures at Black Mountain College in which he described the book's "intuitive" genesis, "how you leap upon yourself before you know who you are." The first lecture, part of an "Institute of the New Sciences of Man" given in the spring, 1953, shortly before Olson studied mathematical topology with Hans Rademacher at the College, included the statement:*

It started, for me, from a sensing of something I found myself obeying for some time before, in *Call me Ishmael*. It got itself put down as *space*, a factor of experience I took as of such depth, width, and intensity that, unwittingly, I insisted upon it as fact (actually tried, there, to bring it down out of the abstraction of the word of it and away from the descriptive error of the illustrations of it I was then capable of — American geography, pre-history, and by way of the test-case, Melville, proto- or archeo-culture — by telling three sorts of stories, by setting in alongside the abstractions and the analogies three documentary narratives which I dubbed FIRST FACTS, to give space, by that noun, and those narratives, the mass and motion I take it to have, the air that it is and the lungs we are to live in it as our element.

I knew no more then than what I did, than to put down *space* and *fact* and hope, by the act of sympathetic magic that words are apt to seem when one first uses them, that I would invoke for others those sensations of life I was small witness to, part doer of. But the act of writing the book added a third noun, equally abstract: *stance*. For after it was done, and other work in verse followed, I discovered that the fact of this space located a man differently in respect to any act, so much so and with such vexation that only in verse did I acquire any assurance that the stance was not in some way idiosyncratic and only sign of the limits of my own talent, only wretched evidence of the lack of my own engagement at the heart of life.

But the mark of life is that what we do obey is who and what we are. And we have no other recourse than to see what we do as evidence of what we are, and use it, for good or worse, (1), to make more use of what we obeyed in the first place, and, thereby, (2), continue the pursuit of who we are (which pursuit seems to me now only a permanent one, if the only excusable one of men so inclined).

Note: About this time, when asked by a lady visitor to Black Mountain College what he taught there, Olson replied, "You might say that I teach posture."[1]

Three years later, in 1956, Olson prepared the first of three drafts of a statement that would eventually be published as the essay "Equal, That Is, to the Real Itself." In its first version, the essay was a lecture preceded and followed by the study of A. N. Whitehead's Process and Reality: an Essay in Cosmology.

Olson's lecture, Black Mountain College, 1956:

I am the more persuaded of the importance and use of Whitehead's thought that I did not know his work — except in snatches and by rumor, including the disappointment of a dinner and evening with him when I was 25 and he was, what, 75! — until last year. So it comes out like those violets of Bolyai Senior on all sides when men are needed, that we possess a body of thinking of the order of Whitehead's to catch us up

---

[1] Olson conversation, June 13, 1968.

where we wouldn't naturally poke our hearts in and to inten-
sify our own thought just where it does poke. He is a sort of
an Aquinas, the man. He did make a Summa of three centuries, and cast his system as a net of Speculative Philosophy
so that it goes at least as far as Plato. And his advantage
over either Plato or Aquinas is the advantage we share: that
the error of matter was removed in exactly these last three
centuries. I quote Whitehead:

"The dominance of the *scalar* physical quantity, inertia, in the Newtonian physics obscured the recognition of the truth that all fundamental physical quantities are *vector* and not scalar."

> (Scalar, you will recall, is an un-
> directed quantity, while vector is
> a directed magnitude as of a force
> or a velocity.)

So one gets the restoration of Heraclitus' flux translated as,
All things are vectors. Or put it, All that matters moves! And
one is out into a space of facts and forms as fresh as our own
sense of our own existence.

In the pleasure of these substantiations of Whitehead I
should like myself to gather up in a basket—or all it will take
is a hand—my own pre-propositions to a knowledge of his
thought. And it might be interesting to someone else in this
sense, that, like violets we are a bunch!

It comes down to fact and form. A writer, I dare say, goes
by words. That is, they are facts. And forms. Simultaneously.
And a writer may be such simply that he takes an attitude
towards this double power of word: he believes it is enough to
unlock anything. Words occur to him as substances—as entities, in fact as actual entities. My words were *space, myth,
fact, object*. And they were globs. Yet I believed in them enough
to try to reduce them to sense. I knew they were vector and
in *Ishmael* treated them as such, but they didn't, for me, get
rid of scalar inertia. Whitehead, it turns out, would say that I
was stuck in the second of the three stages in the process of
feeling:

"The second stage is governed by the private ideal . . . whereby the many feelings, derivatively felt as alien (the first stage of response, the mere reception of the actual world), are transformed into a unity of aesthetic appreciation immediately felt as private."

I cannot urge on you enough to remind you that these stubborn globs one sticks by, and is stuck with, are valid, at the same time that I urge you, one day, to recognize them as "losses" of the vector force in exactly the sense in which Whitehead goes on to characterize this second stage further:

"This (the second stage described above) is the incoming of 'appetition,' which in its higher exemplifications we term 'vision.' In the language of physical science, the 'scalar' form overwhelms the original 'vector' form; the origins become subordinate to the individual experience. The vector form is not lost, but is submerged as the foundation of the scalar superstructure."

So they sat for me, space myth fact object. In fact *myth*, which I guess was the first one, at least in the sense that the word as word had power over me, wasn't even finally home until Tuesday night of this week at about 1:30 am of Wednesday morning, in this sense that Miss Harrison, at that hour, I found attesting what Duncan had told me she did, that the word myth, the Greek *muthos*, is at root the same as mouth! From a root *mu!* At which point I have come to the end of that row. And I remember exactly the place and hour of my first attempt to write down how I understood myth to be —on the Annisquam River, winter, 1939, with Schwartz's mother-in-law, in whom I took great fantasy pleasure, in the same house! The prose of that said piece was, of course, impossible. Or at least was beyond my reach.

Space as such of course I opened *Ishmael* with, wordwise, etc. Yet in that wonderful sense—"marvelous maneuver," Franz Kline, a creature of last night's dream, called the writer's ability to get will ass-backwards—in that wonderful sense that one does what one knows before one knows what one does, I behaved better in *Ishmael* than I knew. Even, for example, to jamming in the other two terms as well as myth and space, hammering object and fact as powers of the com-

position, at least as means of structure if the power of form
is not what the book is conspicuous for. Indeed, *Ishmael* is a
construct, and is thus, creatively, the last term of the syllogism
as passed to me by the fathers in said dream:

> of rhythm is image
> of image is knowing
> of knowing there is
> a construct

(And the boat did swerve then, just because Schwartz's
mother-in-law and I and all my people were, even then, involved in avoiding the

> yelping rocks
> where the tidal river rushes

I mean only to stress blind obedience — or what Whitehead
I now find calls "blind perceptivity." I quote:

"An actual entity, in its character of being a physical occasion, is an
act of blind perceptivity of the other physical occasions of the actual
world."

At which point I should think it might be clear how space
myth fact object, as I had stumbled, and was stumbling,
on them, were, unknown to me, obediences to words which were
my private nomenclature of knowledges as men are violets
and share a hillside at moments of renascence in man the
species' experience of the Real. And I am offering these notes
simply as such, to find out where, now, at what stage I am.
Which, if the obedience is still reasonably exact, ought, still,
to be another season on same said hillside.

It is actually form that I am seeking to draw out of the
thought — to seize a tradition out of the live air, or something,
the Bejewelled Man once said — the thought which, I have
suggested, and Whitehead has the system to demonstrate,
man is now possessed of after the last three centuries once
again. (I suppose because I am a mythologist and least of all
a philosopher I stress the last phrase, once again. The seasons
of man also recur, even if it will be some time before we know
them as deliberately as we do those of nature. Hers are symmet-

rical. Man's like Venus's period of rotation, is asymmetrical.)

That is, I am not aware that many men's acts of form yet tap the total change of stance or posture (postulate or premise) of which Whitehead's "philosophy of organism" is one completed exemplification. Mind you, be careful here. Remember the violets. A philosophy, even of his order, or because of his order, a philosophy, just because it is a wind-up, it does seek, as he says, to be so water-tight that, "at the end, in so far as the enterprise has been successful, there should be no problem of space-time, or of epistemology, or of causality, left over for discussion," form, in the sense in which one means it as of creations, can have no life as such a system. It is like the moon, without air. Or a mother. It has had to be like Whitehead has to find God as wisdom to be, "a tender care that nothing be lost." The creation of form by man could hardly let this statement of his operative growth cover him just because he is not God, and his third stage of feeling — "the satisfaction," Whitehead calls it — can only assert itself, even as a "completed unity of operation," in a new actual entity. In other words has to go back to the vectors of which it is a proof. Taking off from the thought one can define an act of art as a vector which, having become private and thus acquired vision, ploughs the vision back by way of primordial things. Only thus can it have consequence. It cannot, by taking up consequence, into itself. This return to object has a good deal to do with Whitehead's description of art:

"All aesthetic experience is feeling arising out of the realization of contrast under identity."

I mean, discords. The discordant. The want of agreement. The want of concord or harmony. Variance, dissension, contention, dissonance. Contest. The *agon* as well as the *pathos* and the *epiphany*. (The name of the actor in Greek tragedy was *agonistes*, contester.) The shift, from sorrow to joy.

II

The other part of my backwardness was the poetics. I was

stuck with particulars. And am still stuck. And my question is to wonder, what's wrong with The Bunch as the essential principle. At least to urge it on you, even if I might mislead. For what one knows is that valuation is also distinctly blind — blind perceptivity. And so a man has no course but, with care, to propose it, to propose his valuation. Proof is either forthcoming or it ain't. The risk is obvious. It is a good part of the struggle.

I had already practiced the principle of the particular when Creeley offered me the formulation form is never more than an extension of content (sign he too was one of Whitehead's violets!). And in no way does this contradict the literally poetic definition of prosody. Pound's. Prosody is the articulation of the total sound of the poem — if you are prepared, and I mean prepared in the sense we speak of an initiate as prepared, or a man and a woman who approach marriage, or even those who are about to be born: are they prepared? Or like the sign says as you approach the tunnel, are you prepared to die?

are you prepared to see content as equally possessed of sound?????

are you prepared to be enjoined as Achilles was by old Phoenix, who came to him, he said, from Achilles' father, Peleus,

> "to teach him to be both
> of words the speaker and
> of deed the doer"

that they are one and not two things, that one can't do anything right without the right words to go with it. And I mean go with it. Go

                              with

          it

Do it. And say it. Motor speech and motor movement. One sanction and the same binding force. One does not speak of holy things. One does not expose the peyote bundle. The stone is a holy object. It speaks.

What I am losing in phrasing is, to press on you that the actual entity stains the whole performance. If you leave the particular as the occurrence of force — as the vector — you lose the force. And the satisfaction, the crux of vision, is lost. Form is the art of tensor.

Form, in fact, is now definable as tensions. The single word. But the simplicity hides in itself the insistence that the content as actual has the same powers of tension which its extension, form is no more than, also has by a double as pervasive as that by which God has to be seen. The double problem cannot be separated into two distinct problems, to apply Whitehead's thought. Either side can only be explained in terms of the other —

                            either form and content,
in our present context, or word and deed.
                           We are dealing with two
fluencies each time we do a single thing, a primordial fluency
               In comes the roaring tide
and a consequent one:
               Fast falls the even

And each makes up the matter: the objective immortality of actual occasions requires the primordial permanence of form, whereby the creative advance ever re-establishes itself endowed with initial creation of the history of one's self. What makes us want to, a Lady asked me. It is what I mean by no choice. History is to want to. It is the built-in. And as such it is the other time which a man's own time is included in. Or, to take the working dictum and the governing axis, a man's time is at once a center and a circumference, and the drawn, the circumference, is history, the force and tensor, history.

It was also Keats who said, "A man's life is an allegory."

Sources

Butterick, George F. and Glover, Albert. *A Bibliography of Works by Charles Olson*. New York, 1967.

Dahlberg, Edward. *Can These Bones Live*. Ann Arbor, 1967.

Davis, Merrell R. and Gilman, William H. *The Letters of Herman Melville*. New Haven, 1960.

Eliot, T. S. *Literary Essays of Ezra Pound*. New York, 1954.

Emerson, Ralph Waldo. *Selected Writings*. New York, 1950.

Franklin, H. Bruce. *The Wake of the Gods: Melville's Mythology*. Stanford, 1963.

Freud, Sigmund. *Moses and Monotheism*. New York, 1955.

Lawrence, D. H. *Studies in Classic American Literature*. New York, 1955.

Leyda, Jay. *The Melville Log*. New York, 1951.

Matthiessen, F. O. *American Renaissance*. New York, 1941.

Melville, Herman. *Collected Poems*, edited by Howard P. Vincent. Chicago, 1947.

————*Moby-Dick*, edited by Luther S. Mansfield and Howard P. Vincent. New York, 1962.

————"Mosses from an Old Manse." reprinted in *The Shock of Recognition*.

————*Pierre: or, The Ambiguities*, edited by Henry A. Murray. New York, 1949.

Moore, Harry T. *A D. H. Lawrence Miscellany*. Carbondale, 1959.

Olson, Charles. *A Bibliography on America for Ed Dorn*. San Francisco, 1964.

————*Call me Ishmael*. New York, 1947. (The edition currently in print is a paperback published in 1967 by City Lights Bookstore, San Francisco.)

————*The Distances*. New York, 1960.

————*Human Universe and Other Essays*, edited by Donald Allen. New York, 1967.

————"Lear and Moby-Dick." *Twice a Year*, Number One, Fall-Winter, 1938.

————*Letter for Melville 1951*. Black Mountain, 1951.

————*The Maximus Poems*. New York, 1960.

————*Mayan Letters*. Mallorca, 1953.

————*Proprioception*. San Francisco, 1965.

————*Reading at Berkeley*. San Francisco, 1966.

————*Selected Writings*, edited by Robert Creeley. New York, 1966.

Perry, Bliss. *The Heart of Emerson's Journals*. Boston, 1926.

Pound, Ezra. *ABC of Reading.* New Haven, 1934.

Scoresby, Captain. *The Northern Whale-Fishery.* Philadelphia, c. 1820.

Sealts, Merton M., Jr. *Melville's Reading.* Madison, 1966.

Stovall, Floyd, editor. *Eight American Authors.* New York, 1963.

Warren, Robert Penn. "Melville's Poems." *The Southern Review,* III, 4. Autumn, 1967.

Weaver, Raymond. *Herman Melville, Mariner and Mystic.* New York, 1921.

Williams, William Carlos. *In the American Grain.* New York, 1956.

Wilson, Edmund. *The Shock of Recognition.* New York, 1943.